Edmund Bedingfield

The Life of Margaret Mostyn

Edmund Bedingfield

The Life of Margaret Mostyn

ISBN/EAN: 9783744659864

Printed in Europe, USA, Canada, Australia, Japan

Cover: Foto ©Raphael Reischuk / pixelio.de

More available books at **www.hansebooks.com**

Quarterly Series.

TWENTY-FIFTH VOLUME.

THE LIFE OF
MOTHER MARGARET OF JESUS.

ROEHAMPTON:

PRINTED BY JAMES STANLEY.

THE LIFE OF
MARGARET MOSTYN

(MOTHER MARGARET OF JESUS),

Religious of the Reformed Order of our Blessed Lady of Mount Carmel.
(1625—1679.)

BY THE

VERY REV. EDMUND BEDINGFIELD,

*Canon of the Collegiate Church of St. Gomar, and Confessor
to the English Teresians at Lierre.*

LONDON :
BURNS AND OATES, PORTMAN STREET
AND PATERNOSTER ROW.
1878.

✠

DILECTUS · MEUS · MIHI

ET · EGO · ILLI

QUI · PASCITUR · INTER · LILIA

(Cant. ii.)

PREFACE.

[BY THE EDITOR.]

THE Life of Mother Margaret (Mostyn) of Jesus, which is contained in the following pages, is taken from a manuscript preserved at Darlington. The religious of the Carmelite convent in that town form the same community as that in which she lived. It was founded at Lierre, from Antwerp, in 1648, as is related below, she and her sister, Mother Ursula of All Saints, being two of the band of religious who migrated from Antwerp for that purpose. The sources from which this Life has been drawn up were all contemporaneous with its subject. After the death of Mother Margaret, the nuns who had lived with her so long were ordered by the Bishop to write down their recollections of her, and the papers thus produced form a great part of the substance of the following pages. The general narrative is due to the labours of Canon Bedingfield, the confessor of the convent and Margaret's intimate friend, who laid on her the task of setting down on paper the favours which she received in prayer, and who used them along with the other papers already mentioned in the composition of her Life. But his own death came too soon for the completion of the work which he had undertaken. No one seems, for some time, to have continued the work. Its completion, as we now possess it, is owing to a writer—probably, like Canon Bedingfield, a confessor of the community—who finished the compilation as late as 1779. The manuscripts left behind her by Mother Margaret herself, from which so large a part of this volume is taken, exist in a collected form at Darlington, but they are not by any means arranged in order, and there are frequent repetitions in the manuscript. This manuscript, as well as that of the Life, has been kindly lent to me by the religious of the present community, who have also furnished almost all the notes containing personal and historical information which are subjoined to the pages of this volume. The reader will find that I have inserted several passages from the manuscripts of Mother Margaret, which were not used by Canon Bedingfield or his successor in the compilation of the Life.

The manuscript which contains the Life of Mother Margaret also contains four shorter Lives—those of her sister, Mother Ursula of All Saints, called at her baptism Elisabeth, and of her three nieces, Sister Lucy of the Holy Ghost, Sister Mary Anne of St. Winefrid, and Mother Margaret Teresa of the Immaculate Conception, whose baptismal names were Elisabeth, Anne, and Margaret. The present volume would have been inconveniently long if these lives had been added in full to the Life of Mother Margaret. I have therefore contented myself with giving a short account of them, taken from an article lately written for a Catholic Review.

I should have been able to publish this volume sooner, but for several months of ill health, which will, I fear, also have the effect of delaying some other volumes already in preparation for the Quarterly Series. I had especially hoped to be able to finish the new volume of the *Public Life of our Lord* in time for the Midsummer issue, but I fear that that is now impossible.

H. J. C.

London, Feast of St. Augustine, Apostle of England, 1878.

CONTENTS.

Contents.

Contents. xiii

Contents.

THE AUTHOR'S PROTESTATION.

———

"*Whereas His Holiness Pope Urban the Eighth, of happy memory, on the 19th of March, 1625, published a Decree in the Sacred Congregation of Cardinals and Universal Inquisition, and confirmed it the 1st of July, 1634, by which he forbids books to be printed of the actions, miracles, revelations, or other benefits received from Heaven, by men famous for sanctity or martyrdom, except they be first examined and approved by the Ordinary of the place, or, as His Holiness declared, explaining that they have no ecclesiastical approbation, but only depend on the fidelity of the author — in conformity to the said Decree, Confirmation, and Declaration, I most humbly profess that all which is contained in this book does only rely on human authority, which I have most sincerely and candidly delivered, without any ecclesiastical Approbation.*"

PREFACE.

[BY CANON BEDINGFIELD.]

HAVING undertaken to write the life of the venerable Mother Margaret of Jesus, which is replenished with various visions and revelations, things but little understood and less esteemed by many—whose pride perhaps hinders them from experiencing with what familiarity our Lord is pleased to treat His friends—it will be necessary to speak a word or two concerning them. The learned Abbot Blosius admonishes such as attribute these favours to fiction of weak brains, to take care they be not misled by such erroneous opinions, which argue a want both of faith and humility, since they oppose themselves to so many ages' experience, which shows us that Almighty God, from the beginning of the world, has constantly directed mankind by these extraordinary gifts, verifying thereby His affection towards us, having declared that His delight is to be with the children of men. If we look into the Old Testament there is scarce a page which does not bear witness of this truth. We find Him there familiarly treating and conversing with our first parents, Noe, Moses, Samuel, David, who was a man according to His heart; and with innumerable other patriarchs and prophets, to whom He was pleased to reveal the favours He had reserved for the New Testament or covenant, of which He speaks by the Prophet Joel, saying, 'In those days I will pour out

B 26

My spirit upon all flesh, and your sons and daughters shall prophesy, your ancients shall dream dreams, and your young men shall see visions: yea, upon My servants and handmaids I will pour out My spirit.'[1] This was partly accomplished in the Apostles, particularly St. Peter, St. John, and St. Paul—whose visions and revelations were so sublime, that as he says of himself, 'Lest the greatness of revelations should puff me up, there was given me a sting of my flesh, a messenger of Satan, to buffet me'[2]—and in their disciples, and others of the primitive Christians, as Agabus, and the four daughters of Philip the deacon.[3] It has been continually verified in persons eminent for sanctity in all ages unto these latter days, which have been sanctified and illuminated by the admirable revelations of St. Bridget, St. Gertrude, St. Catharine of Siena, and divers others; but chiefly by those of the seraphical mother St. Teresa, whose writings are dignified by the Church with the title of celestial, and greatly tending to excite the minds of the faithful to sincere desires of their heavenly country.

I know that many would fain cloak their incredulity by pretending that these extraordinary gifts are more common to women than men, which is far from being universally true, since in the Old Testament we find but few women endowed with these favours, and in the New they seem promiscuously imparted to both sexes, according to the above-said prophecy of Joel: 'Yea, and upon My servants and handmaids I will pour out My spirit in those days.' For proof of this I shall refer my kind reader to the annals of the different Religious Orders, which have been founded from age to age, who all abound in persons frequently visited by Almighty God with celestial visions and revelations, besides many of the clergy and laity. The Seraphical

---

[1] Joel ii. 28.   [2] 2 Cor. xii. 7.   [3] Acts xi. 28; xxi. 9.

Order of the humble St. Francis alone will be found a sufficient warrant for this assertion. If God at any time has had a particular regard to the humility of His handmaids, we know His Divine Spirit breathes where it pleases, and the humble receive the plenitude of it, according to that of Isaias, 'To whom shall I have respect but to the poor little one, and the contrite of spirit, and him that trembles at My words?'[4] St. Paul in his First Epistle to the Corinthians says that God 'has chosen the foolish things of this world to confound the wise men; and God has chosen the weak things of the world to confound the things that are strong; and God has chosen the mean and contemptible things of the world, and the things that are not, to destroy the things that are, that no flesh may glory in His sight.'[5]

I mean not here to patronize the too great credulity of many, who are always disposed to believe anything that is given out for a vision or revelation, but only to prevent the obstinacy of some who refuse to credit any. Both extremes are equally odious, and both justly corrected by the seraphical mother, St. Teresa, in her ninth advice or admonition to the Rev. Father Jerome Gratian, where amongst other things she says, 'Although it be certain that there are some true revelations, yet it is well known there are an infinite number of false ones, which are only composed of lies. Now it is a very hard and difficult matter,' concludes the Saint, 'to draw one truth out of a hundred lies.' To proceed therefore with some security in these dubious and extraordinary ways, it will be necessary to weigh attentively the admonition given us by St. John in the fourth chapter of his epistles, where he says, 'My dearest, believe not every spirit, but try the spirits if they be of God.'[6] This has ever been the practice of the most learned, many

---

[4] Isaias xxvi. 2.   [5] 1 Cor. i. 27, 28.   [6] St. John iv. 1.

of whom, as St. Bonaventure, Cardinal Turrecremata, John Gerson, Chancellor of Paris, John of Avila, and others, have given certain rules or signs whereby to discern true from counterfeited spirits, the substance of which I shall briefly here set down under four heads. The first is to consider the nature, condition, and temper of those who receive these visions and revelations. The second is to examine the effects they produce in the soul, because, as Christ said, 'By their fruits you shall know them.' St. Gregory had a particular esteem of this proof, so that speaking of a religious man called Peter, who whilst he lived in the world was carried in spirit to behold the pains of Hell, he says, 'This person chastised himself so severely with all sorts of penances, that had he been silent his manner of life spoke sufficiently to witness he had seen those torments, and to express the horror he had of them.' The third is to observe whether they consist of solid and profitable matters, or of vain and frivolous things. The fourth is to weigh attentively whether they agree in all with Holy Scripture, and contain nothing contrary to the received doctrine of our Holy Mother the Church.

All these articles are so advantageous in our venerable Mother's regard, that they exclude all reasonable doubt of illusion or deceit. For, as to her personal qualities, she was of a quick and solid judgment, which was tempered with simplicity and sincerity. She was of a cheerful and merry disposition, free from melancholy or passion, and of so equal a temper that no circumstances or trials ever seemed to alter it. The effects her favours produced were a sorrow for her past crimes, as she termed them—which never exceeded a venial sin—and a daily advancement in humility, knowledge, and contempt of herself, so that she was not only an utter enemy to pride or ostentation, but I may say a stranger to it, not being able to conceive how it was possible so vile a creature as she esteemed herself could find anything to take satisfaction in. She was so far from setting her heart upon these extraordinary graces, that it was her constant prayer to be freed from them, and to walk the beaten way of the Cross. Her obedience was equally singular, which was put to no small trial when I ordered her to write down the particulars of her life and favours, to which she had an extreme repugnance and aversion, yet complied so exactly with it as to descend to the minutest circumstances; and this she did with so much secrecy that, although she only employed herein spare times, and though many of the things here mentioned passed thirty years before her death, the community was entirely ignorant of them, till I gave them life after her departure, she apprehending nothing more than to have them divulged; so that on her death-bed she earnestly charged the Subprioress never to permit the religious to say anything in her praise. As to the favours themselves, it is to be observed that the gifts or graces of Almighty God are generally divided into two heads—the one, according to the scholastic term, is called a grace given *gratis*, which commonly regards others, as the gift of prophecy or miracles, which are of no real benefit to the persons endowed with them; the other is called a grace rendering us pleasing to God, and this has for its chief object the sanctification of the person to whom it is particularly imparted. Of this last sort principally are the favours received by our venerable Mother, who, by a kind of intimacy and innocent familiarity with the Sacred Infant and His Blessed Mother, was wholly inflamed with the love of God, which worked so powerfully in her as not to allow her any content or satisfaction but in labouring and in suffering for His sake.

As the advice of the Holy Ghost, ' Before death praise

no one,' has sealed up my lips for above thirty years, and hindered me from publishing to the world the singular perfections and graces of our venerable Mother Margaret of Jesus, who during this time sincerely disclosed unto me all the hidden secrets of her happy soul, now that she has yielded up her blessed spirit into the hands of her Divine Spouse, I think my obligation equally great to comply with the impulse of the same Holy Spirit, Who, as St. Maximus, a learned prelate, commentating upon the same place, avouches, requires that we should praise men after their consummation, because then, as the Saint says, there is neither danger of adulation in the person who commends, nor of vanity in the person commended. Having therefore kept these just and approved measures, I hope no one will impute either of these vices to my charge: for although I propose in this relation to follow the accounts I have had from herself, either by word of mouth or in writing (during which she has sometimes been visibly seen to be assisted by our Blessed Lady standing by her side), she cannot be justly censured either with levity or ostentation, since she had no other motive than purely to comply with obedience, which we may look upon as in some degree heroic, on account of the great interior confusion and humiliation she suffered in acquitting herself of this task, neither ought such description to appear anyways strange, since the wonderful lives of St. Bridget, St. Gertrude, St. Teresa, and others, have been delivered to us through the very same means, by which this is transmitted to those who are to come after us, notwithstanding they have met with universal approbation. I may perhaps be suspected of searching herein my own credit; but I think with little reason. For when I began this work, my age and daily increasing infirmities allowed me no other prospect than an approaching death, which may probably reduce me to a desired oblivion before I complete it. My only comfort is that I am in the hands of a merciful God, Whose honour is the only object of my present undertaking, which I commit entirely to His providential disposals, being assured there is nothing in this narration but what greatly tends to encourage those who are already engaged in a spiritual life, to persevere faithfully in it, and to draw others, who have not yet experienced how sweet the service of God is, to fervent desires of giving themselves wholly to it, where they will also find traced out by a living example the most efficacious means of obtaining it. Amongst others, the principal is to have a particular devotion to the ever Blessed Virgin Mary, of which they will find most wonderful effects in the life of this dear Mother, who from her infancy was singularly protected and assisted by her in all her actions and frequently recreated and comforted with celestial apparitions, which, though noways to be wished for or expected by others, show what our Lord has reserved for those who sincerely honour His beloved Mother, by whom He will have us seek access to Him. Therefore, laying aside all further suspicions, I shall submit myself and this small work to the charitable thoughts of my pious reader, who, I confide, will easily pardon all its defects, considering me as a stranger to my own language and country even from my youth, and also remember to pray for a miserable sinner,

EDMUND BEDINGFIELD.

THE LIFE OF
MOTHER MARGARET OF JESUS.

.

CHAPTER I.

The birth, parentage, and education of Margaret Mostyn.

THIS our venerable Mother, called in the world Margaret Mostyn, was born at Hurst in Shropshire, near Shrewsbury, in the year of our Lord, 1625, on the 8th of December, being the feast of the Immaculate Conception of our Blessed Lady, of whom she soon became a true devotee, and afterwards a zealous promoter of her honour in the illustrious Order of Mount Carmel, whose splendour had no small addition in the possession of so noble and virtuous a person. Her father was John Mostyn, Esq., of Talacre, in the county of Flintshire, in North Wales; her mother, according to her maiden name, was Ann Fox, daughter to Henry Fox of Hurst, Esq.—both ancient and Catholic families. She had three brothers, and four sisters, one of whom died in her infancy, two were married and remained in the world, and the other called Elisabeth, in religion Ursula of All Saints, became religious with her in the English Monastery of Antwerp. They had ever a great natural affection for each other, and their virtuous inclinations rendered them inseparable, so that in many circumstances their lives are so interwoven that it is hard to write the one without mixing something of the other. Two of her brothers died young and unmarried, and the eldest, Sir Edward, was created first baronet of the family, which has ever since wonderfully prospered, and still continues to be an exemplary support and protector of the Catholic religion. Partly on account of her having been born in her grandmother's house, and partly for her amiable and sweet and grateful disposition, which appeared even from her cradle, this virtuous and grave matron would never be prevailed upon to part with her, and therefore had the sole care of her education, which was most pious and edifying. She had scarce arrived unto full six years, when she began to be greatly delighted in adorning, with her bracelets, chains, and other curiosities, a picture of our Blessed Lady with the Infant Jesus in her arms, in which she often spent much time, and was once so seriously occupied in the innocent devotions that she forgot her dinner. This loss however was abundantly recompensed; for she was assured that from that time our Lady took her under her particular protection. At this picture, as long as she remained in the house, which was upwards of ten years, she daily asked our Lady's blessing, said her beads, and other little prayers, which if at any time she chanced to forget, she found within herself so much disturbance and remorse that she could not be easy until she had taken some occasion to supply for them.

As she was observed to be much inclined to fearfulness, to overcome it, a Father of the Society of Jesus, who lived in the family, would often send her errands alone to the most remote places of the house, promising pictures and medals, or to teach her some devotions, to which she would most willingly attend for a long time together, if she would but venture, which, notwithstanding her repugnance, she readily did; and on these occasions was often favoured with the visible presence of her angel guardian, who sometimes led her by the hand, sometimes carried her, and that even until she arrived to

the age of eleven or twelve years, which greatly augmented her devotion to, and confidence in, this heavenly
guide. She was also blessed with an early faith and
affection towards the Blessed Sacrament, which made
her greatly envy those who had the happiness to receive
It, and to lament her own want of age. These desires
increased with her years, and were much enlivened on a
certain occasion, when, being present in the chapel whilst
her grandmother communicated, she thought she saw
the Infant Jesus in the Host, at which sight she could
not contain herself, but began with prayers and tears to
beg that she might also receive the Child Jesus, and was
so importuning, that they were obliged to carry her out.
Another time, having been left alone in the chapel on
Holy Thursday, she had got a chair and was climbing up
to the chalice, but fortunately some one coming in, took
her down, and asked her what she meant to do. To
whom she sighing answered, 'I wanted to see my dear
little Jesus.' These innocent and tender sentiments drew
her to make frequent visits to the chapel, where her
great uncle, Mr. Layton, having been somewhat vain in
his youth, but now blind, and a very holy man, was
accustomed also frequently to retire himself. Here she
had her set devotions, and sometimes getting up in the
middle of them, she would go to him, and desire him to
intercede for her to her grandmother, that she might
obtain leave to become a nun, for she feared if it was
deferred too long she might lose her good vocation.
This good gentleman, more pleased with the humour
and manner of her request than at the petition itself,
generally put her off by telling her he did not think she
was cut out for a nun, and therefore must have patience
till she knew better what was required for such a state of
life. But neither these, nor other repeated denials, were
able to extinguish the good desires which the love of

God had enkindled in her tender breast. She seemed still to languish after this happy state, and being now admitted to her First Communion, at which she was again favoured with the visible presence of the Sacred Infant in the Blessed Sacrament, she received such sensible impressions of the veracity of her vocation, that she became daily more importuning to put it in execution. She informed her confessor of what had passed, and solicited his interest in her behalf. But he, taking the thing in ill part, and supposing it the effect of imagination, told her with some displeasure, that if she continued to entertain such fancies as those, she should not go to Communion again for a long time.

These inclinations were no less disagreeable to her grandmother, who had quite other views for this darling child, whose absence she could not suffer so much as a day. Calling her therefore to her, she represented in the strongest terms the unreasonableness of such designs, which beside being immature, could not fail of being both prejudicial to her own constitution, which was too delicate for a religious, and to the whole family, which seemed to have great hopes in her. The good lady also laid before her her own distressed situation, which was really moving, she being afflicted with the gout, dropsy, stone, and other infirmities, which confined her to bed, where she lay entirely helpless, and continued so for many years, to the great wonder of all who knew her. To these she added many other endearing expressions, as well as threats, assuring her grandchild she would never agree to any such proposals; and therefore commanded her to be henceforth silent on that head. Margaret, who amongst other virtues possessed also that of a dutiful affection towards her parents, did not long defer to give the desolate matron all the consolation and comfort she could expect, by promising to remain with

her as long as she lived, and render her during all that
time all the service that lay in her power, on which
account she resolved to suspend all thoughts of what
had passed. Her grandmother, to confirm her the more
in these dispositions, and to give her an occasion of
more dissipation, charged her with the care and management of the house. This employ, if we consider her
age, was liable to difficulties, and might have been
attended with many inconveniences, had not her good
qualities, discretion, and prudence surmounted them :
for at that time there were several near relations, her
cousins german, in the family, much superior to her in
years, who might have thought themselves more fit for
such an office. Yet her virtue, innocence, and good
nature had such an ascendant over them, that, far from
repining, they seemed to have a pleasure in being under
her direction and seconding her proceedings, which were
the admiration of all about her, as also her talent in
pacifying quarrels and composing disagreements that
were sometimes apt to arise from the different humours
and interests of those she lived with, who were always
satisfied with her mediation, she being ever looked upon
as an angel of peace.

In the midst of these domestic and charitable offices
she employed much time in reading the saints' lives and
other spiritual books, which she sometimes read to the
servants, some of whom being Protestants, she explained
to them the ceremonies of the Mass and other solemnities observed in the chapel, which had so good an
effect that two of them became Catholics. They could
never sufficiently express the efficacy this innocent and
pious practice had over them, which she has since been
assured by our Blessed Lady to have been highly agreeable to her Blessed Son.

But the solicitude she had for her suffering grandmother was what chiefly occupied her tender mind. On her account she deprived herself of all kinds of pastimes and recreations suitable to her age, and when invited by others to any little party of pleasure, her answer was, that she could not possibly be easy or take satisfaction in anything if absent from her afflicted mamma, apprehending that she should need any comfort that lay in her power to give her. For this reason she constantly attended her day and night, making it her business to dress, feed, and turn her in her bed, for which purpose she used frequently to rise in the night three or four times. For although there were always two strong maids in the chamber to assist her in what she wanted, nothing was done to the good lady's satisfaction unless Margaret had a hand in it, so passionately did she love her company and conversation.

At last, finding herself mastered by her many long infirmities, and ready as it were to yield up the ghost, she called this darling child to her bedside, where she expressed to her, in such terms as her circumstances would permit, the gratitude she owed to her for such a cheerful and faithful attendance, assuring her she had received more true comfort from her than from any of her own children, and that her greatest affliction was to be obliged to depart from her. She said she was sorry for having hindered her from advantageous matches, which her other friends had so much desired should take effect; but above all she greatly regretted her unreasonable proceeding in declining her from a religious state, for which, being only the effect of a blind and fond affection, she begged her pardon, and desired that after her death she would faithfully comply with her happy vocation in case she still found herself thereto inspired.

CHAPTER II.

How she struggles for a long time against her vocation, but is wonderfully confirmed by the Blessed Virgin.

SOON after the funeral of her deceased grandmother Sister Margaret went home to her mother, by whom she was received with great joy and tenderness. As she had been some time a widow, she entertained great hopes of comfort and assistance from this her so long absent daughter, whose views also were now no other than like a dutiful child to attend and wait upon her parents, for which purpose she applied herself, by her mother's direction, to the different charges of the family in which she gave general satisfaction. However, she had not been long here before her former thoughts of becoming religious came fresh again to her mind, which being now prepossessed with the plausible appearance of assisting her mother, met with some resistance, yet so, that the more reasonable her charitable undertaking appeared, the more violently her interior call to a more perfect state preyed upon her. The contrast she experienced became so great, that it rendered her quite uneasy and comfortless. In this disturbance she disclosed all her intentions and difficulties to her confessor, in hopes of some relief. He, considering all her circumstances, the loss of so dear a friend, the change of abode, where she was now like almost a stranger, and

the circumstances of the house, in which she was yet
necessary, put her off by telling her such melancholy
thoughts ought rather to be slighted than taken notice
of. This answer, suiting well with her present inclination, satisfied her so far, that it enabled her to make
head for a while against these importuning thoughts,
during which time she began to amuse herself like her
equals in dress, she got a liking for gay company and
other innocent diversions, in which being joined by her
sister, Ursula,[1] they contracted such a love and friendship
for each other as to come to a mutual promise, that
whenever the first of them should be married, the other
should use her endeavours to marry some one in the
same neighbourhood or county, so that they might in
some sort enjoy each other's company. By little and
little her thoughts were so far taken up with worldly ideas
that those of being a religious were kept at a distance.
She could no longer bear to hear the name of a nun,
and if by chance any one began to speak of the advantages and blessings of a religious state, she was accustomed to leave the company, lest such discourse should
make any impression on her. This apprehension went
so far almost as to deter her from reading spiritual
books, on account of the remorse and uneasy consequences it sometimes produced. These efforts were too
weak to withstand the impulses of the Divine Spirit.
All the reasons she could find out to persuade herself
of being able to serve Almighty God in the world,
appeared empty and insignificant when compared with
the many perfections of a religious state. All her
precautions to prevent these pious thoughts from entering into her mind were in vain, they had already full

---

[1] [This sister's name was Elisabeth, and she took the name of Ursula
in religion. She was fourteen months younger than Margaret, having
been born February 14, 162$\frac{6}{7}$.]

possession. Moreover, the last recommendation of her dying grandmother seemed still to sound in her ears, so that she thought her spirit haunted her. This filled her with new perplexities and extreme fear, which being unusual, she was much ashamed that it should be perceived by others. Nevertheless, she durst not be anywhere alone; and, when in company, although of such as were highly pleasing to her inclination, she often found herself suddenly disgusted and dissatisfied without being able to give any reason for it.

On one of these occasions she was so overpowered, that she hastily withdrew herself, and went into the garden, there to give scope to her tears and vent her affliction. Her oppressed mind was at once agitated with a hundred thoughts, and a constant wish to find out something that might make her easy was what interrupted her desolate sighs. In this condition, many projects presented themselves, some seemingly indifferent, others less so. The most innocent, as it then appeared to her, was to divert herself in reading idle books, which she had some thoughts of doing, when behold, the Mother of Mercy, the ever Blessed Virgin Mary, vouchsafed to comfort this her adopted child, and in a seasonable time to reward her many devotions towards her with a visible apparition, attended by St. Teresa, saying: 'My child, if you will be happy, follow your first vocation—St. Teresa will help you.' She was startled and amazed at the novelty of this vision, which, although it passed in an instant, she could not doubt was real; for from that moment she seemed quite like another person. All those clouds of worldly affections were dissipated, her mind was freed from its vain alarms, and an interior peace ensued, she found her former sentiments, vigour, and resolutions renewed, and thought only how she might put them in execution.

Had she followed courageously these first steps, and sought advice therein, it would have been more to her advantage, for her backwardness in manifesting what had happened became a stumbling block to her designs. She kept all to herself for upwards of two months, waiting for a proper occasion to declare it. During which time the common enemy of all good was not failing to renew his wonted attacks, by laying before her many apparent difficulties, which being aggravated by some pusillanimous thoughts, greatly slackened her proceedings in this happy enterprize. One great thing was, how to disengage herself from her usual company and conversation without rendering herself particular and liable to strange remarks, especially if she gave no reason for it. Another obstacle arose from the consideration of the many austerities of a religious life, fasting, mortification, self-denial, and other hardships came all at once to her mind. Silence and retirement had a very lonesome and melancholy prospect. But what made the most impression on her was the thought of parting with her sister, Ursula, who she supposed would remain in the world. The remembrance of her former promise to her, which she must now break, brought her to the fierce trial, the thoughts of that last adieu shook her strongest resolutions. In this wavering condition, as she entered the chapel one day to acquit herself of her usual devotions, our Blessed Lady appeared again to her, and commanded her to make known what had passed to her confessor, and then to inform her sister of her resolution, assuring her that a religious state was equally fit for both.

Margaret, struck with her confusion and sense of her own weakness and inconstancy, demurred now no longer to comply with these celestial admonitions. She repaired immediately to her confessor and declared to him all that had befallen her; she communicated to her sister her present intentions, and the assurance she had from our Blessed Lady that a religious profession was also required of her. What greatly astonished her was to find that Ursula made no particular difficulty or objection to the proposals, but seemed willing to engage herself in the same state of life which she had resolved upon. This facility gave occasion to further inquiries, and these again to a thorough opening of themselves to each other, by which, finding their sentiments and proceedings to have been in many things the same, they mutually congratulated one another on this happy event, which set them quite at liberty and freed them from all restraint. Their former union and friendship became as it were cemented by a more virtuous and lasting bond of reciprocal love and affection, which rendered them ever after inseparable. They concluded, therefore, immediately to send for Father Platus' book, treating of the happiness of a religious state, which Ursula had some years before caused to be put out of the way, not to be tempted with.

By this and other proceedings their design was soon published, nor did they any longer seek to make a secret of it. Their chief concern being to meet with some speedy occasion to put it securely in execution, which by several accidents was put off a whole year, so as to give occasion to new trials. Margaret's person, carriage, conversation, and other accomplishments had made such an impression on some that they began to make proposals of marriage, and left no means untried to prevent her undertaking. One in particular, who thought his pretensions could meet with no refusal, finding all his artifices unaffected, carried his passion so far as to make use of charms, of which she felt the effects for many years after, being frequently assaulted by most violent temptations which caused her unaccountable sufferings. During this said delay she applied herself much to prayer, mortification, and other austerities, in which guiding herself more by her own fervour than proper advice, she sometimes greatly exceeded : such was the sense of her great ingratitude and past infidelity to Almighty God in resisting so long her vocation, that it was always before her and prompted her to a most severe and rigid repentance ; whilst the great favour she had received in the garden, by which she clearly saw all the helps and advantages she had received from Him moved her to the most affectionate acknowledgment of His goodness, which went on increasing at the remembrance of the many occasions she had thrown herself into, and by His grace had been mercifully preserved from, grievous offences. Here we may note, that although her gay and lively disposition led her into pastimes and diversions, they were always such as are looked upon as innocent and harmless, and no way misbecoming a young lady of her condition. But as they had been many ways instrumental towards the rejecting her vocation, and deluded her so far as to desire Almighty God to withdraw it from her, they became now the constant object of her grief and affliction. These pious reflections, and the disgust she had to all that was worldly, grew so familiar to her, that even in the midst of company, which she could not always avoid, she continually found a particular attraction to the divine presence of God in her heart, and such tender sensible feelings of Him that she could hardly dissemble it. Thus she went on, preparing herself for the great sacrifice which she was shortly to make, trampling under foot all vanity and worldly expectations, despising the solicitations of friends, and mollifying the grief of her dear mother, and the importunities of her relations, who were yet unwilling to part with her, at least so soon, little reflecting that every delay was a new trouble to her, who, although she had still apprehensions of what she was going to undertake, aspired after nothing more than speedily to accomplish thereby the will of God.

CHAPTER III.

Her journey to Antwerp, and the many dangers she wonderfully escaped in the course of it.

ALL obstacles being at last surmounted, and everything in readiness, Sister Margaret, with her sister Ursula, after tenderly embracing their disconsolate mother, and bidding adieu to their little brothers and sisters, who with the rest of their relations stood bathed in tears, left their native home and paternal habitation, in search of a more happy and lasting one in the land of Carmel. The nation then being miserably involved in civil war, for greater security they were accompanied by their confessor and eldest brother, Master Edward. But their greatest confidence was in the protection of the Blessed Virgin Mary, to whom they committed the chief care of their journey, who on her side did not fail to answer their expectation by an extraordinary assistance. The war here mentioned broke out by mutual hostilities in the year 1640, during the sitting of the Long Parliament, which not only refused to assist the King in reducing the Scotch to their duty, but even declared their rebellious proceedings against him just and advantageous to the nation ; thus it also released by its own authority, all those whom the King had imprisoned, and condemned several of his Majesty's Ministers and officers to occupy their places, and finally declared itself indissoluble till such time as the grievances of the nation were fully redressed.   Charles had long been sensible of the disaffected inclinations of his Parliament, and therefore for some years had kept it from meeting, which gave great umbrage, and his being at last obliged to convoke it made it become insolent.   His Majesty at the same time had rendered himself odious to the people by his own great zeal for the uniformity of litur- gies and for supporting the authority of the bishops in opposition to the Presbyterian party, which would not hear of either.   In these circumstances he found himself greatly distressed, yet was resolved to maintain his authority and reduce the Parliament to reason by force of arms. The want of subsidies seemed the greatest obstacle. This was, however, supplied by several coun- ties, towns, and others of his loyal subjects, who declared themselves in his favour, and enabled him to take the field with a promising appearance.   But the Parliament- arians, who on their side had been equally vigilant and active, being also prepared, he foresaw nothing could be concluded without much effusion of blood, which made such an impression on his mind as showed him to be a true father to his people and moved him again to propose and listen to conditions of an accommodation, till, finding all mild means ineffectual, his goodness abused and imposed upon, he was necessitated to have recourse to his first resolutions, which gave occasion to many battles that were carried on with great vigour and various success for upwards of nine years, till the King, who had generally the misfortune to lose all that was decisive, fell at length into the hands of his enemies and came to the tragical end of being beheaded on a scaffold by a cabal of some mean rebellious subjects.

At the height of this general fermentation it was that these two courageous young ladies began their journey. It had been an occasion of more than usual company at home, and was no less a just cause of fear for them whilst abroad, had not their zeal and resolution exceeded their sex. After having passed through many dangers they arrived at Weymouth, a seaport town in the county of Dorsetshire, looked upon at that time as the most convenient for their taking shipping, on account of its remaining faithful to the King. For such as were in the interests or subject of the Parliament had general orders to stop all passengers, so that the greatest forecast and precaution was necessary to avoid meeting with any of this party, to whom their being Catholics would have rendered them more suspected. Many narrow escapes made Margaret and her companions think themselves more happy in their present apparent security, which in reality was only the beginning of danger. For whilst they were waiting for a ship the town was surrounded by the Parliament army, which immediately cut off all communication with the sea. The news of this filled them all with a general consternation, not knowing now what course to aim at. However, after some deliberation most of them resolved to return back and put themselves under the protection of a loyal company of horse commanded by Lord Wardour,[1] which was posted here to escort the Queen as far as Exeter. This seemed chiefly advisable for Master Edward, since it might have cost him both his estate and life to have been found there. But as it was also attended with difficulties it could not be so soon put in execution.

In this interim Margaret could not hear of going

---

[1] [Lord Arundell of Wardour. This was the second lord, who was wounded in the royal cause at Lansdown and afterwards at Oxford. He died May 19, 1648.]

back, and used all her endeavours by tears and entreaties
to dissuade them from this enterprize, in which she had
the good luck to prevail. For, seeing all sides hazardous
and uncertain which to take for the best, as people in
a desperate case, they left her to decide her lot. Upon
which she desired them to join her in saying our Lady's
Litany, and then to act accordingly as they felt themselves inspired. Meantime secret intelligence came of
a loyal frigate that lay a good distance from the town
and was to set sail in the night with despatches for
Holland. This immediately determined them to make
use of the occasion and to engage themselves as passengers. So soon therefore as the night was a little
advanced, they set off from their inn to go to the ship,
full of fears and repeated alarms, the whole town being
then in an uproar. They saw some as they went along
the streets abused and tossed about by the rabble, and
others seized and detained by the guards, whilst to their
great astonishment they were permitted to walk on peaceably without the least molestation till they came to the
boat which was to carry them to the vessel. Here a
sentinel who was posted not far off hailed them, and
after the usual repetitions of 'Who's there?' offered to
shoot, but could not get his musket to take fire, although
he tried a second and third time, at which being struck,
he bid them go in God's name, for He was surely with
them, otherwise they had perished. Having cleared all
these dangers, they got safely to the frigate, where they
fell to their prayers, beseeching our Lord and His
Blessed Mother to protect them also in passing through
the Parliament fleet that had blocked up the haven ;
which as wonderfully happened, yet not so secretly but
the enemy perceived something, so that towards morning,
looking sharply out, they discovered the vessel at some
leagues distance, and sent two swift frigates after it.

Which the captain seeing, in great perplexity changed his course and put for the coast of France, saying that if they came up with him he should be obliged to fight and rather let himself be sunk than taken.

This caused new terror in all, but was not the only one, for there sprung a leak in the ship, which threatened them with more present danger, it being as much as they could do to keep it above water by pumping. The two sisters, however, in the midst of the confusion were greatly comforted, for being still at their prayers, our Blessed Lady appeared to them and told them they were hers and she would preserve them, which fell out accordingly. For having been chased the whole day in this distressed condition, towards seven o'clock in the evening they got strangely into the Bay of Havre de Grace, where luckily the French fleet lay at anchor, otherwise the Parliament frigates would have forced them again out of the harbour as they had done some others before. All things falling out so unexpectedly made the captain think his voyage more than natural, so that he became inquisitive about his passengers, who, although they kept their disguise, were not less persuaded of the hand of God having been with them than himself.

Sister Margaret and the company having, as we may say, miraculously escaped so many dangers, here determined not to go any more to sea, and therefore began to think and form a plan of the route they should take by land, which, although liable to hardships, was at least safe. But before they set out, as they had been much fatigued and frightened, they stayed some days at Havre to refresh themselves, during which time, going to the Catholic church to hear Mass, and being in some anxiety about their journey, they were again encouraged by our Lady, and assured as she had hitherto assisted them so she would continue to do till the end. Religious houses and dresses being a novelty to them, they were curious to see as much as they could, by which they got into a conversation with a venerable Father of the convent, who after some discourse very much surprised them by saying he knew they were going to be Teresian nuns, which puzzled them much more because they had always been careful to conceal their designs as much as possible, not being willing to be suspected on such an errand. Much the same thing happened to them at Pontoise, when going to see the Teresian monastery there; the Prioress, a person esteemed for her sanctity, and daughter to the Venerable Sister Mary of the Incarnation,[2] since famous for miracles, who received them with all marks of civility and friendship, was very earnest to know whether

---

[2] [This was the famous Madame Acarie, in religion Mary of the Incarnation, who was beatified by Pius VI. in 1791. Under God, she was the principal instrument of the introduction of the Teresian nuns into France. In 1604 she obtained, by means of the Holy See, power to bring to France six Discalced Carmelites from Spain, some of whom had been companions of St. Teresa herself. In 1615 she became herself a Carmelite lay-sister, and died at Pontoise, April 18, 1618. She had three daughters in the Order, whose names in religion were Mary of Jesus, Margaret of the Blessed Sacrament, and Genevieve of St. Bernard. They were all Prioresses in different houses in France, and remarkable for sanctity; but none of them were either religious or Prioresses at Pontoise. The two sisters, Margaret and Elisabeth Mostyn, very probably visited Pontoise to venerate the remains of Sister Mary of the Incarnation, to whom the Queen had erected a magnificent monument, and at whose intercession miracles were often granted. If they also went to Paris on their way to their destination, they might have seen the second of the three daughters of Madame Acarie mentioned above, Margaret of the Blessed Sacrament, as she was then Prioress of one of the houses in Paris. Mary of Jesus had died in 1641, and Genevieve of St. Bernard died this same year, 1644, Prioress at Sens. Margaret of the Blessed Sacrament was a wonderfully favoured soul, and her mother said of her that our Lord had revealed to her that Margaret would be greater in glory in heaven than herself. It must be remembered that the account of this journey of the two sisters Mostyn is not related by themselves, and that Canon Bedingfield may very well have misunderstood what he had been told about their visiting Pontoise and Paris.]

they had no intention to become religious, and freely offered to receive them there without any fortune; which she frequently repeating, they smiling thanked her for her kindness, and made appear as if their inclinations were not fixed on that state of life. But her reverence, not satisfied with their dissimulation, told them she knew very well they would both become religious, and that of her holy Order.

Their journey, although tedious, continued prosperous, as appeared by different accidents, one of which I shall here relate. The two sisters, their confessor, and brother, Master Edward, travelling in a coach in the heat of the day, were much overcome by it, so that Master Edward, to refresh himself, proposed getting out and walking, but the coach not stopping so soon as he desired he tried to jump, in which his foot slipping he fell under the wheel, which ran over him and much alarmed the company, who expected to find him either dead or lamed; when to their great surprise he got up himself, without having suffered the least scar or bruise, or any other damage than a rent in his clothes; for which they all gave praise to our Lord and His Blessed Mother, to Whom they attributed so wonderful an escape. Notwithstanding all these singular marks of God's protection, Margaret and her sister were troubled from time to time with their former apprehensions of the difficulties attending a religious state, and the nearer they approached the town of Antwerp the more these fears preyed upon their spirits, so that they partly dreaded the hour of their arrival. But, as soon as they entered the church of the monastery, whither they went first to return Almighty God thanks for all His mercies to them in rescuing them from such eminent dangers, all their diffidence vanished; they found themselves animated with new courage, and became so solicitous to be admitted amongst the community that

they had scarce patience to wait till their habits and
other things were in readiness for their clothing day.
Meantime they were received and entertained with all
the marks of joy by the religious, particularly the Reverend
Mother Anne of the Ascension, who soon discovered their
interior spirit. Grace and nature, she saw, had plentifully
bestowed their favours upon them, but were exceeded
by the rare endowments of their mind, which might have
caused her not only to love but to respect them greatly,
so that she was no way surprised when their confessor
told her that he had brought her two great treasures, and
that the eldest from her childhood had been singularly
favoured by our Lord and His Blessed Mother, the Virgin
Mary.

This venerable Mother, who had experienced no less
things in herself, and been brought to embrace a religious
state of life in much the same marvellous manner, took
the holy habit and was professed at Mons under the
Spanish Mothers, from whence she accompanied venerable Mother Anne of St. Bartholomew to Antwerp, where
she lived with her for some years, and contracted such
an affection and esteem for her as to be unwilling to
leave her, till she was ordered by obedience to go and
found the monastery of Mechlin, where she was chosen
Superioress and Mistress of Novices. From this employment she was called to make a foundation for the English
at Antwerp, where again she had the pleasure of seeing
her beloved Mother Anne of St. Bartholomew, with whom
from the time she knew her till her death she kept a
sincere and constant correspondence, for she was the
only religious she had ever been able to make free with.
This English monastery was begun by such as had been
brought up under the Spanish Mothers, who had lived
with and received their instructions from St. Teresa herself, and Mother Anne of the Ascension was chosen first

Prioress, in which charge she was continued by re-elections for the space of twenty-six years, till her death.[3] In this time she underwent many troubles and fatigues, and laid in this house such a foundation of perfection and religious observance, according to the spirit of St. Teresa, as has, and will be, famous to future ages, of which the life I am here writing is no small proof.

[3] [Mother Anne of the Ascension was the first Englishwoman who became a Teresian nun, and is the connecting link between the companions of St. Teresa, who began to found houses in Flanders, in 1607, and the English monasteries of Discalced Carmelites. Her family name was Worsley. Her father was attached when very young to the service of Philip II., and followed him to Spain on the death of his wife, Queen Mary of England. There he married a lady of high birth, and afterwards came to reside in Flanders. He had two daughters, both of whom became Carmelites. Mother Anne of the Ascension was the eldest. Her sister was many years younger, and was called in religion Teresa of Jesus Maria. She was the first novice received by Mother Anne at the new English foundation of Antwerp. Mother Anne of the Ascension made many Teresian foundations in Flanders, Holland, and Germany, and was universally venerated and beloved. She was much favoured by our Lord, as is shown by her Life, which exists in manuscript.]

CHAPTER IV.

Her Clothing and Noviceship, during which she is encouraged by her Angel Guardian in the practice of self-denial. She obtains the gift of prayer, and is comforted by an apparition of our Saviour.

HIS Lordship, Gasper Nemius, Bishop of Antwerp, being informed of the arrival of these two young ladies, and acquainted with their intention of becoming religious, was so obliging as to take upon himself the trouble of examining and clothing them, a thing so unusual to him that it was justly looked upon as a particular honour, by which he was pleased to distinguish them. On the feast of St. Laurence, the day appointed for their taking the habit, they were dressed out as is customary for such a solemnity, and adorned with the costly jewels of Lady Catharine Howard and the Countess of Arundel, who attended at the ceremony and led them into the monastery, where they were received and clothed by the venerable Mother Anne of the Ascension, who afterwards declared to many that when she put the blessed habit on to Sister Margaret she felt to herself such an unusual joy and satisfaction as she had never before experienced. This she looked upon to presage some particular good that was to come to the house and to the whole Order by her means.

Although it be the devotion and practice of young ladies who enter into the holy Order of Mount Carmel

to change their names, Sister Margaret, as St. Teresa
and others had done before her, retained her own, which
was sanctified with the title of Jesus, by Whom she had
the happiness on this occasion to be wonderfully favoured.
For, in receiving the Sacred Host from the hands of
the Bishop, she saw our Lord there present, as an Infant
all in glory, but had the simplicity for some time to
think it a privilege belonging to the Bishop as such,
supposing that all whom he communicated partook of the
same blessing, till an innocent mistake made her better
informed. She was also greatly comforted throughout
this ceremony by the visible presence of our Blessed
Lady, whom she always beheld on her right side; which
neither change of posture, nor others that were stirring
about her, were able to intercept or hinder. So that
we need not wonder at Mother Anne of the Ascension
being so particularly moved in the midst of such company, nor at the esteem she expressed for this her dear
novice, whom, as she said, she never looked upon
without receiving some new degree of comfort and
satisfaction. Nothing can express this holy woman's
sentiments better than a letter which she wrote to a
monastery that by her own industry had been lately
founded in Germany, in which, after rejoicing with
them on their prosperity, she says: 'I know no greater
happiness to wish you than two such novices as
I have lately clothed, whom I look upon as my
greatest treasures, because I am confident they have
the spirit of our holy Mother. The eldest is endowed
with such admirable parts and perfections, both of
nature and grace, that she will be able to advance
our Order greatly, which I would not have you look
upon as written by way of compliment, but upon
just and reasonable motives; so that I hope you
will join us in praising our Lord for so singular a

D 26

blessing.' How prophetical these lines were the sequel will show.

Sister Margaret being of a sweet docile temper, easily accommodated herself to those she lived and conversed with. The austerities of the Order at first fell rather hard upon her complexion, which was inclined to be delicate; for naturally she had an antipathy to fish and eggs, and such an aversion to woollen, that the mere handling of it made her flesh creep upon her bones, so that it is easy to guess how she was affected with wearing it. Yet such was her fervour, that far from complaining or showing any uneasiness in these regards, she made appear as if all was according to her inclination, and did not spare herself in the practice of many other self-denials, in which she was much encouraged by her angel guardian. For, in the first month of her noviceship, by chance looking out of her cell window upon an apple tree loaded with green fruit, she fixed her eye upon one fairer than the rest, and felt a longing inclination towards it. But, thinking it an inordinate piece of sensuality, she said within herself: 'I will mortify myself in this for the love of God.'

Upon this immediately her good angel appeared, and gathering it, seemed to turn it into a beautiful crown, assuring her that no action of that kind, however small, should pass with a less reward. By this pious disposition in lesser things she soon became a proficient in greater. Spiritual reading, of which she was always a lover, rendered her familiar with the lives and maxims of the saints, where amongst other things she learned that the way to perfection is mortification: as she, therefore, seriously aimed at the one, so she zealously applied herself to the other, searching always after some occasion to bear in her body the mortification of Jesus. With leave of her Mistress [1] she frequently humbled herself by extraordinary penances. She also exposed herself to the inclemencies of the seasons' heat and cold, never coming so near the fire as to receive any good of it, but only to save appearances. In choir, or in cell, she generally kept herself in some painful posture; and, in regard of diet, commonly chose what was most disgustful, and of that ate but a small quantity. Neither was she less exemplary in point of charity and willingness to assist and prevent, if possible, her sister novices in the most laborious and loathsome employments, which virtue made her looked upon amongst them as a second Magdalene of Pazzi. This fervour, however, gave occasion to many other trials, in which her Mistress of Novices, witness of what passed, prudently exercised her, thereby to discover more thoroughly the spirit from whence all proceeded, and if she could leave herself as easily as her meat; knowing well that the mortification of the will is of more importance than exterior show, which is liable to deceit and illusion. But in these our novice gave evident proofs that she was carried on by the Spirit of God: her patience and humility, like the gold that is purified by the fire, became more and more conspicuous, she cheerfully went through all with a true religious simplicity, taking other people's faults and aspersions upon herself, without the least reply or excuse, as if she had been really guilty. In the midst of this progress, her greatest discouragement was in regard of prayer, in which she found herself so dull, as she says, that she could neither frame to herself any imaginations belonging to the mysteries, or help herself therein by way of discourse, which made her look upon this duty rather a loss of time than of benefit to her.

---

[1] [Mother Margaret of St. Teresa (Downes) was her Mistress, and was Vicaress of the foundation made at Lierre, 1648.]

Yet she continually endeavoured to break through the difficulty, and to stick punctually to her Mistress's directions, oftentimes humbling herself before the Divine Majesty of God, Whom she adored as present to her heart; touching which verity she received much light and more clear knowledge than before. She seemed, at the same time, to hear our Blessed Lord speak to her these words: 'I have established My seat here,' bidding her also to endeavour to recollect herself thus, and behold Him in the most interior of her soul, and to keep this manner of His presence, without afflicting herself with other representations. This appeared to be very evidently required of her by Almighty God, and she found much satisfaction and benefit by it. So that her way of making prayer was to recall the mystery to her mind, and proceed quietly to ruminate upon it as in God in Whom all things are, without framing any imagination belonging to it, there being nothing in her power, for the most part, but to leave herself in the will of God. This was more or less, according to the favour Almighty God was pleased to grant, for when extra-ordinary graces were absent and withdrawn, she was only able to make acts of faith, and spend her time in seeking out means to practise virtue, mortify her passions, and to bear with due resignation the troubles and contradic-tions she met with.

The unexpected death of Venerable Mother Anne of the Ascension[2] had made much impression upon her, so that she stood in need of all her virtue to conform with the consequences. She had a singular esteem and affec-tion for this holy Mother, who was no less dear to the rest of the community, which universally regretted her loss as their greatest misfortune. There being no one in

---

[2] [Mother Anne of the Ascension died December 23, 1644, aged fifty-four years.]

the house that could equal her in the important charge
of Superior, and few or no one but what others made
objections against, gave occasion to some little disunion,
which Margaret easily perceived; and as she herself was
much esteemed and beloved by all, many had the im-
prudence to communicate to her their respective grievances and uneasiness, which went so far in some as
to make appear a very great disgust. This struck our
inexperienced novice to the heart, and made her reflect
that, even in religion, there was danger of falling into
great miseries; and since an accident of this kind had
been able to make such a change, she apprehended it
might also one day be her case to experience the same
melancholy effects. These and other sad thoughts
worked much upon her, neither had she the confidence
or resolution to mention them to any one; within doors
she knew it was unfit, and others were wholly strangers
to her.

Amidst this trouble the time of her profession also
drew near, which altogether made her abound with
many dubious and pusillanimous thoughts. In this
dejected state, prostrate one day before the Blessed
Sacrament in sighs and tears, imploring Almighty God's
assistance for herself and her sister Ursula, who was in
danger, as she thought, of being affected by ill-advice,
our Blessed Lord appeared and comforted her, saying
He would not forsake her, but she must know that
Heaven suffered violence, and was not gained at an easy
rate; that what had happened was permitted for a greater
good, and was no prejudice to the house, in which He
should still be well served, nor any great motive to make
her quit her vocation; that she should therefore confide
in Him, and make so free with her confessor as to let
him know her difficulties. This last article she had
some repugnance to, yet she faithfully complied, and

declared all her doubts, in which she received great
satisfaction, being assured by him that her vocation was
sure, being confirmed by so many favours was un-
questionable, and as to the rest her fears would preserve her from those apprehended evils, if she only
took care to keep herself disengaged from all particular
attachments, and in a due conformity to the will of God,
in which religious people sometimes forget themselves,
and thereby give occasion to the common enemy to
tempt and deceive them.

These singular favours, and the advantageous parts
we discover in this fervent novice, will be greatly confirmed and heightened, if we consider the contemptible
and low opinion she had of her own person and proceedings, treating herself as the meanest of the house,
as one unapt to learn the duties of a religious state,
of which she feared she should be thought unworthy.
This appeared particularly when the time came for her
admission by votes, being then in great concern lest
the community should reject her, on account of her many
defects and imperfections. But as she had the happiness to be the only one who could discern them, she
was unanimously received by the religious, who were
entirely satisfied with her performances and behaviour;
so that having thus laudably accomplished the year of
her probation, she was admitted to her profession, which
she made at the age of twenty, in the hands of the
Reverend Mother Anne of St. Austin, on St. Clare's day,
the 12th of August, 1645.

CHAPTER V.

Her Profession, and her interior disposition after-
wards. Her mortifications, and a dangerous sickness,
of which she is miraculously cured.

BEING thus happily enrolled amongst the spouses of
Jesus Christ, she began to run in the odour of His
sweetness. 'A bundle of myrrh my Beloved is to me,
I sought for Him and could not find Him.' This she
experienced at her profession, which she performed with
many fears and little or no sensible devotion, but with
an heroic resignation of herself into the hands of God,
to suffer and endure whatsoever He should please to
impose upon her.

After this she had the comfort of our Blessed Lady's
presence who greatly encouraged her, assuring her that
her sins were now forgiven her, and that by making this
great sacrifice she had completed the will of God, and
deserved her special protection, which she and her sister
Ursula should always enjoy. This favour was again
renewed presently after Communion, when our Blessed
Lady appearing, sweetly admonished her to render herself up to her as her slave, by a voluntary renunciation
to all satisfaction in anything she did, giving her at
the same time to understand that no creature could
imagine the high reward those should have who cheerfully offered themselves to serve her in this humbling
way.

She was much struck at the proposal, yet, as she thought, made the same oblation of herself, although with great anxiety; for reflecting on her own weakness in lesser matters, she apprehended she should never be able to comply with so arduous a task. But our Lady soon dissipated her fears, by assuring her that if she only endeavoured to go on with humility and confidence, when she least looked for it, she herself would furnish her with strength sufficient, whilst at the same time if she did but study the way of the Cross and sufferings, by striving to master her lesser imperfections and difficulties, she would enable herself by degrees to overcome greater. From this time in all she does or desires she has experienced a want of satisfaction, so that when anything of importance happens to her, this double sacrifice she has made of herself to our Lord and His Blessed Mother immediately comes to her mind, by which patience and love of sufferings seem to be required of her. And if at any time she shuns any occasion of self-denial or mortification, or seeks her own satisfaction, she finds such a reprehension within herself, that whether she will or no, she cannot rest, but is forced to beg more patience and more sufferings. Once it happened that something being spoken of her that troubled her very much, she intended to say something of that person equally to their disadvantage, being something transported with passion: but suddenly she heard a voice, which said, 'You are not despised as I have been,' and though she saw nothing, the sufferings of our Lord were in a lively manner represented to her mind, and the fault she had committed appeared very clear, which wrought so good an effect in her soul, that she has oftentimes since taken content in being thus slighted, and found herself greatly strengthened in her endeavours to behave the most obligingly to those she conceived least liked her proceedings. This as she said was in little things, for she knows not how it would have been in greater, which never offered themselves: but she still finds in herself a will and desire to suffer, and put up with all kind of humiliations, although both now and heretofore, when Almighty God seems to leave her to herself, she falls into divers miseries and pusillanimities, especially in times of little bodily indisposition; for when she is vehemently sick, she finds herself most particularly favoured with a desire to suffer.

She also found a great desire to frequent the holy Sacraments, not so much for her own satisfaction, as on account of the strengthening graces she experienced they left in her soul, so as to enable her with alacrity to accept of all with a true conformity to the will of God, and to overcome the tediousness and pusillanimities above mentioned. Yet, notwithstanding this benefit, were she not advised to communicate often, her sins and imperfect life would deter her from it, especially when she finds herself in a heavy dry humour. It has also pleased Almighty God to give her sometimes such a particular knowledge of His greatness in the Blessed Sacrament, of which we shall speak in its place, that although she ardently desired to receive Him, she greatly apprehended to approach His heavenly table, on account of the extreme reverence and respect to which she was moved, till His goodness did show itself in a more than ordinary manner, and thereby made her understand how so poor a creature as she was permitted to treat with His Divine Majesty. The knowledge of which, and that her whole dependence is upon so good a God, has been of great help to her, and lets her clearly see that of herself she is more poor and miserable than any creature, and that if she be saved, it must be through the singular mercy of Almighty God. This reflection often causes in her a certain interior joy, because she is certain that all those that know her miseries, and see how great an object of His mercy she is, will be moved to love and adore His infinite goodness the more.

She often on these occasions finds herself so much recollected, and her soul in such quiet and solitude, that she is only able to give herself up to be disposed of by Almighty God, and to neglect what impertinent fancies may arise; which when our Lord is pleased thus to favour her, she finds more advantageous than vocal prayers, or other endeavours to entertain Him; for though she thinks not upon any particular virtue, nor is able to give an account of what passes, yet she finds herself much more disposed to the practice of good works than at other times; and the means to overcome her passions are more clear to her, than by many other considerations, so that frequently the whole time of preparation, or thanksgiving, is past before she is aware of it; which gave her scruples of omitting her ordinary prayers. She frequently also found herself moved and excited to perform several sorts of penances, so that besides those of the Order, in which she seldom failed, she was accustomed daily to take a discipline, or wear a chain for some hours. On Friday nights, when she could get leave to sit up, she made three or four hours prayer on the Passion upon her knees, and when leave was refused her, she used to compose her bed in such a manner as not to be able to sleep, and thereby oblige herself every time the clock struck to meditate as long as she could upon the said sacred Passion. She often mortified herself in kneeling in some painful posture, especially in the choir, hoping such penances would satisfy for the many deficiencies in her prayers. So likewise in her cell she would place herself in some cramped situation, and though never so weary, not change it until the bell rang to some act of community; in which things she was so indiscreet, as to make no scruple of prolonging or augmenting these, or any other invented penances, without letting any one know of them. In point of diet she always mortified herself as much as circumstances would allow, making appear as if she liked that the best which she fancied the least and was most disgustful to her; besides, she was so sparing in it, that for the most part her whole day's diet was only a couple of eggs, which she always ate with great aversion.

To contradict her fearful inclination, she went every night after Compline into the dead-cellar alone, where she performed several penances and devotions for the poor souls in Purgatory. She exposed herself day and night, as much as she could, to the inclemency of the season, heat and cold, and never came near the fire only by way of formality to save appearances. If she found any one bore more affection to her than another, she would seem insensible towards them, and say ridiculous things to them, that so they might less esteem her. Whilst she thus rigorously treated herself our Lord was pleased to try her in another way: for some time after her profession she fell into a violent sickness, which was attended with a continual fever for upwards of twelve days, without receiving any help from the most experienced doctors, who after having ineffectually tried various remedies gave her up as incurable, which occasioned great concern in the community, by whom she was generally beloved, and looked upon as a person of great expectation. In the midst of this alarm, one of the religious bethought her of a picture they had in the house, which Reverend Father Morse going to martyrdom took out of his breviary, and sent to the Prioress of Antwerp Monastery by a friend that was near him saying: 'Remember me to those good Religious, and tell them when I come to Heaven, whatsoever they shall ask of me, if it be pleasing to God and for their good, I will obtain it for them.' Upon which the whole community assembled, and with great confidence calling upon the holy martyr, laid the said picture upon the sick person's breast, and having some of his blood, gave her a little of it mingled with wine to take inwardly; which was no sooner done but she found herself wonderfully eased, and when the doctor came he found her without fever and out of danger, to his great surprise, for he said he expected nothing less than to have found her dead.

This miraculous recovery gave great satisfaction to the community, but proved a heavy cross to Sister Margaret. She was so racked and weakened by the violent remedies they had forced upon her, that she never regained her strength and health, but from this time, in the flower of her age, became subject to all sorts of infirmities, having no part of her without a particular pain, especially in her head, which was in a manner never free. Her stomach was also grown so weak, that for a long time after she could not digest anything, not so much as the quantity of an egg, but vomited instantly, so that her whole sustenance for many months was only raw orange-peel. Yet, as soon as she got about, she was the first at all religious duties, and could not endure to be dispensed from the rigours of the Order, nor from any acts of community, in which she often forced herself beyond her strength.

CHAPTER VI.

Sister Margaret made Mistress of the Infirmary, in which charge she is wonderfully helped by her angel guardian. An apparition of a soul in Purgatory.

THE charge of Infirmarian was at this time of great importance, there being upwards of forty religious, and frequently many of them sick, which required a person of no less charity and sweetness than Sister Margaret, who on this occasion fully answered the opinion each one had of her abilities and tenderness. Amongst others there was one blind, in a deep consumption, who by the vomiting of corrupted matter was so insupportable that it was as much as any one could do to remain with her. This poor creature was Margaret's chief care. She constantly cherished and tended her, with all the love and charity imaginable, washing with her own hands her dirty linen, and performing all other disgustful things about her with such cheerfulness and alacrity, as if she had no feeling of it, whilst at the same time she had an interior aversion and almost a horror of coming near her, for her infirmities had also hardened her humour, which was not naturally the most agreeable. Being once much pressed with temptations of this kind, and having some thoughts that it was a slavery to be confined to such a person, Margaret presently saw her angel guardian, who mildly reprehended her, saying, if she could not perform such charitable offices for her fellow-creatures, he would do

them for her, since he esteemed it an honour to serve
the spouses of Christ, and did she herself but know the
beauty of that poor creature's soul, she would think it
the greatest blessing on earth to be near her. Such was
the effect of the apparition, and so great the change it
wrought in her, that afterwards she had a comfort in
performing difficult things for her, yea, those that before
she abhorred to name were now most grateful to her, so
that henceforth she attended her night and day till her
death, and ever after retained a veneration for her,
having been afterwards assured by our Blessed Lady that
Sister Dorothy was in great glory, far above divers others
who were held in greater esteem of sanctity; 'for you
must know,' said the sacred Virgin, 'that those who
are visited with afflictions, and thereby obliged to lead a
hidden and contemptible life, if they make but a right
use of it, as she did, are great in the court of
Heaven.'

Oftentimes, both then and since, her good angel
admonished her of deficiencies in point of observance,
and also when she was dilatory in putting away distractions, which may convince us of the attention these
heavenly spirits have towards us, and the regard they
have for the minutest things which concern regular and
pious practices; since, as she says, having twice or thrice
forgotten to say the *Ave Maria*, she heard it repeated by
her guardian angel, who assured her such devotions
performed with a spirit of obedience were more grateful
and acceptable to God than great penances, or other
extraordinary works. Some time after this, upon an
Ascension Eve, at night, having been during the day
employed, and much fatigued, in serving the sick, she
was sent to her cell to take her rest, where she had not
been long before she suddenly heard herself called upon
by her worldly name, 'Miss Mostyn.' As she knew all

the sisters were in choir, she was much frightened, but after some little consideration, having blessed herself with the sign of the Cross, she rose up, went and opened her door to see if there was any one about that wanted her; where finding all quiet, and nothing to be seen, she returned again to her bed, in which she had scarce composed herself when she heard her religious name twice repeated most distinctly. This gave her new uneasiness. However, she endeavoured to pacify herself, thinking it might be only apprehension; thus she let it pass on without saying anything, till at length it grew so constant that she was every night wakened and frightened, sometimes by noises in her cell, sometimes by rustling of papers, and sometimes a cold air would seem to blow upon her, as sensibly as if one had made use of a pair of bellows, but when these disturbances were past all her fear immediately ceased, which made the thing appear more wonderful. Having, therefore, casually spoken of it to some of the religious, they advised her to speak of it to the Reverend Mother, which she did, who thereupon ordered her to change her cell, and appointed some religious to watch by her at night; yet still about the same hour she was awakened and frightened as usual. Upon this the Reverend Mother consulted the Confessor, who, after he had informed himself of all the circumstances, gave orders that she should speak to the spirit, for he was confirmed that it must needs be more than fancy. For greater security, and to diminish her apprehension, she was laid in the upper choir before the Blessed Sacrament, and the Subprioress Margaret of St. Teresa, afterwards Mother Prioress at Lierre, being looked upon as one of the most courageous, was appointed to watch by her, accompanied by another sister, and to give her the words, lest through fright she of herself should forget them. When the time came, which was always between twelve and one, she was suddenly awakened, according to custom, trembling with fear; yet after a little pause she was able to say the words after the Subprioress, which were these : "In the name of God, if you have leave, show what you would have." And presently was represented unto her a book with her own handwriting in it, and signed with her name, which made the whole story clear in an instant; for in the twinkling of an eye she was gone.

This spirit was a maidservant of her grandmother, that had waited upon Sister Margaret, and died three or four years before she came over to be religious. She was of a very melancholy humour, and scrupulous, but had an extraordinary genius in dressing ladies according to the mode, which gave occasion to endless scruples and difficulties when she had done. Having once spent much time in dressing her mistress, who was then to go abroad, a Father of the Society who lived in the house coming into the chamber, she began to complain to him, and lay out her grievances. But he being desirous to have her mistress speedily with him, without listening further to her ditty told her if she would only make haste he would pray her out of Purgatory, and promised her three Masses, which she writ down, and he signed it, at the beginning of her little English prayer-book. This, when it was represented to Sister Margaret, was dashed out, and only her promise was there clearly to be read, which she had inconsiderately made for her maid, who at the same time took up a pair of beads of fifteen tens, and desired her to say them for her when she was dead. She replied, "Make but an end of dressing me, and I will say them fifteen times for you," which the maid also writing down, she immediately signed, but never had more thought of her promise till she saw the book again in the manner above mentioned. Whereupon she carefully in all haste fulfilled her promise of saying the rosary fifteen times. The night following, as in a dream, she saw again this servant-maid, who seemed to be under a curious green apple tree, and appeared as green as the tree itself, where making a low bow in sign of thanks, she grew instantly white, and so vanished. The explication of this last extraordinary sort of apparition, as far as one can conjecture, may be attributed to the maid's indiscretion in eating green fruit, for the doctors were of opinion that she killed herself by it.

NOTE I.

Extract from a paper of Resolutions by Mother Margaret when at Antwerp.

' I WILL endeavour to serve Christ our Lord in the sick (she was Infirmarian), doing all things concerning them in the same manner as I would do actually to the person of our Blessed Lord ; since I have used this practice I have found much benefit, for by knowing how easily I am effused,[1] and apt to grow cold in spiritual things, and having difficulty in conversing with some persons and much inclination to others, I was much troubled, fearing that this office would be of much hurt and absolute disadvantage to my soul, and being so much distracted that passing by the Blessed Sacrament I forgot to make any reverence or adoration according to our custom. I was suddenly struck with fear and as though I had been asked what I meant, and I kneeling down, our Blessed Lord seemed to be present and bid me 'to look upon Him, and all things would be easy to me, that He had brought me hither to serve *Him only and to love Him only*, and that I must not incline to whom I have inclination or contradiction, but behold them all in Him. This passed presently away, but when I recollect myself never so little,

---

[1] Poured out exteriorly.

or am in presence of the Blessed Sacrament, my soul is humbled even to nothing in the presence of God, yet, though unworthy, moved to a great admiration of His mercies and goodness to me, and a sincere desire to please Him. When I am in presence of the Blessed Sacrament ever since this time, I see clearly my faults and infidelities, and this not with any devotion, for that I seldom have, except sometimes when I communicate, or of late when I have confessed ; and also I have never since this time had any difficulty that I could not overcome in performing this office, nor difference of persons, but all are alike dear to me in my care. To the best that I know of myself I have not lost by this occasion,[2] for whether I will or no I find myself carry a reverence to the Sacred Humanity of Christ our Lord in all persons, and this causes recollection in me as long as it lasts.' So far Sister Margaret's own words ; and then she continues to say how this favour of specially feeling this recollection is obscured if she commits any infidelity, and proportionably to its being great or less, and then concludes this part of her resolutions thus, ' But I will never cease to confide in His mercies, and only desire that I may not offend His Divine Majesty, and then to be disposed of as His will shall ordain.'

Mother Margaret in the same paper speaks as having found by her own experience, that oftentimes when we are in great temptations, and great danger of offending God, yet we are *more secure* than when we are tempted to curiosity in small things, silence, custody of eyes, which we look on as trifling imperfections, but which are great hindrances to our spiritual advancement, and hurt us more often, for we easily yield to them, than those to us more apparent sins and dangers.

[2] Of being Infirmarian.

CHAPTER VII.

She is comforted in dejection, is forewarned of a cross, which she afterwards understands to be her leaving Antwerp to come to the new Foundation of Lierre, where she is again visited with a dangerous sickness.

IT was Sister Margaret's ordinary custom to spend the half hour between Compline and Matins in meditating upon the Prodigal Son, to which Gospel she had a particular devotion, as it excited her to acts of humility. However, being once in a dry dejected humour, in which all that she did appeared as though done through human respect and vanity, she thought it would be much better to humble herself in fact, by leaving off all particular devotions, and so let each one see what a poor creature she was, who had hitherto not only deceived herself and others, but even Almighty God Himself. She resolved, therefore, to begin with this meditation of the Prodigal Son; but in going out of the choir she heard distinctly these words—'Go on with your devotion, and teach it to your sister Ursula, for it is very pleasing to Me to be deceived by such humble prayers.' Startled at these words, which she understood came from our Lord, she returned to her place, where she was assured so many humble acts helped to satisfy for her many imperfections, which made her careful afterwards to continue this pious practice.

Upon St. Teresa's eve, almost a year before the foundation of Lierre began, being much oppressed with her usual apprehensions and fears, sometimes for herself and sometimes for her sister, our Blessed Lady appeared to her, accompanied by St. Teresa, who seemed to require of the Virgin Mother of God that she should bring to effect what she had proposed to do and to accomplish by them, which the sacred Virgin graciously promised, saying they were both under her protection, and would do well, thus leaving Sister Margaret comforted for the time, but in a great uncertainty what this might mean. Her apprehensions were renewed the Good Friday following, when praying according to her custom before a certain crucifix, to which she had a particular devotion, she was suddenly forewarned of a very difficult cross she would meet with, to which she should now begin to resign herself. As she could no way conjecture what this cross might prove to be, she was in new concern lest something or other should go amiss with her or her sister.

She continued in this suspense for some time, till one day after Communion our Lady appearing to her let her understand that this cross was to be her leaving Antwerp to go to a new Foundation, concerning which the Prioress would soon speak to her, and charged her to offer herself to be of the number of this holy colony. Some time after the Reverend Mother, who found a difficulty to meet with such as were willing to go, amongst others called for Sister Margaret, and laid open to her the whole affair, which had hitherto been a secret, upon which she immediately made use of the occasion, and presented herself, as she had been commanded by our Lady, though with great reluctance and violence to her inclination; to which the Reverend Mother replied that such was not her meaning, but she wished she would endeavour to persuade her sister Ursula to it, for she thought it would be good and proper for her. To which Sister Margaret answered, that she knew full well her sister would never agree to be separated from her; however, as her Reverence desired it, she would not fail to propose it to her.

Meantime she again consulted the whole affair with her confessor, Father Andrew White, a very holy man, whom she found greatly changed in his sentiments, for in place of being against her removal, as he had a little before signified, he now assured her it was the will of God, and would be greatly to His honour and her own good to go to the Foundation, which he said he had understood in time of Mass. He told her also of many things that had passed in her soul, and others she would in time experience, which she had found to be true, and said if she were but humble and free with her confessor there would be no danger of her being deceived. All this gave her a better heart, and diminished in part the reluctance she had to quit her mother-monastery, but she was much perplexed how she should bring things about with her sister, to whom she had difficulty in opening them, not knowing what the effect would be, till our Blessed Lady, after her accustomed manner, appeared unto her, and confirmed all that her confessor had said; adding that Lierre was the directed way for her to Heaven, no less than for her sister, whom she might assure in her name, that it would be a house wholly dedicated to her service.

In consequence of this, informing her sister Ursula of what had passed, and repeating to her the above-said words of our Lady, Ursula was immediately reminded of a vision she herself had also had on St. Teresa's eve in time of the *Te Deum*, when our Blessed Lady appearing reprehended her for a certain conversation she kept with

one of the religious, and having that night spoken too
freely with her, which she ordered her to confess before
she went to Communion, and said she might prepare
herself to be removed to another house, where she
should be well served by her. The reflection of this
made her beyond expectation willing, upon condition
she might have Margaret's company, to which Sister
Margaret could give no answer till she had informed the
Reverend Mother Prioress, who accepted of their proffer,
but commanded them to say nothing of it, which was
almost as great a mortification to her as leaving the
monastery, not being able to mention or take notice of
it to some particular persons, whom she knew would be
most sensible of her departure, which was to be in so
sudden a manner as only must be published three days
beforehand. This was so sensible to her that she could
not entirely dissemble it, not being able to refrain from
tears as often as she came into their company, which
made them sometimes ask her if they had been the
occasion of her affliction, little thinking of her removal
to the new Foundation. However, these affections and
other repugnances she had to leave the community, insensibly diminished by prayer and serious consideration,
so that when the names were publicly read of those who
were to go to this Foundation, she found her difficulties
to leave her friends not so great as she had imagined,
but became rather ashamed of her seeming insensibility,
not expressing the least trouble to leave those who were
the most solicitous, out of kindness for her, to keep her
amongst them, not listening to any reasons they could
allege to dissuade her from abandoning her mother-
house.

She had scarce been a full month at Lierre before she
was confined to her bed by a violent fever, which continued many weeks without ever going off, and brought

her to such a degree of weakness that the doctors apprehended that she would not be able to get through it,
which had doubtless proved too true if she had not been
wonderfully assisted by our Blessed Lady, through whose
means, as she was afterwards assured, she unexpectedly
recovered. In the beginning of the Foundation there
was no convenience to treat so dangerous a sickness,
where there was want of all things for that purpose in
every kind, which put the religious to great distress, and
caused no less concern amongst those of their mother-
house of Antwerp, by whom her departure was greatly
regretted, having been in general against their will. As
they were, therefore, desirous to have her back again,
they thought this a fair occasion, and with that view
represented to Superiors her uncomfortable and neces-
sitous situation, which could not at that time be other
ways relieved than by her return, for which they earnestly
solicited. But Sister Margaret could not be brought to
accept of their kindness, saying, with many tears, 'Why
do our dear Sisters regard so poor a creature? if I die it
imports little where; and for convenience, I have more
than I desire. Nothing grieves me but the trouble I
give. I hope, for our dear Lord's sake, you will have
patience with me, and then I can affirm all sufferings are
a pleasure to me.' This, indeed, manifestly appeared
to each one, for all acknowledged that her patience and
edifying behaviour rendered it a pleasure to be about
her, especially to hear her speak of spiritual things, for
she ever held the world in great contempt, whilst the
joy and satisfaction she took in sufferings was so great
that she has been oftentimes heard to say, that to love
God and not to delight in sufferings and afflictions for
His sake seemed impossible.

NOTE II.

From the account of the foundation of the English Discalced Carmelites in the City of Lierre.

THE English Monastery of Antwerp, notwithstanding the foundations to which it had given birth, still increasing in number, so as not only to exceed that appointed by our holy Mother, but also the convenience for lodging them, began again to look out for a convenient place, wherein to establish a new monastery. After some deliberation the city of Lierre was providentially pitched upon as the most proper, and Mother Margaret of St. Teresa (Downes) as the most capable to head so great an undertaking, and therefore was secretly designed to be the future Vicaress of it. She was a woman of great prudence and virtue, and had formerly been employed in such and other important affairs, which rendered her able to form a just notion of what was most necessary in them ; that is, virtuous and exemplary religious.

This was her first care ; and though she could not fail of being abundantly provided in a community so renowned for sanctity, yet she was no sooner informed of her destiny than she began to solicit Superiors, to let the two sisters Margaret of Jesus and Ursula of All Saints be amongst the number of those who were to accompany her. Their virtues rendered them conspicuous in the midst of virtue ; and although young, their humility and other good qualities moved all to presage they would prove great supports and promoters of St. Teresa's spirit and Constitutions ; which was the opinion venerable Mother Anne of the Ascension had of them even during their noviceship. For writing to a monastery of the Order lately established, she said, the greatest blessing she could wish them was, to have two such novices as she had lately clothed, whom she looked upon as sent by Almighty God to procure some particular good to the Order.

They were of the noble and religious family of the Mostyns, and seemed chosen by Heaven to promote and sanctify this foundation. They were unwilling at first to quit their mother-house, and the community was more so to part with them, but afterwards knowing it to be the will of God, both sides made Him an agreeable sacrifice of their respective interests.

Things being in this favourable disposition within the monastery, and the city of Lierre fixed on, as the properest place, the affair was represented to his lordship the Bishop of Antwerp, at that time Gaspar Nemius, who having maturely informed himself of all its circumstances, was no less satisfied than zealous to have it put in execution, being convinced he should thereby procure to his diocese another most valuable treasure. He, therefore, used all his interest for to accomplish so laudable a work, and after having consulted his Highness the Archduke Leopold, then Governor of these countries, without whose permission nothing of that nature could be undertaken, on account of the King's edicts forbidding all new establishments of religious, and having obtained from him not only a license thereto, but also a recommendation in their favour to the clergy and magistrates of the town, his lordship communicated the same to them by a letter, wherein he represented in the most tender expressions the necessity of so many young ladies, who had sacrificed their ease and fortunes for the sake of religion, and chose a voluntary exile from their country and friends, so as to be more at liberty to serve Almighty God in the most perfect observance of a religious profession ; concluding with the inconveniences they were put to for want of a proper settlement, which was the chief object of his petition, not doubting but they would grant it ; since such a charitable action, as giving refuge to these pious exiles, could not fail to draw down God's blessing and protection over them.

The Reformed Order of Carmel was then in such repute in these countries, that provided they had but license from the Court, most towns were ready to receive them with open arms, each thinking it a happiness to have a house thereof within their walls. Such were the dispositions of the citizens of Lierre, who readily acquiesced in the pious remonstrances of their virtuous prelate, and assured him they were willing to admit the said religious, upon condition, however, that they should not be any ways burthensome to the town by begging, or any ways molest the burghers thereof by their buildings or enclosure. These conditions being accepted of, they were drawn up in proper form, signed and sealed and given to the religious as a security for their admittance, after having been registered in the town's books.

There might have been some difficulty or retardment for want of a confessor had not Providence interfered ; for it accidently happened that there was an English priest at that time passing Antwerp, of whom his lordship the Bishop being informed sent for him, and desired him to accompany in that quality these good religious to their new settlement. At first he made some difficulty to accept of the charge, but being more fully informed of their circumstances and looking upon them as professed servants of the Blessed Virgin, to whom he had a particular devotion, he accepted of his lordship's proposal. This priest who might justly be called venerable, was Mr. Edmund Bedingfield, distinguished by his birth, but much more so for his prudence, learning, and purity of life, which was so remarkable as to make him appear angelical to men, and odious to the devils, which they publicly showed on several occasions. His disinterestedness was extraordinary, for although he served the community gratis and entirely at his own expense, both as to victuals, lodging and other necessaries, for the space of thirty-two years, he could never be prevailed upon to receive any small presents they were often out of gratitude solicitous to give him. Which makes them look upon this as one of the least acknowledgments they can make to so signal a benefactor, who was and is still esteemed to have been one of their principal helps in the beginning of this foundation.

All things being now in readiness, this little community, which consisted of twelve persons, namely, nine choir nuns, one novice, and two lay-sisters, set out for Lierre on the 26th of August, in the year of our Lord 1648, accompanied by the Reverend Mother Teresa of Jesus, Prioress of Antwerp monastery.[1] They arrived in the town the same day and repaired immediately to a house they had agreed for some time before ; but unexpectedly finding the owners thereof run from their bargain, and ready to drive them away with threats that, if they endeavoured to make good their pretension to it, they would soon find means to break their intended foundation, the poor religious were obliged peaceably and patiently to retire to a large house, which, after some inquiries, they had found in a bye-corner of the town at that time casually empty. As they had neither money nor sufficient interest in a strange place, to maintain their right to the above-mentioned house, they were glad to hire the one they were in possession of at the rate of four hundred florins a year, till such time as an occasion offered of pur·chasing another more to their liking and convenience ; for this, besides being incommodious and such only as their present necessity obliged them to put up with, was also in a manner unalienable, it being the Refuge of a neighbouring Abbey of Bernardine Dames called Nazareth.

Here they might justly lay claim to, and comfort themselves with, the expression St. Teresa made use of at her foundation of Medina del Campo, who, being much in the same circumstances and disappointed in her expectations of finding a house ready to receive her, and hindered from it also by a community of religious men, said before one who brought her the unexpected news : ' Now I know, my God, how vain and insignificant the resistance of man is against those whom Thou hast undertaken to protect, for in place of being dejected at this accident, I am rather encouraged, since I look upon this trouble, which the devil has raised against us, as a sure mark that Thy Divine Majesty will be served here with great fidelity.'

Meantime, workmen were procured and the house laid out, and fitted up, in the most convenient manner it would allow of : which at best was poor, since with all their contrivance and industry, it was a full month before they could get a place decently adorned and proper to put up the Blessed Sacrament in. This memorable action, which

---

[1] They were also accompanied by the Bishop's Vicar-General.

seemed to be St. Teresa's greatest comfort and satisfaction, and what encouraged her most to go through with the many difficulties she met with in her foundations, was here completed on the 4th of October (1648), being St. Francis the Seraphic's day, who afterwards revealed to Mother Margaret of Jesus that he had it under his particular protection.

The ceremony was performed with all the solemnity their poor circumstances would permit, and attended by a concourse of devout people, who as they gradually grew acquainted with the house, became also the admirers of the spirit of poverty, mortification, and patience, which remarkably appeared in all they heard or saw of it, so that the community soon gained the repute of sanctity, and was spoke of by all with the greatest veneration.

The names of the religious that came from Antwerp to the foundation of Lierre were (1) Vicaress, Mother Margaret of St. Teresa (Downes); (2) Sister Catharine of the Blessed Sacrament (Windoe); (3) Sister Mary Anne of Jesus (Foster); (4) Sister Mary of Jesus (Powderle); (5) Sister Elisabeth of the Visitation (Emery); (6) Sister Eugenia of Jesus (Leveson); (7) Sister Margaret of Jesus (Mostyn); (8) Sister Ursula of All Saints (Mostyn); (9) Sister Jeronima of St. Michael (Winter); (10) Sister Margaret of St. Francis (Johnson), lay-sister; (11) Sister Alexis of St. Winefride (Harris), lay-sister; and lastly (12) Sister Mary of St. Joseph (Vaughan), novice.

(1) The Vicaress, Mother Margaret of St. Teresa (Downes), was a person of great talent and energy as well as remarkably holy. She was ever considered the right hand of Mother Anne of the Ascension, and had aided her in many of her foundations, and had also been Novice Mistress to the greater part of the Antwerp religious.

(2) Sister Catharine of the Blessed Sacrament (Windoe) who came as Sub-prioress, was an eminently holy and contemplative soul who had the privilege of pronouncing her vows at the early age of fifteen. A saying of hers is recorded and which she frequently repeated to the Prioress : 'Mark me well, dear Mother, those that don't like recreation, don't

like mortification,' not only because recreation in due time is the spirit of St. Teresa, but also because it often gives occasion or opportunity of practising both self-denials and self-sacrifices, all most pleasing to our Divine Lord.

(3) Sister Mary Anne of Jesus (Foster).

(4) Sister Mary of Jesus (Powderle), a soul most pleasing to her Spouse, Who, in order that the Lierre foundation should possess her, worked no less a miracle than that, when the Antwerp Prioress read out the list of the religious who were to be sent to that filiation, to her great astonishment the name of Sister Clare which had been written down was effaced and that of Sister Mary of Jesus appeared in its place. To this evident manifestation of God's will Superiors deferred, and she accordingly accompanied the religious destined for Lierre instead of Sister Clare.

(5) Sister Elisabeth of the Visitation (Emery).

(6) Sister Eugenia of Jesus (Leveson), a very humble courageous and favoured soul, she received the habit of Carmel at Antwerp, in 1634, aged sixteen, but was forced to leave on account of her health, but again returned in 1640, and was clothed a second time, and 1641 professed. To be helped by her suffering, which was always very great, and to secure her prayers, the holy souls in Purgatory often visited her. Her esteem for obedience was very remarkable, and often she used to say: ' It imports much for the obtaining of perfection to perform and observe the least inclination of my Superior's will, for in doing her will I am sure to do an act of obedience, and in doing the least thing though seemingly better according to my own will and judgment I am sure of doing a great imperfection.' She was the first who died at Lierre, August 18, 1652.

(7) and (8) were the Sisters Margaret and Ursula (Mostyn).

(9) Sister Jeronima of St. Michael (Winter). She was professed at Antwerp, June 29, 1648, the same year the Lierre foundation was made. She soon won her crown, dying in 1655.

(10) Sister Margaret of St. Francis (Johnson), was a lay-sister, a most holy and simple soul, and so pleasing in the eyes of our dear Lord that in one of the revelations of

Mother Margaret He said that He was impatient to have her with Him in Heaven, but He allowed her to live because she merited so much.

(11) Sister Alexis of St. Winefride (Harris) was also a lay-sister. A particular providence watched over this simple and fervent soul. Born of Protestant Welsh parents, her father, a labourer, was accidentally killed while employed on the Marquis of Worcester's estate. The latter provided for his widow and children, and the future Teresian fell to his lordship's daughter, Lady Anne Somerset's lot as we are told, 'to take care of, bringing her up a good Catholic,' which she did, instructing her, and having her, in quality of maid, always about her, and when Lady Anne went to the English Monastery at Antwerp of Discalced Carmelites, she took her with her, and she was received on her lady-ship's portion as a lay-sister, and professed at the age of twenty, 1626.

(12) Sister Mary of St. Joseph (Vaughan), of Courtfield, Monmouthshire, novice, made up the number of the twelve religious destined for Lierre, and she was professed the following year, 1649, at the age of seventeen (without a dispensation Teresians, according to the Constitutions, cannot be professed till seventeen), and died at the ripe age of seventy-seven, 1709, having during the whole of that long religious life, as is related in her life, 'never lost her first fervour, but going on from one virtue to another, increased every day in a continual tendency to religious perfection.'

It was at last resolved to purchase another house, and having found one which was esteemed too small and incapable of being rendered fit for their use, as experience afterwards convinced them to be true, at this time was, however, purchased, and some little accomodations being made, sufficient for the speedy reception of the religious, her Reverence with a companion (Sister Margaret) went to see it and take possession of it. Sister Margaret from her first coming to Lierre had a kind of instinct that this house should be their convent, and that our Blessed Lord and His good Mother would be well served there, which she would often say, though all others were of a contrary opinion to hers, especially the Superior, who would not hear of it, alleging it was small and close, with many other inconveniences, which made it appear very impossible; notwithstanding, it fell out as Sister Margaret had foretold, to the great amazement of all.

They had scarce entered the room which was afterwards the Chapter-house, but there arose on a sudden a violent storm of wind and thunder, which shook the whole building, and filled the place where they stood with a most horrid stench of brimstone, which the religious in the monastery also experienced in such a degree as almost suffocated them. This storm lasted a considerable time, and raised so much dust in the streets that they were scarce passable, and in many places barrels and other things were blown up into the air, which caused great confusion and fear, all affirming they had never seen the like before, nor could conceive how the weather, which was fine and settled, should so suddenly change.

The religious were in the utmost fright and concern. Reverend Mother Prioress and her companion Sister Margaret were at the new house, the Confessor, Rev. E. Bedingfield, was gone to Antwerp to obtain leave of his lordship to remove to it, who returning in the midst of the storm, also in great amaze at this extraordinary change of weather, which he thought more than natural, repaired immediately to the monastery, though with great difficulty. Here, finding all in disorder, and so much smoke and dust that we were scarce able to see one another, he called for holy water, said St. John's Gospel, and then sent for an image of our Lady which was held in great esteem in the house; but the Sister who ran for it in coming back was thrown downstairs by the force of the wind, and the statue dashed against the pavement in the middle of the court. Yet neither the Sister nor the image, which was small and curiously carved, were the least hurt, nor the crown or sceptre, which were loose, removed from their places, to the great astonishment of all, who expected to find it broke in many pieces. This statue is still extant, and preserved with great care and veneration. This wood statuette is still in our possession, inclosed in a reliquary in our choir.

It was then carried to the choir, where, with much ado, a blessed candle being lit, the Confessor began the Litanies of our Lady, during which the storm seemed to abate, and by the time all was ended the air reassumed its former calmness and serenity, and our Reverend Mother returned home with her companion Sister Margaret of Jesus, who affirmed she had seen the devil in one of the greatest claps. On this she comforted herself and the community with hopes that it was his last piece of spite, and that Almighty God had finally freed them from his tyranny.

Next morning Reverend Mother went again to the house with six or eight of the religious, leaving Sister Margaret of Jesus, with some of the most courageous, to order and regulate the transporting of their goods and furniture. This change happened in the year 1651, but we cannot find out either the day or the month, which we only conjecture to have been either July or August. The house, or rather houses, for there were different straggling ones, were bought with the fortunes of four novices, and put the community to great expense in uniting and rendering them tolerably convenient, by the good contrivance of Reverend Mother Margaret of St. Teresa (Downes), who had a particular genius in such things.

———

NOTE III.

Margaret's devotion to her Angel Guardian.

In a paper given by Mother Margaret to Father Beding-field soon after she came to Lierre, she mentions, 'Lately as I was present at Mass, and begging of our blessed Mother[2] to prepare me for her feast I suddenly seemed (to have) present my good angel, and yet I cannot say I did see anything, for my eyes were shut, neither did I hear anything, yet it seemed to me he said, *Do what you do*,[3] and I will

---

[2] She always calls our holy Mother St. Teresa thus.

[3] Here we cannot but remember the golden sentence of old, *Age quod agis.*

take care for the rest, since this time I carry another kind of devotion to my Good Angel, and whatsoever I am doing or desire, methinks before I am aware, or without any reflection, I am referring it to his care, and so am out of pain with the event.'

On the same paper she mentions she would beg every day Almighty God to prepare her heart for *sudden* sufferings; and again she writes, 'When I find fear and apprehension of suffering, I will presently before a crucifix offer myself to suffer what it shall please God to permit to fall upon me, and offer it in union with our Saviour's Passion.'

NOTE IV.

A Favour received from our Blessed Lady.

On a loose piece of paper in Mother Margaret's hand is the following short account of a favour received, written to give Father Bedingfield. It must have happened soon after she came to Lierre.

'Upon the Conception Eve of our Blessed Lady, when I had begun to speak to your Reverence, being to go to the noviceship at the ordinary hour, and finding myself all oppressed and overcome by ill thoughts and desires of all kinds, especially against my vocation, and that ill affection; as I was passing the refectory and begging of our Blessed Lady (whose feast was begun) to help me, I heard in a loud sweet voice these words, "*Adsum*," which all changed me into a great deal of peace and joy; and though I understood it not till your Reverence told it me and disposed me to believe and submit, I now understand that it was our Blessed Lady who was present, and did then (because I had a sincere desire to help myself), give me that comfort, and after that I was enabled to be daily more and more sincere.

CHAPTER VIII.

Sister Margaret made Mistress of Novices: she is relieved in her distress for them by our Blessed Lady, who blesses their beads. New sufferings, in which she is again comforted by our Blessed Lady.

THE Mistress of Novices is at all times a charge of much importance, in which a great deal of prudence, mildness, and patience is requisite, having to deal with young, inexperienced persons, whose passions are in their prime, of quite different humours and dispositions, each of whom must be discerned, considered and treated accordingly, and by degrees formed and trained up to the same common way of life, and if possible to the same way of thinking, in which is required a total reformation, interior and exterior, so as to make an undisciplined worldling into a regular and perfect religious. An office of itself so arduous must needs be much more so in the beginning of a new foundation, which totally depends upon these new plants, by whose lives and example it is to be regulated in future ages, and a beaten path formed for all their followers to guide themselves by in spirit and truth. This employ was therefore intrusted to Sister Margaret of Jesus, and certainly no fitter person could be found, who, from her first entrance into religion, was looked upon as a pattern of all religious virtues, chosen by Almighty God to cultivate the vineyard of Carmel, and to uphold the spirit of St. Teresa's holy reform. The circumstances the foundation was in at this time were very disheartening : at home, the religious infested with malign spirits, that haunted the house and gave them no respite night or day, which was no small discourage-ment to the novices, who, besides their exterior fright, were interiorly tempted to pusillanimity and to waver in their vocation. They had also much trouble to undergo on account of objections which had been raised to the foundation of more Teresian convents which were subject to the Bishops. Prayers and tears, fastings and mortifi-cations were made use of to withstand the fury of their domestic enemy, which they never could have sup-ported had they not been supernaturally assisted, as we find they were, and that even in a visible manner. For Sister Margaret, who was in great concern and apprehension for her dear novices, fearing that at last their constancy should be overcome, praying one day earnestly for them, was favoured by a vision of our Blessed Lady, who assured her they were all under her protection, and ordered her to bring their beads, to which she would give a particular blessing, of which each one should be sensible ; if they only wore them about their necks at night, they should find solace, and feel the effects of her assistance, which they truly ever after experienced till their troubles ended.

Sister Margaret, in the meanwhile, had by this an occasion of fresh sufferings: for from that time the enemy sought to revenge himself by all manner of ways, and all kinds of temptations, as was visibly seen by a pious young carpenter, who was then working in the house, and was so alarmed at it, that he immediately informed his confessor, who was a Capuchin Father, charging him to admonish the religious of the dangers he saw they were exposed to, and particularly one, meaning Margaret, who seemed to have no respite, which she experienced to be too true ; for as she herself acknowledged, through the extreme melancholy and variety of other temptations, with which she found herself grievously oppressed, she was almost reduced to despair, not being able to obtain any peace or rest either night or day. So that Mother Lucy of St. Ignatius Bedingfield,[1] elected out

[1] [This Lucy of St. Ignatius, who died the following year (1650) of small-pox, aged thirty-six, after nineteen years of religion, was a Professed Sister of the English Monastery of Antwerp, and was daughter of Francis Bedingfield, of Redingfield, Suffolk, and Katharine Fortescue his wife. It is related that just before her marriage ' Katharine began to repent, and said she would prefer being a religious ; but her father told her had she expressed her wishes sooner he would willingly have yielded to her, but now he considered it was too late to change her mind, for her portion was half paid. She consented, and God seemed to reward her love for the religious state by giving her, besides other issue, ten daughters, who became religious in different orders'—two of them, Katharine, in religion Lucy of St. Ignatius, and Magdalen, in religion Magdalen of St. Joseph, became Teresians at the English Monastery of Carmelites at Antwerp. Both were very eminent for their virtue and holiness, but especially Mother Magdalen of St. Joseph, who became very renowned for sanctity ; she founded the Monastery of Neuburg on the Danube at the wish of Duke Philip Count Palatine, A.D. 1661, and died Prioress of that monastery in 1683 or 1684. In 1727, her coffin having been accidentally opened while some repairs were taking place in the nuns' dead vaults, her body was found perfectly incorrupt, without a trace of corruption, which was still more astonishing as two measures of quick lime still remained in the coffin. The mantle, habit, veil, tuck (head-dress), even the bouquet of rosemary, were all perfectly preserved ; the tuck (white linen) especially was as unsullied as if it had only just been placed there. There are at Darlington some interesting letters written on the occasion of Mother Magdalen of St. Joseph's body being found, and miracles worked by it, to the then Prioress Mother Margaret Teresa, of the Immaculate Conception, Fettyplace, widow *neé* Mostyn, a relative of hers, the Bedingfields of Redingfield and the Mostyn families having intermarried. There were two other bodies of Teresians of Neuburg found incorrupt at the same time, and it was so well known in the town that, in 1804, when the convent was suppressed, all the coffins of the religious in the vaults were burnt except the three containing the incorrupt bodies, which were placed in a tomb apart. The Bishop of Ausburgh offered to have the body of Mother Magdalen of St. Joseph given to her family if they wished to translate it. An account of the above convent and incorrupt bodies appeared in a German magazine called *Of Sion*, A.D. 1852. The Francis Bedingfiel of Redingfield, father to the above Carmelites, was grandson of Edmun Bedingfield, Knight, of Oxburgh, who died A.D. 1585.]

of Germany to be Rev. Mother Prioress of the English monastery at Antwerp, passing through Lierre, and on account of these disturbances not being able to sleep, wondered how the religious could withstand such terrible noises as she had heard, and warned the Prioress to have great care of the community, for she feared they would all be sick. It is almost incredible what she underwent in this terrible conflict, in which it seemed as if all Hell had broken loose upon her, and that the devil made it his only business to afflict her in all kinds of ways. For he would sometimes beat her to such a degree as to leave marks and bruises on her body ; at other times he would throw her down stairs, and when she was in the garret or other offices alone, the doors of a sudden would be fastened, and the place filled with a horrid darkness, like to a thick smoke or black cloud, so that she could not see or imagine where she was. In this frightful situation the devil would trail her about for a long time together, till she could scarce any longer fetch her breath or recover so much strength as to call upon the sacred names of Jesus and Mary, or make the sign of the Cross. Then he would frighten her with the most odious and disgustful shapes, amongst which he would sometimes appear like a furious wild horse, coming so fiercely towards her, as if he would run over her which also he often did, leaving the print of his feet on her legs and other parts of her body, another time like a strange monster with fiery eyes. What she dreaded the most was when he would lift her up into the air, and threaten to let her fall, or carry her away, for then she was in a kind of agony, so great was her anxiety and apprehension. Besides, she was often molested in her cell with hideous screeches and howlings, and such violent offensive stenches as to bereave

her in a manner of her breath, and almost of life by
suffocation.

These trials lasted a long time, to her own and the
community's great concern, yet could she scarce be prevailed on to believe them, unless she found evident
signs of them, or herself so spent and reduced that she
could hardly stir. The same spirit of incredulity seemed
also to prevail over her with regard to the favours she
had received from our Lady, particularly this of blessing
the beads, which the devil continually suggested to her
as a mere fancy, and a thing made up of her own
head, that she might be esteemed a saint. From this
temptation she suffered much, on account of the perplexity with which it oppressed her mind, always apprehending she had been deceived, till our Lady was
pleased to succour her by another appearance, telling
her not to fear, nor doubt of what she had done for
her, since she could bestow her blessing where she
pleased, and that without any regard to her merit or
virtue, but out of her own pure goodness ; that she had
not only blessed those beads, but was ready to do the
same to any others she should ask her with humility and
confidence, ' For,' said she, ' you must know, my child,
I have many other blessings in store for you. If notwithstanding the devil still continues to tempt you,
know it is for your greater good and his confusion, and
by leaving you in these uncertainties with regard to my
favours, I do you a greater favour than by giving you
a further assurance, which you shall only receive from
your confessor. This will keep you both humble and
obedient, be a new torment and confusion to the devil,
to whom it is worse than Hell, to have leave and power to
tempt you, and yet find himself unable once in a
thousand times to effect anything. The worst he can
do is to vex and trouble you when you are unfaithful or

disobedient; his power shall not be more, because my honour is concerned in making you happy. Therefore, if you are victorious, you know it is owing to me, and not to yourself, so you need not apprehend your confessor thinking you a saint, he knows sufficiently your misery, and my charity who am the Mother of Mercy.'

The Foundation being now happily established, and the rage of its interior enemies at last efficaciously quelled, the religious were at liberty to give more scope to their fervour and attention to the pursuit of virtue and regular observance, in which they shortly became so eminent, as to excite the admiration of all about them, and deserve the title of holy nuns, out of the veneration each one had for them; whilst Margaret, whose rare virtues rendered her conspicuous in this saintly abode, went through all the duties of her charge with universal satisfaction, doubtless bringing down many blessings upon the house, being frequently so particularly favoured by our Blessed Lady, and on all occasions so zealous and eager in procuring its good. For her abilities in the management of temporals were no ways inferior to her talents in the spirituals, having been brought up to housekeeping from her youth. In consideration for these qualifications, she was charged with the office of Procuratress, which at that time was a tedious burthen, being low in circumstances, and obliged to consider all expenses in repairing and accommodating some houses the community had lately purchased, wherein they might have a fixed settlement; for hitherto they had been obliged to put up with a hired house, on account of some disappointments they met with at their first coming to town, which put them to great inconvenience, till they met with the occasion which, although indifferent, they found then necessary to make use of.

CHAPTER IX.

She is forwarded in obedience and religious observ-
ance by several particular favours, amongst which
she had a glimpse of heavenly glory, sees the Order
of Carmel, and receives instructions for her novices
from St. Teresa, who assured her that her spirit was
in this house.

SISTER MARGARET being sometimes favoured with
heavenly music, it happened on this occasion that her
mind became more than usually elevated by it, and her
desires drawn earnestly after it, so that in the midst of
her admiration she begged of our Blessed Lady to
obtain for her through the sacred merits of her dear
Son, that she might eternally hear it. On which our
Lady appearing to her, said : ' Fear not; as long as you
obey, and know you are poor and deserve nothing,
your desires shall be granted, in pledge of which I here
bring you my Son. Keep Him company, and desire
Him to prepare your heart for Communion to-morrow,
when you shall hear a Mass with as much jubilee as
can be imagined, and more than you ever conceived
Heaven itself to be.' But she thinking within herself that
nothing surely could exceed this music, our Lady answered, ' My child, how little do you know what is to be
enjoyed there !' Then laying her hand upon Margaret's
head, she said, 'You shall hear and know other manner
of comfort, even in this life, for I cannot withhold my
favours from you.'

The bell ringing for Vespers, she immediately rose up to go to that act of community, but seeing our Lady did not move, she was dubious what to do, yet went straight to the choir, where our Blessed Lady met her with the Sacred Infant in her arms, said, 'Because you left me to obey the bell, I bring you my Son; if you had done otherwise, you would have lost this pleasure, take Him, He shall remain with you till I fetch Him,' and so vanished. She saw, indeed, the Infant, yet did not know how, for He seemed to be in her heart, and at the same time embracing her, and as she was adoring Him, and calling to mind her wicked life, He, smiling, said all that should not hinder Him from obliging His Blessed Mother and comforting her, that she must now imagine herself a little child, since His delight was to have her so, which she understood to consist in an innocent simplicity and entire unconcern for what the world might think of her, forgetting all things thereof for His love.

Thus the time passed from two o'clock till three, when she went up to the novices, where kneeling down with them to say the Litany of our Blessed Lady, and her heart being full of her former wickedness, for which she again begged pardon of the Sacred Infant, Whom she constantly beheld within her, He put His finger upon her lips, and said, ' They are pardoned ; you would force Me to go away from you, but I must and will obey My sacred Mother, though you will not. We must not now speak of sins ; I am here to comfort you, and let you see what My Mother enjoyed, when she had Me so long in her arms, and to show you what it is to become a child for My love, which you thought to be but a trifling matter when your confessor recommended it to you ; but know that such alone are My true favourites.'

At the time of the Litany our Blessed Lady appeared accompanied by an angel, and asked her if she was willing to part with her Son; to which she, through the amaze and confusion she was in, not being able to make any answer, our Lady took her Blessed Son into her arms, and desired Him to make Margaret content. But He, turning to His Mother, said, 'She is unwilling to let us go,' on which our Lady questioned her again if it was so, but she could say nothing, only in her heart she desired to be taken out of this uncertain and dangerous world. To which thought our Lady replied, 'You know not what you desire, for if you understand but the value and merit of one act of obedience, neither human respect, nor anything in any way whatever you suffer in this life, would ever be able to hinder you from practising the most difficult ones, or to prevail upon you to omit the least, or most insignificant.' Then turning towards the angel, 'Do you know this angel?' which Margaret remembering to have seen before, our Lady told her that in all her necessities he should be with her, and that she should often see him with the names of Jesus and Mary in glory, which when she had said, the little Infant held up his hand, and gave her his blessing.

In the morning, whilst she was saying the Hours in the choir, finding one of the novices absent, she thought to go and call her, but our Blessed Lady appearing, bade her not go, but tell her of it afterwards; and immediately, as she thought, she saw all Heaven open, then she instantly heard most delightful voices, but observed no motion of their mouths. At which our Lady, answering her thoughts said : 'Though you see and hear this harmony, yet it is not as things are in this life, for Heaven is all in God, and in Him we have all we desire, so that if there be anything we do not enjoy, it is because we do not desire it.' All which she seemed to understand for that present, and yet could no way express, for all seemed to keep order, and yet to pass without any motion or change, and all kind of varieties that she could imagine were represented before her in one instant. Our Blessed Lady then told her that all things in this world were equally in God, even in the same manner as those Divine things she had seen here, and that if we could see how all things in this world are in God, we should see no world in the world, which at that instant seemed so to her, for she saw all was in Him, and otherwise nothing, but only inasmuch as He gave it being. Then our Lady said, ' I have showed you all this to convince you what blessings are to be obtained in the next life by the exercise of your obedience and faith in this, for according to what it is here, so will it be there, more or less known. If the world did but see and comprehend this truth, as I have, and show it sometimes by extraordinary favour, it would be Heaven, and there would be need of no more faith ; but this is a blessing only enjoyed in Heaven, since all this human life is capable of understanding is a mere shadow of what a soul there experiences ; but as they grow here more and more perfect, they come to a clearer knowledge of this truth, so that in this life there is a kind of Heaven for pure humble souls, who give up their wills into the hands of my Son, Whose delight is to be known and conversant with the children of men. This, by my advice, you gave Him at your profession, and this is all He requires of you : be but humble, and then you will become as simple as a dove, and as wise as a serpent.'

After this our Lady bid her go and call the novice to Mass, which being begun before she came back, she saw the angel with the names of Jesus and Mary in her place; but at her arrival, making a bow, he left her place, and immediately our Blessed Lady seemed to fill the whole choir, and was attended with most delightful music. All the Order of Carmel did seem present, and were occupied in singing the praises of our Blessed Lady and her dear Son. Our Lady, as she thought, said, 'She is of our number,' and as she asked within herself to know as much for all the sisters, she instantly saw them in the very breast of the Sacred Infant, from Whom she heard these words : ' I repose in their hearts, and My lodging is in their breasts, and therefore their place of rest is in Mine, as you see.'

At the Elevation, all the altar seemed to be encompassed round about with Heaven, and the mysteries of our Blessed Lord and all His sacred Passion were represented to her most clearly, and He said : " Thus every time Mass is celebrated I am offered to My Eternal Father for you, and how little does the world reflect upon it ! here are all My merits, be you then content in offering them up, for you may obtain all you please by them.' In the midst of her amazement, a thought occurring, whether this glory was with every priest that said Mass, although they should not be in a good state, our Lord answered, He was there only till the Sacred Host was consumed ; but with those who were grateful to Him He stayed according to the knowledge, faith, and affection which they carried towards Him, and according to the favour He pleased to do them, since He could not leave a soul that was truly humble, and desired to keep Him company.

Being once at work with the sisters in the recreation, when the bell rang the *Angelus,* she happened to rise up first, and whilst she was saying it, our Blessed Lady appeared with the Sacred Infant, Who gave His blessing to all. And our Lady said to her, ' Because you stood up first at the sound of the bell, I will give you my Son the whole time of recreation.' This filled her with so much joy that she was inclined to leave off her work, and discourse, that she might attend with more earnestness to this Divine Guest; but He let her understand that she pleased Him best when she was serious in performing the present action, and in so doing she should equally enjoy His presence, which she experienced on this and many other like occasions when, engaged in this celestial company, her duties called upon her. What she found the hardest in this point was going to rest, which she looked upon as the greatest misery of human life, being obliged thereby to interrupt her conversation with our Lord. But He was pleased to assure her that this action was as pleasing to Him as any other, for though she slept, He could watch in her heart, where, according to her obedience, He would impart His graces, and make her sensible that His spouses' hearts, if they endeavoured to be humble and obedient, are more pleasing to Him than His imperial Heaven. He then showed her how every little act of obedience was an act of adoration unto Him; and how little things, done purely for the love of Him, are of great moment, but both in such a manner that she could not express it.

On another occasion, having forwarded her novices to go to Communion, she was favoured with a vision of St. Teresa, who commended her for it, and assured her that frequent Communion was her spirit, so that although persons be very imperfect, or can use little or no preparation, provided they be but in the state of grace, and free from any wilful attachment to venial sins, if they do it to conform themselves to the community, and because it is the spirit of the Order, they participate of the devotions of all the rest, whose preparations do satisfy for the negligences of others; and oftentimes such weak members merit more, if they have but a sense of their own infirmity, than those who feel in themselves much fervour and devotion.

Then St. Teresa showed her how this community was like to her first religious, letting her see their hearts, and how they behaved in every act of community, and with what simplicity and love to God she and they passed their lives. 'Therefore,' said she, ' my child, as you see, my right spirit is this, that by your simplicity and fervour, you inflame one another, and by your alacrity of spirit, which ought to appear in all your words and actions, you render the service of God sweet and light to each other. You must be so all one heart in our Blessed Lord, as to partake of each other's consolations and tribulations, of which every one ought to have as sensible a feeling as if they were their own. You are to rejoice in the perfections you see in others, and bear a real esteem for all in general, for if you do not esteem one another you will not love one another, nor pray for, or comfort one another in your afflictions. This tenderness and union amongst yourselves is so very much my spirit, that I would have it practised even to an excess, as it was often in my time, when the simplicity of my religious was such that the least sickness or indisposition of any one was sensibly felt by all the rest.' Then she said: 'This house shall be my particular care,' and so disappearing left in Margaret's breast a lively picture of the life and duties of a reformed Carmelite, the sole idea of which inspires a certain air of happiness more than terrestrial, and truly greater than all the world can afford ; for here we see that happy age of the primitive Christians renewed, in which all had one heart and one mind.

CHAPTER X.

The repugnance she had to declare her particular favours, which she is many times ordered to do by our Blessed Lady, who with her Son divers ways caresses her, lets her know the state of her parents in Heaven, gives her a clear sight of our Lord's Nativity, and helps her to surmount a strong temptation.

SISTER MARGARET being one day at her prayers in the choir, and recommending to our Blessed Lady a particular friend of hers, by whom she had been much obliged, suddenly she imagined to see our Lady holding a beautiful crown in her hand and heard her say: 'This I have prepared for his[1] reward.' But reflecting upon a command she had lately received from our Lady, which was, with much sincerity and simplicity to inform her confessor of all, and then only credit what he approved of, to excuse herself from speaking of this, she endeavoured to look upon it as a mere fancy: yet could not so entirely free herself from a scruple of this omission, but that the fear of proving disobedient perplexed her the whole day, which hindered her from applying to her usual prayers, and made her grow so weary, that she knew not how to employ her time. But our Blessed Lady appearing again, bid her say her beads for such poor souls, who are devoted to her, and yet remain in an ill state, earnestly recommending her to make frequent use of this devotion; for she assured her that it was of

[Father Bedingfield.]

all others the most grateful, since there were divers she desired to help, who on account of their demerits did not deserve it, therefore she required to be moved to assist them by the prayers of others.

Then our Lady showed her again the crown above mentioned, and bidding her observe well asked her if she thought it still a fancy, and chiding her for not having told her confessor, said, she never let her know anything however simple it might appear but what she would have exactly related to him, without any formalities in composing her words, and that when she keeps anything to herself, she has then just reason to fear being deceived by the devil, who would try her several ways; but as long as she was faithful in obedience by sincerely declaring her interior he could have no power over her. As Margaret still found a reluctance, she seemed to propose in herself a question, why so many others more virtuous, observant and perfect than herself were privileged to serve God peaceably and happily in a religious state, and were freed both from the assaults of the devil, and from those fancies and favours which she imagined to experience. But our Lady immediately reprehending her again, bid her serve God, and be humble, for she did not bestow these favours upon her because she was more pleasing to her than others, but because she would mortify her in all, and she must know that others had strength and love to suffer for, and serve her dear Son, but that she without continual help could do nothing, and so vanished.

The next day following, some time after she had communicated, she was troubled with fears of several kinds, especially concerning her confessor, which made her wish with great anxiety that she might never more have any of these fancies of our Blessed Lady's appearing to her, promising to serve her in the best manner

she could, if she would only do her this favour; but
these prayers were ineffectual, for she instantly beheld
the Blessed Virgin in a silver cloud, with the Sacred
Infant in her arms attended with numerous angels, and,
as she thought, St. Teresa. Our Blessed Lady then laying her hand upon her head, said : ' My child, what are
you afraid of? May I not bestow my favours where I
please? if it be that you apprehend the mortification
of speaking of them, because that you will be thought
simple and apt to fancy, or that they will not be believed,
your mortification is what I propose and you shall therefore experience things incredible to all whom I do not
inspire to believe ; for I am resolved to let you see how
I can and do reward those who give themselves to my
service.' But, first, she sweetly smiling, said : ' Why do
you not make the sign of the Cross as your confessor bid
you?' which she had wholly forgotten, and our Lady
immediately supplied with her sacred finger, making a
cross upon her forehead, and bid her tell it to her confessor and ask him if she had reason to fear its not
being she. Then she caused her Blessed Son to make
the sign of the Cross upon her, which He did by way of
giving her His blessing.

After this, our Lady taking Margaret's beads[2] into her
hand, gave them to the Sacred Infant, Who, as she
imagined, returned them unto her, and said He would
give them another benediction, which was, that as before
they only gave her a lively presence of our Blessed Lady,
so now they should make her see and know Him
present in her arms. All this, as she thought, and much
more, passed in one instant, and our Blessed Lady, with
her hand still upon her head, asked her what she desired,
to which she answered in thought, for she did not speak,

[2] [These beads are still in the possession of the community at
Darlington.]

' Most sacred Mother, let me be an angel belonging
to your throne;' but she replied : ' You know not what
you desire, for if you continue to be faithful to me, you
shall have a place as much higher, as Heaven is from
the earth.' As she seemed to doubt of this, on account
of her great sins which were then clear before her eyes,
our Lady bid her think no more of them, according as
her confessor had advised her. Then, turning to her
Son, she said, ' What shall I do to convince her that she
shall be eternally happy? Give You her a sign of it.'
At which the Infant with a joyful countenance showed her
her place in Heaven, not far from St. Teresa, but nearer to
our Blessed Lady, who said, that at that time when she
offered up herself to be her slave, she had exalted it so
much nearer her, as it was now further from St. Teresa.
She showed her likewise a place for her mother, and told
her she should have a higher one in Heaven than her
grandmother, whose greatest imperfection, as she then
understood, and for which she had suffered in Purgatory, had been her hindering her from being religious
and bringing her up in some vanities. Finding herself
troubled at having been the occasion of her grandmother's demerit, she heard a sweet shrill voice which
said, ' I am well and have all I desire :' this comforted
Margaret, who was assured by our Lady, that her grandmother received new glory by every virtuous action she
performed which any ways proceeded from the pious
principles she had instilled into her by her instructions,
and care to have her well educated.

Then our Lady told her she let her know these particulars, that the world might see how much it imports
to learn children vocal prayers, and teach them to be
devoted to her : and also that parents might take warning how to bring up their children, and on what account
they hindered them from religion. Our Lady likewise

assured her that all her brothers and sisters were in her care, and had always been so, because her father and mother had dedicated them to her before they were born. Here St. Teresa seemed to admire our Blessed Lady's goodness towards them, and told her if she did but know how our Lady was honoured in Heaven, and would be glorified on earth for what she had done in particular for her, she would have a Heaven upon earth. Then our Lady said, she was resolved to communicate herself to her in all ways that might comfort and mortify her too, for this point of humbling her should be the effect of all favours, and bid her read the seventeenth chapter of St. Teresa's life, where she would find much help; so, giving her benediction to the whole choir she disapppeared.

Margaret after this remained full of joy, and desirous of praising our Blessed Lady, though she said nothing, nor at that time could doubt of what passed being true, but when it afterwards occurred to her mind with how much familiarity and sweetness our Lady had treated her, as if a mother was talking to her child, she thought it was impossible for the thing to have been so and began to imagine it all a fancy. However, she told it all to her confessor, and the day following after Communion our Lady appeared to her again with the Sacred Infant in her arms, and thanking her for her obedience said: 'What the worse are you for being thought a fanciful creature, or simple? I shall be honoured by your simplicity, and you shall be rewarded; see, here is my Son become a little one for love of you. Tell me, now, what you desire;' which she said with so much tenderness that it moved her to tears, and not being able to make any answer, our Lady said: 'As long as you obey me, I am forced to find out new ways of comforting you,' and, as she imagined, for she knows not whether

it was so or not, she took her little Son's hands, and
with them He touched her eyes, saying : ' These eyes
shall never see anything grateful to them but Me, nor
shall ever offend Me in anything considerable.' Then,
as she thought, He embraced her, adding : ' From this
time forward you shall have a particular impression and
memory of Me and My Blessed Mother ; My name and
hers shall be engraven in your heart, where I have
always been, though you knew it not, since the time
you fancied to hear those words " I have established My
seat in your heart," ' which happened in time of her
noviceship. Then He told Her she was in His favour,
and her soul without spot, and showing her the place
above mentioned in Heaven, He pointed to a particular
glory there, on which our Lady said : ' See what esteem
you ought to make of obedience, since you have merited
that for overcoming the mortification you had in giving
your confessor those papers he exacted of you.' Then
our Lord asked her again what more she desired, to
which she answered : ' Lord, to be eternally happy and
not to deceive others in this life,' for her heart was so
full she could say nothing else. Whereupon, He replied :
' You are Mine, and shall deceive no one.' On the
same day at Vespers when the Psalm *Credidi* began, our
Lady showed herself again with her Blessed Son in her
arms, with the same impression as in the morning, and
let her see her heart, with their names, *Jesus*, *Maria*,
imprinted in it, and the sweet Infant said He would
always live there as He had promised her formerly.
Then our Lady said : ' Do you believe now ? Can you
think this a fancy too ?' and reprehending her for not
having spoken of certain harmonious music she had
heard, said : ' I require nothing particular of you, but that
you be faithful in declaring all to your confessor, in
which if you fail, I tell you again, you will be in

danger of being deceived, and can never proceed with security.'

The morning after she had told her confessor of the music, and acknowledged her fault in time of the Hours, she heard the same, and our Blessed Lady seemed to be there according to her usual way, and said: 'Do you know what you hear? See, here is my Son, as He was newly born, and this music is the same I heard and saw at that time,' all which passing in an instant, and a thought occurring lest she was deceived, she made the sign of the Cross. Then our Lord said: 'Do not fear, be but humble and obedient, have no choice in anything, and you shall see what blessings I have in store for you, this day you shall experience more of My favours in this kind,' which was soon verified. For having communicated she heard the same angelical music, and our Blessed Lady appearing in great brightness showed her again the mystery of the sacred Nativity in her heart, assuring her that her Blessed Son was there, and she, both highly pleased. Then she told her the devil had tempted her much in point of declining her devotion from that feast, but henceforth she should carry in her heart a constant memory and presence of that mystery, and notwithstanding all her doubts she was resolved to let her always enjoy the same favour, which was fully attested by the singular devotion she had all her life long to the sacred Infancy of our Lord. All this filled her with much joy, nor could she then doubt, having newly received, but that our Lord was really in her heart caressing her with such affectionate expressions as would appear incredible. Then she thought our Blessed Lady put the Sacred Infant in her arms and said: 'Is not this a reward above all expectation? this you would have lost had you not acknowledged the music.' After this she desired her little Son to bestow some particular benediction upon her, that so she might never forget this favour, on which the Blessed Infant said : 'From this time she shall never take vainglory in anything, but know Me as the cause of all good, either in herself or others.'

Having afterwards written all down according to orders, she went to perform her devotions before a favourite image of our Lady, but was stopped in her road by a thick black cloud which she supposing to be the devil, she offered to bless herself, but could not stir her arm ; at which being frightened, and turning to go back from whence she came, she saw an angel who told her that the devil was in that cloud, and would carry her to Hell if she wrote or spoke any more of those fancied favours and apparitions. Supposing this to be the false angel as formerly, she resolved rather to pass through the cloud than encounter him, and bethought herself to make a cross with her head, which she had no sooner done but her arm was free, with which making the sign of the Cross, the cloud dispersed, and she got into the room, but was still afflicted with divers apprehensions by that false angel, who suggested to her that her confessor was pleased to hear those things out of condescendence to her great weakness, and that all spiritual directors must do the same by persons in her miserable situation, since they knew it was better to have those fancies than worse, which she herself might see if she had but the humility to remember her former wickedness, and then consider if such sins, and such favours, were likely to stand together. Therefore, to put herself in a secure way and avoid being puffed up with pride and vanity, she should burn those papers, and undeceive her confessor by letting him know the falsity of all that had hitherto been said, and then think of doing penance for what was past, according to the example of that great penitent Thais, who for forty years

together was never permitted to look up towards Heaven,
nor to say or use any other prayer than this humble
petition : 'You Who created me, have mercy on me.'
If she were only put in such a way she might have some
hopes of salvation, but as she continued to deceive herself and others by these holy fancies, although she had
no such intention, the pride and satisfaction she took
in being thought very holy and a saint should be all
the Heaven she was to expect.

Having said her beads, full of these thoughts and
fears, and earnestly imploring our Lady to help her, and
not permit her to be a lost soul, since she desired
nothing more than to obey, she saw the Blessed Virgin
standing as it were upon a curious bed of most odoriferous flowers, who bid her take courage, for it was only
the 'devil who would persuade her not to acknowledge
her favours; but as she felt in herself no particular
comfort, and the temptations above mentioned had
wholly obscured and possessed her mind with fears of
new deceit, she apprehended this, and wished within
herself she had not seen it. As she had these thoughts
our Lady drew nearer, and seemed to put her hand
under her chin, saying : 'Fear not, though you would
leave me, I will not leave you, those acts you made of
believing nothing but what your confessor bids you have
brought me hither, and as long as you continue to do so
you shall see that I will be your Mother and will defend
you.' At this her apprehensions were changed into joy,
and wished she was but so happy as to be always equally
certain that it was our Lady, she should then be freed
from all further molestations of the devil ; to which our
Lady answered her, she should both free her and give
her that certainty, but as it was not so good for her,
she would only secure her by such mistakes from all
pride and false confidence in herself. Then she showed

her the angel like an ugly black dog, and said : ' This
is he who would hinder you from crediting my favours.'
She was much frightened at this sight, and began to
creep nearer the place where our Lady was, but seeing
the devil did not move, she began to doubt whether
it was our Lady or not, till she mercifully casting her
mantle over her right side said : ' It is I, my child, I am
the Mother of God, and know, this devil is forced to stay
here to his own confusion, and from this time in token
of my presence, I commanded him never to come upon
your right side, so that let him be in never so much
glory, as long as you obey and are faithful to me, you
shall never be so far deceived as not to be able to help
yourself and discern his illusions.'

CHAPTER XI.

She is favoured again with a sight of the Order of Carmel, and beholds our Lady as in her triumphant Assumption, by whom she is clothed, girded, and crowned. She sees also the Blessed Trinity and our Lord's Humanity. And throughout the whole chapter is taught humbly to abandon herself to our Lord's disposal.

THE community having been engaged to sing a Votive Mass in honour of our Lady's Assumption, in thanksgiving for some favour received, on the same morning early our Lady appeared to Sister Margaret, and giving her her blessing, bid her to prepare herself to receive her Son: for that she was resolved to mortify her to-day, by giving her a taste of what she was to enjoy in the next life; she must therefore, notwithstanding her unmortified disposition, be contented to speak of incredible favours, and to become a child in all respects. Our Blessed Lady continued present with her all the time of the Hours and afterwards till Mass, which so occupied her thoughts betwixt amazement and confusion, that she scarce knew where she was, expecting with great apprehension to know what our Lady intended to do for her.

When the Mass began it seemed as if Heaven itself was opened, so glorious did the choir appear and every person in it. She heard the angels tuning most curious music, yet could not distinguish whether there were

instruments or voices only: all she could say of it
was, that it excelled everything of the kind she had
ever heard before. In the meantime our great Queen
sat upon a majestical throne of glory, and asked what
she thought would give her the greatest consolation,
and embracing her said : 'Fear not, you shall experience
that I am your Mother, and who can wonder at it, since
you are the spouse of my Son, and a child of St. Teresa.'
This put her in mind of wishing to see the Order, what
place it had in Heaven, and instantly it was represented
to her, on one side of our Blessed Lady. The place
seemed so large that she could see no end of it, and
withal so glorious, that she thought it impossible to
imagine more. But, not seeing any of the deceased
Sisters she had known, a doubt occurred whether the
religious women under the Ordinary were as agreeable
to our Lady, as those under the government of the
Order: on which our Lady showed her Mother Anne
of the Ascension, with all her other Sisters, and said :
'They are as dear to me, for I take them wholly into
my care.' Dear Mother Anne of the Ascension said
she had no reason to repent separating herself from
the Order, which she thought much the fittest for the
English ; but she told her not to pray any longer for
more foundations of that kind, to wit, under the bishops,
because in Catholic countries it was much better for
the religious to be under the direction of the Order,
which being wholly dedicated to our Lady, was most
pleasing to her: and although some particular persons
had suffered much from certain rigorous proceedings,
yet what the Order had done was more conducive to
the better observance of the Rules. St. Teresa, at the
same time, in a most affectionate sweet way, said she
had obtained her this favour in reward of her fidelity
and moderation in times of trouble, in speaking with

a due esteem of the Order, and, as she said, taking
things right without prejudice, by which way of proceeding she would become serviceable to her neighbour, please God, and promote His honour. After
this, our Lady told her it was in some sort a sign of
predestination to be of this (Lierre) house, and in
some sort of the Order, and that her children had a
particular privilege of not being tempted in point of
purity, for, as she said, it was as common to have that
favour in her Order, as it is in the world to have the
contrary. Then she showed her divers persons in
Heaven, some for having overcome the devil, amongst
whom she saw, in great glory, Mother Teresa of Jesus
Maria, sister to Mother Anne of the Ascension, who
had suffered great temptations : others, and those in
great number, who had been so happy as never to have
understood anything against that virtue. All which,
as she observed, had a particular privilege to be near
our Lady.

This sight filled her with much joy, and yet she was
struck with a deep sense of her infidelities to God in
that point, and thereupon desired our Blessed Lady not
to permit that her former sins should prove any obstacle
towards worthily receiving her Sacred Son, for she saw
clearly what purity of soul was requisite to perform that
great action. Whilst trembling she expected to hear
what our Lady would say, dear Mother Anne of the
Ascension kneeling to her said : 'Sacred Virgin, since
you were pleased to assure her, when I gave her the
habit, that she was without stain or blemish, now vouchsafe to confirm the same.' On which immediately our
Blessed Lady and St. Teresa drew nearer to her, and,
together with Mother Anne, clothed her with a white
garment, which she could compare to nothing better
than to a clear crystal, and said this was given her in

token that she was one of our Lady's number, by whom she had been particularly preserved in the virtue of purity. Then, as she thought, our Lady took a girdle from about her own waist, and put it round her, saying: 'This shall preserve you from ever experiencing any impure cogitation, for you are now girded with my girdle, which you have often worn before and been protected by it in dangers, when you little thought of me or it. You have formerly taken all my favours for fancies, but know they were real, and that the dove you took for a dream was a true emblem of your soul.'

This dove she remembered to have seen when she lived at Antwerp; it was white, and most beautiful, only the two wings were clipped, which Father Andrew White told her was like her soul, for there was nothing betwixt her soul and God, but want of speaking her conscience freely, which would make her a perfect dove, and give her wings to fly to Almighty God, where she must only rest. After this, our Lady putting a glorious crown upon her head, or rather, as she thought, rays of glory, for it did not seem like a crown, she said: 'This is for all those victories you have gotten over the enemy, and for the many times you have overcome yourself, which I have numbered and will reward them all: for as your former temptations were unavoidable, and out of your power, so are also my favours or the contrary, as I shall think best; and as long as you do it, I shall always show myself a true mother; for a soul thus disengaged from herself, who goes on acknowledging my Son in His ordinary gifts, humbly believing herself ignorant of all good, and yet desiring nothing but to remain so, supposing His will is thereby accomplished in her, shall be ever filled with a plenitude of His graces; and when He finds it fit and agreeable with His honour, He neither will nor can forbear doing her favours in abundance, for her humility will ever draw Him out of Heaven, and when He bestows His graces in earnest, He will be sure that the soul shall not only in words say : " Lord, all that is good comes from you," but He will have this stamped upon her heart, and every motion of her mind shall be still inclining her to think and desire that all the world may know she is nothing, nor deserves anything. When she can thus not only wish, but take pleasure and satisfaction in being deprived of all extraordinary graces and comforts, because from her heart she deems herself unworthy of them, then she is in a disposition ready to receive the impressions of my Son, Who when He bestows His favours does not give them with a view either of rewarding our long services or other good works, for this would make us think it in our power to command His favours at our discretion ; but we must do all on our parts, and then know that His Divine favours are given or taken at His own pleasure.'

Then our Lady bid her go to Communion ; after which, she was favoured with a vision of the Blessed Trinity, in such glory that she could form no likeness of it. She saw at the same time our Lady, as she thought, ascending on a throne of immense majesty and glory, whereby was represented the triumph of her glorious Assumption, and though this seemed to be above the clouds in the empyreal Heaven, for she thought not that she was in the choir till all was over, yet she seemed to be present with our Blessed Lady and near this glory, which so infinitely exceeded all she could imagine to have seen before, as if some poor bit of glass had been compared to the richest diamond. Being struck with amazement and reverential fear at this extraordinary sight, our Lady seemed to have compassion on her, and drawing nearer to her, showed her again the same white dove above mentioned, only she observed that its wings were now their natural length, telling her she must henceforth be as simple as a dove, for in a true simple heart her Son did dwell, and would then teach her heavenly wisdom.

Then showing her our Lord upon a glorious throne, she said: 'See here is Christ our Lord Whose spouse you are.' But Margaret being startled at this unusual appearance, betwixt fear and reverence, began to exercise herself in various acts of humility; on which our Lady turning towards our Lord said: 'See she is more afraid of you now than when she enjoys you a Child in my arms.' Then leading her nearer to our Lord, He said: 'I will be to her what she desires, for I cannot forbear multiplying My graces upon her: so that those humbling thoughts have now brought both Me and My Father, with the Holy Ghost, into her very heart, and from this time we will ever remain there.' And instantly she saw distinctly the Three Persons of the Blessed Trinity in her soul: and He made her understand how He proceeded from the Father and the Holy Ghost from them both, and how they Three were but One, and that she was equally dear to them all, and now possessed in her soul her Father, Spouse, and Com forter. Since she, therefore, knew herself poor and frail, she must leave herself wholly in His holy will, which as long as she did, He would seal up her heart, so that nothing should ever enter but Himself, and laying His hand upon her breast, He said: 'I am and will ever be well pleased here.' Margaret being interiorly desirous that the Sisters might also share in these favours our Lord was doing her, He answered: 'I am come to grant you all you desire.' And immediately she saw our Lord in every one, or rather as she thought every person and all she could wish in Him, Who several ways showed most dear expressions of affection to each one in particular, and asked her if she now believed all was contained in Him.

He told her this favour of showing her His Sacred Humanity was one of the greatest He had done her, and that she should often see Him in this manner in others, which would work such effects in her soul, that if she was but faithful to Him and humble, she would become adorned thereby with strong virtues : and having flowers in His hand of great beauty, He strewed them upon her, and said, 'As I now adorn you with these flowers, so and much more will this favour, which My Father and I with the Holy Ghost have bestowed upon you, become ornamental to you.' In this interval beholding the Sisters encompassed with glory of different sorts, a favour she had enjoyed on other occasions, she observed that some who were formerly endowed with extraordinary splendour were now in a much inferior degree, and others on the contrary, who had appeared less glorious, were now so far superior to all the rest, as Heaven seems different from earth, of which not being able to conceive the meaning, our Lord told her this was to let her see that all was in His own hands, and that He can as well take as give : 'The reason, therefore, why persons appear to you at one time more glorious than another is, that you may know I am the Author of nature and grace, Who can in one instant, by a simple act of the will, exalt them even into the third heaven; by which you may also learn that even the most dear unto me and the most consummate in perfection, as long as they are in this life, must experience changes, that being at times thus humbled here, they may become the higher exalted hereafter, in the next life, where they will be freed from all further vicissitudes. Be you therefore humble, do simply what you are commanded by your Superiors, remember the instability of your condition in this mortal life, and then visit Me with the rest.'

Having the little cross in her hand that hung at her beads, and was without either image or picture of our Lord upon it, a thought occurred whether this was as pleasing to Him as another, but He immediately asked her why she did not look upon the living Image: then, showing her Himself in her heart, He said: "Here as long as you are faithful to Me you shall ever find My true image engraven.' From which time she saw Him no longer by her as before, but found His presence by that other impression in her soul, which remained with her.

CHAPTER XII.

She sees our Lord as at His glorious Ascension, attended by eighteen souls released out of Purgatory. She is admonished how liberal our Lord is of His favours on great feasts, for which He would have His servants particularly prepare themselves. She receives also other favours and useful instructions.

A LITTLE before the first Vespers of the Ascension, having finished writing some of these papers, she found herself so quiet and peaceable in all kinds that it gave her particular satisfaction, so that in a sort of transport, addressing herself to our Lady, she cried out, 'Most Blessed Mother of God, what have you done for me? I have now by your favour all I desire, being able to rejoice on this great feast of our Lord.' But reflecting on her great unworthiness, and recalling to mind the sins of her former life, and the miserable manner in which she had let pass so many solemn feasts, her poverty and ignorance, as she thought, made her unfit for anything but to say her beads, with which she was content, provided she could equally please and serve God thereby. Whilst she was thus humbling and resigning herself to all, her whole cell seemed to be filled with a pure white silver cloud, of such brightness that she had never seen anything like it, and our Lady appeared close by her and said, ' I will now let you see the glory of my Son's triumphant Ascension, for whilst you are humble and desire nothing I will make you partaker of all.'

After this she saw in the said cloud our Blessed Lord, in the same manner as when He ascended into Heaven, with a great number of saints all in glory, amongst whom our Lady pointed out eighteen who by her means had newly been freed out of Purgatory ; they seemed to be in great joy for being released from their torments, but our Lady let her know that the joy they expressed was only to make her more sensible of their happiness, for, as she said, from the first instant that a soul enjoys God, all memory of past pains is as wholly forgotten as if they had never suffered any, and the glory they enter into so entire and complete as if it never had a beginning. She said that all the feasts of our Blessed Lord, and every action of His life, were now as present in Heaven as when He actually performed them on earth, as were also the good actions of the saints, which were constantly seen in Him, and this made the Church upon earth and in Heaven so much one and united, that though it is always in Heaven where the feast of feasts is kept together, yet our Lord is so much pleased with the solemnities that are kept of them here, that He has a singular satisfaction in granting and bestowing blessings upon the faithful in general, but particularly on those who He finds have disposed themselves to receive them ; because He is honoured by their petitions and glorified in granting their requests, which if made in a due manner in things that are to their advantage, He never refuses, so pleasing it is to Him to have these mysteries of His sacred life and actions commemorated.

This is in proportion equivalently the same with the saints, who receive an accidental augmentation of glory as often as we imitate their examples, solemnize their feasts, or perform other acts of virtue in their honour ; and their charity is so infinitely perfect that if there could be pain in Heaven they would suffer extremely to find people indisposed for receiving their favours. Our Blessed Lady then assured her that she always obtained some favours for her clients on these occasions, and had now on this festival procured the freedom of those eighteen souls out of Purgatory, who were all of different conditions and states of life ; and that she now thus favoured her, that she might thoroughly be convinced of the great good that might be obtained by the disposing ourselves for the keeping of all feasts, as also in reward of the diligence she had hitherto used in this point. Then our Lady asked her what she would have, and it should be granted her ; to which Margaret, betwixt fear and perplexity, could answer nothing, but thought she should be happy to be out of this world, where there was no security. On which our Lady told her she knew not what she desired, nor how to value the happy state she was in, by being in a condition of meriting; 'For,' said she, ' if my dear Son, of His infinite mercy, draws a poor sinner from the bottom of Hell, as it were, and by one act of His will, or a thought of His mind, raises him to become a glorious saint in Heaven, as He frequently does, what will He then do for those who endeavour faithfully to serve Him ? with how many crowns shall every good action and work they do be rewarded ? Fear not, therefore, your want of security ; for those who trust in me, and acknowledge me for their Mother, shall find by experience that I will carry them through this world in my arms.'

As Margaret, in the depth of confusion, was thinking herself unworthy of such favour, our Lady said, ' Do you still doubt of my affection towards you ? ' and immediately she let her see the Infant Jesus in her arms, and as she thought she saw herself in Him, and our Lady again said, ' Now do you believe you are in my arms ? see here ; it is in the strength of this Lord of ours, in Whom and by Whom I can do all for you and my dear servants.' At this Margaret, adoring, said : ' You are indeed my Mother, and the Mother of all poor sinners ; your mercies have no limits.' To which our Lady replied, ' You say well ; I am the Mother of Mercy, and help of sinners ; but I am also the strength and comfort of the perfect, and of all those who faithfully serve my Son. There is only this difference, that sinners come to know me by the necessity they have of my help, and by knowing me come to the knowledge of my Son ; whilst others, by knowing my Son, come to a perfect knowledge of me, as they become enriched with my favours. You must not, therefore, think that those who have sinned are less dear to me than those who have led an innocent life ; for if the sinners' repentance be such as to exalt them above others in my Son's favour, then they are most acceptable to me ; and if the others' good works and humility exceed, then believe they are most in my favour who merit most before my Son, Who is never found without me, nor am I ever applied to with an humble confidence and sincere heart but my Son is found, and sooner or later becomes the only aim and sole possessor of their hearts.'

All this she understood as clearly as if it had actually passed in her own soul, which received such a sensible impression that she shall never forget it, yet it seemed to pass in one instant of time. Having been greatly troubled all the afternoon with various temptations, she found herself much indisposed, yet not so as to be any hindrance to her duties. At night, after Compline, as she was saying her beads, our Blessed Lady appeared again to her, and said she knew she wished to do something by way of preparation for this great feast, and bid her make use of sickness and indisposition in place of penances ; then bid her go and ask Reverend Mother's leave to drink and refresh herself, that she might be better able to assist at Matins, during which she herself would accompany her. This Margaret visibly experienced all the time, and at the end our Lady gave her blessing to the whole choir, and told her to go to rest. This made Margaret again uneasy, for reflecting on some prayers she had not said, and which she was unwilling to omit, being devotions she constantly used, she was dubious what to do; but remembering the advice her confessor had before given her on the like occasion, which was, in case of indisposition or other hindrances, not to force herself beyond her time, but rather to leave her prayers, she resolved to do so and follow obedience. She was no sooner in bed, but she saw our Blessed Lady with her Son in her arms, in the act of giving her His blessing, a favour she has often received from Him, Who has more than once closed her eyes to sleep. Then our Lady said this act of obedience was more grateful to her and her Blessed Son than all her prayers; 'therefore I here give you Him into your arms; take Him, for He shall rest with you this night. Your devotions are performed by another servant of mine, and you shall enjoy the merit both of those and this act of obedience, which is the cause of this particular brightness in which you see my Son; not that any glory is added unto Him thereby, for He has all glory in Himself from all eternity, but that you may understand something more of that immensity which is without limits in Him.' Thus she left Margaret in great amaze, with the Sacred Infant, as she thought, in her heart, where He imprinted a more clear understanding and esteem of obedience than ever she had felt before.

The next morning when she awoke, our Lady seemed present with the Infant in her arms, and after having given her their blessing, bid her prepare herself to communicate, in which she would help her and remain with her till that time. During the Hours Margaret found herself much comforted, and yet greatly humbled at the memory of what had passed the night before; for it seeming impossible, she was almost ashamed to reflect upon it, and so endeavoured to pass it over by believing our Lord could do what He pleased. At Mass she found no great devotion, so that she could only occupy herself in saying her beads and some other ordinary prayers, and therefore as the time of Communion approached she endeavoured to help herself, as usual on such occasions, by offering up her obedience, which she hoped would supply for her unworthiness and want of preparation.

After Communion she saw an extraordinary glory, which she understood to be the Blessed Trinity, and our Lord appeared to her in great splendour, assuring her that she was now in the very bosom of His Eternal Father, and though she knew not what she saw, nor how this was, she was sure she found herself there. Our Lord, continuing to caress her, said He had many truths to engrave in her soul, and, taking her by the hand, seemed to let her touch His Sacred Wounds; but she in great fright recalling to mind her many sins, by which she had so often wounded Him anew, would have drawn it back, but our Lord forced her nearer to Him, and said, 'I have pardoned all, and you have now become the daughter of My Father, and My spouse, and the Temple of the Holy Ghost.' It seemed to her that she then saw the Blessed Trinity all glorious, and in this mystery all Heaven, but could distinguish nothing only our Blessed Lord, Who strengthened her to behold so much—for it far exceeded her natural faculties—that she desired Him either to enlarge her heart or to withdraw His favours, which she thought im-

possible longer to support, at which she saw her heart
enlarged, and vastly great, with our Lord in it, and all
in Him, and then He said, 'Are you content with this?'
to which she could answer nothing but, 'What You
please, Lord, only let me be Yours entirely.' Immediately her heart became as little as before, and yet she
saw our Lord in it, and all in Him, as clear and distinctly as in the great heart, Who told her He showed
her this that she might see His power, and that He was
as much and as great in a little as a large compass, and
therefore hoped she would hereafter believe that though
her heart was narrow and little, He could be in it.
Then laying His hand upon it, He said, 'Now I have
put My seal upon your heart, and know I am wholly
yours, and have made you Mine, and no other shall
ever have place in you.' Then our Blessed Lady embracing her, said, 'You are my sister, the daughter of
my Father, and as the spouse of my Son I crown you
and will ever respect you as much.' And putting the
crown on her head, said, 'Now, see I am your Mother
and Sister, and will ever be your help and strength; be
sure you endeavour to keep your soul pure.'

After this our Lord again said, 'My dear child, the
reason why I have thus comforted you is, because when
you made your vows, which were accepted of in Heaven,
you did faithfully correspond with My will and inspirations, in resigning and giving yourself up into My hands,
for the suffering whatsoever I should impose upon you,
which was so grateful to Me, that it has in a manner
obliged Me to make you entirely Mine. To the end,
therefore, that this may be wholly accomplished, observe
what I now tell you, and let it be an instruction for your
whole life. To be in My favour and to deserve much
from Me, does not consist in having great satisfaction
and sweetness in what you do, but in a readiness of

your will to suffer and labour for love of Me; for you only read once of My great Apostle enjoying celestial delights, whereas he was many years in great suffering. I was only once on Mount Thabor, but oftentimes I suffered for you : do not always consider Me in My Mother's arms, but frequently accompany her under the Cross, and remember the sword of grief that pierced her afflicted heart during My Death and Passion. How many saints have been left to themselves numbers of years, striving both against nature and the devil without any spiritual comfort? Believe Me, My dear child, that the love My Father bears His servants is according to the measure of sufferings He sends them, and according to the love and resignation your soul has towards sufferings such is the true measure of your love towards Me. Now what can I do more, or better for you, than to provide you the same I chose Myself?' Then showing her His Sacred Wounds, He said, 'See here, nothing you have hitherto suffered has come thus far; stick close to My Cross—this is the only way of truth.'

He continued to speak so much of divers kinds of the dignity and value of sufferings, that all that she had ever heard or read could form no comparison, and the impression it made on her mind was beyond all she could express, and as she thought must needs forebode something our Lord was intending for her. He also sweetly reprehended her for having often begged and desired to suffer for Him, whilst at the same time she looked upon trifles as insupportable; then said, 'My child, I have always dealt with you according to what I knew was your rational and true will, and not according to your inordinate suggestions.' He further admonished her that it was not agreeable with our miseries in this life of temptation to be always in one humour, but that she must expect a time of consolation and a time of

desolation, but was in all to confide and trust in Him,
and look upon His sufferings and precious Wounds, which
would make all light, for according to the measure of
her sufferings, such should be her reward; that true
suffering is the denial of our own will in strong temptations, of which He told her she had met with many,
and such, that if He had not, through the intercession
of His Blessed Mother, helped her, she would not have
got the better of them. This said, He gave her the
comfort of His blessing, with an assurance that she was
in His favour, and that He would continue to help her,
and so disappeared.

At which, coming to herself, she could not conceive or
understand what had passed, neither could she believe
what she had heard and seen, as it were in an instant,
was possible. During this surprise our Lord appeared
again, though not as before, for she could not see
anything distinctly, or the place where He was, only
she was assured of His presence, and interiorly heard
Him say it should be impossible for her not to believe,
that so she might acknowledge that both seeing and
being deprived of Him were both in His hands and not
in her power. 'Have I not told you you must be
sometimes comforted and sometimes the contrary?
Remember My words, and know both comes from or
by permission, for your humiliation or greater good. I
often show My favours more unto you by leaving you in
this sort of darkness, and letting you be thus tempted,
than if you did always with certainty enjoy them, for by
that means you come to see how little you can do in the
absence of My extraordinary graces, and how very much
I do for you when I tie the hands of the devil, and am
present with you. The pride and malice of man is such
that if I did not sometimes withdraw Myself you would
begin to think My presence was your due, and that your

own great virtue had deserved it, and so lose all. Beware, therefore, and put your trust in Me by a lively faith, which will strengthen and confirm you in the belief of what I say and do for you.'

As she was in her own thoughts desiring our Lord to give her this lively faith, He replied, 'You must know that although faith be My gift, I require all your desires to obtain it. When you have Me you have all; and if you only believe what your confessor approves, you do as much as My Mother and I desire, and have faith in that kind as will be most agreeable with My honour and your true good. This day you shall experience what it is to believe and enjoy Me;' which was accordingly accomplished, for the whole day she had the presence of our Lord in all she did, and was most sensible of His being very near her. Hearing some one repeat a story of a certain gay lady that was high minded and ambitious of honour, she had a thought that it was a good gallant humour, but our Lord immediately reprehended her, saying, 'Let it be your ambition to love and serve Me, and endeavour to advance My honour, by making that your sole business.' This presently gave her a clear knowledge and contempt of all vanity, and made her see the misery of the world, and her own happiness in being freed from all its snares.

CHAPTER XIII

She is elected Subprioress, admonished of the advan-
tages of corporal infirmities, and forewarned by our
Lord of a cross which she understands to be her
election as Superior, and in all He requires of her
silence, patience, sufferance, and prayer.

THREE years after this new Foundation began Sister
Margaret was elected Subprioress. The many rare
virtues that daily manifested themselves in her performance of other employments moved the community to
promote her also to this, by which she became intrusted
with the care of the choir, which properly belongs to
the Subprioress, who there regulates all that concerns
the Divine Office, and the ceremonies that are to be
observed in the saying and singing of it, which are such
as truly inspire devotion, and were observed in those
happy days with so much exactness as to move all those
who heard or beheld them to admiration and veneration
for those Church duties. The Subprioress has also
another charge incumbent upon her, which is to preside
in other acts of community in the absence of the
Reverend Mother Prioress. This requires her constant
presence in the refectory and at recreation, where she is
to correct any faults or oversights that may escape the
religious in their behaviour or conversation. So exactly
and so well regulated are these reformed houses, that
even the shadow of anything defective is not permitted
to appear. Truly may these blessed inclosures be com-

pared to the 'garden inclosed' mentioned in the Canticles, whose offspring is a 'paradise of pomegranates with orchard fruit, where cypress with spikenard, sweet cane and cinnamon, myrrh and aloes, where all the chief ointments grow.'[1] For to such may their virtues be compared, whose fragrancy and variety no less delight their Spouse Christ, yielding Him an agreeable retreat and secure shelter from the many injuries and offences with which the world is hourly insulting Him. But as we observe in those delicious gardens amongst the most delicate fruit and odoriferous plants the bitter myrrh and thorny aloe, we are hereby admonished that no happiness in this vale of misery, however complete it may appear, can be long enjoyed without a mixture of some kind of adversity, since even the consolations of the saints, which exceeds all that the world can boast of, are frequently interrupted by tribulations and trials, that make them taste of the bitter chalice which our Divine Master, after His glorious Transfiguration, so cheerfully accepted of from His Heavenly Father.

This was to be Margaret's portion, and a new pledge of our Lord's affection to her, as He Himself was pleased to reveal to her. For one day after Communion our Lord appeared visibly to her, and showed her a most beautiful cross, saying, 'I am now coming to plant the love of the cross in your soul.' He appeared all-glorious, and she had a thought that as long as she could see Him thus, all crosses would be beloved by her; to which our Lord replied, 'Although you do not see Me, I will teach you how to make all crosses beloved by you; look only upon My will in them, and they will always be grateful to you. My will is that you and all My servants bear their cross with joy, without adding to its burden by their want of resignation. For to accept

[1] Cant. iv. 12—14.

of what I send them, and in the manner I send it them,
with tranquillity of heart, as coming from Me, is the
completest act of love you can make, for then let what
will happen, though never so contrary to your own will
and sensible content, you will still love Me and My cross
which I am come to bring you.'

Having some apprehensions what this might be, and
reflecting on herself on different subjects, she thought
she did not much fear sickness; to which our Lord
replied that He knew she would make good use of it,
and therefore was resolved she should have her share
also in that kind of suffering, for from this time she
should only enjoy such health as was convenient and
suitable to the designs He had over her, which being to
His greater honour and glory she must be contented to
accept of, but she might be sure that whenever it should
please Him to visit her with sickness it was a favour
tending more immediately to her own good, because
the merits thereof were wholly hers, and a direct means
of uniting her more closely to Him.

At this time He let her understand that religious
persons do lose much for want of making right use of
corporal infirmities and sickness, showing her how these
indispositions, if received with due resignation, do more
sincerely unite a soul to God than the exercise of high
prayer, 'For,' said He, 'all prayer consists in a simple
act of the will, so that a will and a desire to suffer, if
compared with an act of resignation to the real sufferings
God is pleased to send us, differ as much in value and
merit as the dying a martyr for the love of God and
living to serve Him in a pious way.' He also said that
an inordinate desire of health was a great impediment to
religious persons, because it was impossible for them to
be perfect, but that to a proportion they must be visited
by corporal indispositions, especially if they had not

courage to exercise themselves in penitential works, which she saw our Lord required of those whose constitution of body was able to bear it.

On another occasion, having heard Mass, as she says, without being either particularly distracted or particularly devout, after Communion she was able to recollect herself awhile, but not long, for she suddenly grew heavy and weary of prayer, but remembering she had newly received Communion, she endeavoured to stir herself, for which purpose she took hold of her beads,[2] and as she began to say them our Blessed Lady appeared to her, and said, 'No wonder you cannot pray, since you are so dilatory in your recourse to the helps prescribed you. Have I not told you you are to use no other means to recollect yourself than that of saying your beads, unless your confessor orders you the contrary, or you find yourself so taken up with me and my Son, that you forget all other things?' This recalled to her mind the lively impressions these same orders had formerly made upon her, and whilst she was humbling herself for her negligence she saw our Lord most distinctly, and He seemed to stand by her, holding the same cross in His hands she had so often seen before, though she could not conceive how this was, for she likewise saw and knew Him to be at the same time in her heart. These frequent apparitions of our Lord with His cross put her into great anxiety, not being able to imagine what it might mean, or how it would end; as for censures or such-like trials, although she knew herself to be unmortified and easily dejected, she hoped she should be able to bear with

---

[2] [These beads, as is stated elsewhere, are still preserved by the community at Darlington. Canon Bedingfield mentions that our Lady promised that many miraculous favours should be bestowed by their means. They have attached to them the 'Thunder-cross' and two medals, of the Blessed Sacrament and of St. Teresa, worn by Mother Margaret.]

them, and so offered herself to bear any cross except
that of superiority, which her confessor had told her
perhaps might be meant by it, to which, considering the
consequences, she was wholly averse, and so afraid of it
that she could not forbear crying out to our Lord, saying:
' Lord, as for great humiliations Your goodness can make
me strong enough to go through with them. But if You
put me in that other occasion I fear lest I should get a
liking to it, and so fall into pride, offend You, and lose
my soul.' But our Lord said, ' My will must be
embraced without any limitation, how and what are to be
left to Me, Who am ever greatly pleased to see souls
consecrated to My service pass their lives in silence,
patience, suffering, and prayers, and such are obliged to
banish from their hearts all other desires, affections, and
interests, so as to forget themselves entirely, to obey and
honour Me. If you leave the peace and solitude of a
cell to be employed in exterior occupations because such
is My will, and not of your own seeking, although you
should suffer thereby many inconveniences they will only
add new lustre to your crown ; whilst you resolve to
follow Me, you must never seek repose, but continued
labours, in all which have recourse to Me, and behold in
Me the virtues that are opposite to the imperfections
you are assailed by ; for, if you cease to mortify your
too eager desires of peace and security, My grace will
retire itself, for then you abandon its works ; neither are
you to be discouraged at the imperfections or faults that
may ensue, but rather humbled, since it is natural for
the children of Adam to fail; but whilst you depend upon
Me by a simple obedience to My will I shall raise you
up so as even to draw profit from your faults. It imports
not whether you be in action or repose, but it imports
much that both in the one and the other you be separated
from yourself. I will not have you either demand or

refuse anything, but disposed to do all I command and obedience appoints, by a thorough submission of your own will to Mine, for without that you cannot conform yourself to My words, where I teach, ' He that renounces not himself cannot be My disciple.' Suffering is the lesson laid before you in My life, actions, and bitter Passion, and what I have left to sanctify My servants, particularly those who are to appertain to Me by a more elevated state of grace and glory. Follow exactly and carefully My inspirations, and comply with them faithfully, whatever it cost you, for perfection does not consist in great desires nor fair words, but in perfect works and suffering much for Me. Those whom I love, and who I am resolved to make entirely Mine, I purify by these means, and if they are but faithful in following My steps, I favour them with a particular respect and homage to My life and suffering in their heart.'

All this, as she said, was represented and spoken to her in one instant, with such an impression that it moved her to a total resignation of herself to whatsoever our beloved Lord should please to impose upon her, embracing in her heart any cross however difficult. On which He said, ' My child, I have divers kinds of crosses by which I purify My servants. You have experienced some of them, but not all ; let Me, then, do with you what I please. I am able to defend you in all your apprehended dangers, so that you need not fear that any employment I may put you in shall expose you to the loss of your soul, for I can find means in all, even My greatest favours, to humble you and make you suffer.' Then immediately He let her see His Sacred Soul, and how it was sorrowful unto death, which in some sort she seemed to experience in herself; she also clearly beheld the mysteries of His Sacred Passion and Death, and though all seemed glorious, the impression it left put her to much pain, which our Lord assured her was one of the most forcible effects of His favours and grace, and yet the most dissatisfactory and least known, since few can understand how in the midst of so much glory a soul should be susceptible of pain which she then experienced, and of which she can give no account. For all that glory did not give her any motion of joy, but much sorrow, without trouble, or desire of anything, for nothing as she thought was then in her power, but she understood this sensible suffering and sorrow were given by our Lord, not only to purify souls from all self-satisfaction they might take in His other favours and graces, but also, as He signified, to bring them in this life to be continually adoring His sacred sufferings, and in some sort also experiencing them, whilst they are not able to comprehend how or by what means they come to have this impression. Then our Lord said to her, 'You shall be able to say little, nor well understand what I am doing for you, nor even to know when I am with you, as you will not so often sensibly experience My presence, which is as great a favour as any I have done you, and so long as you strive to advance in embracing My will faithfully and patiently, this pure Soul of Mine shall not only remain with you, but by a special union become united, and in some sort one, with yours, which is to participate as far as earth will permit of the happiness the saints enjoy in Heaven, whose glory and bliss is completed by this happy union.' She thought our Blessed Lord now imprinted His sacred sufferings upon her heart, and said He would always be there; but being inclined to think this a fancy, He answered again her thoughts, and said, Is anything impossible to Me? have I not told you I can and will do you favours, which shall even rend your heart to speak of, and when you have said what is required of you, it shall give you no more satisfaction than if you had said nothing; neither will I at any time have you to expect either ease or solace from declaring your conscience, but to be silently contented with the humiliation and confusion that attend it, simply believing what is told you, and adhering to the advice which is given you by those on whom your soul depends. Thus you will live in the constant exercise of silence, patience, and sufferance, which will keep you in a certain obscurity, and free you from all pride, since at times the impression of My suffering and of My joys will be equally dubious to you, and the remembrance of your past ingratitude and great poverty will overshadow and darken all sense of love towards Me. This will bring you to be in continual prayer, either seeing your own nothingness and the much I have done for you, or else in sighing and thirsting after the accomplishment of My will, without seeking to rest in My consolations. For, whilst you see Me suffer, your only desire will be to share in My sufferings, on which account you will always choose the most humble and mean things, and rejoice in all that renders you contemptible.' She felt during this a most sensible impression of Christ's sufferings, and saw at the same time His Sacred Soul in great glory, which struck her with an unusual kind of fear, yet when it was past she became again very peaceful in herself, and retained no other effects of what she had seen. But our Lord said, 'Now, My child, I have showed you how I can make My servants suffer even in the enjoyment of My greatest favours. Continue to be faithful in the sense of your own nothingness, and resolve to obey them, whatever happens will be easy to you, and your cross light, because if you generously accept of it, neglecting your own inclinations, and slighting all that the world may say of you, you will always find Me in this cross, and see therein the excess of My goodness towards you. For one that

is truly simple and humble is so pleasing to My Heavenly
Father that He communicates to her greater lights, and
lets her see more in one instant with the eyes of her
soul than she can behold sensible objects in many years
with the eyes of her body, a thing which is not to be
comprehended or understood but only by those to whom
My Father is pleased to impart it.'

Here our Lord continued to show her much favour,
and assured her He would never leave her, and that her
affections and desires should henceforth be wholly fixed
upon Him, and as long as she kept her soul pure and
humble she should clearly comprehend what she had so
often read, that His delight is to be with the children of
men, leaving her thereby much comforted.

NOTE V.

Margaret's Devotion to our Lady's virtues.

BEING at Mass, and saying my usual devotion of beads,
meditating upon the Passion, during the time of the Epistle,
which was of St. Paul, it being Quinquagesima Sunday,
I was wholly carried away with devotion to St. Paul, who
was present with me the whole Mass, and expressed the
words to me, and showed me much favour. And when the
Gospel was read, our Blessed Lord showed Himself to me,
and seeming to encompass me in with His glory, said,
' My Spouse, I come now to invite thee to the feast of My
Sacred Passion, where thou shalt not only see My pains,
and understand what I have done for thee, and the love
wherewith I did it, but also be enriched with My sacred
merits, and enabled to rejoice in afflictions for My sake.
And now, as thy whole heart and thoughts and affections
shall by My favour be employed upon this mystery of My
Passion, so shall the glory and benefit of it be present
with thee, and I Myself and all I have is thine, to dispose
of for My greater honour, the which in all thy petitions

shall ever be thy only aim.' When the Gospel was
finished, I found my beads also finished, and was troubled
to think whether I had said them or no, because my
thoughts had not been upon them, and immediately our
Blessed Lady, who was present, showed herself, and embracing me showed me my heart with all the mysteries of
the Passion in it, as I have seen it formerly, and said,
'My child, see, you have visited all the Sacred Wounds
of my Son, and done all the devotions required of you,' and
taking the thunder-cross which is on our beads into her
sacred hands she bid me say my *Ave Maria*, and said,
'I will teach you a devotion most pleasing to me, which
you shall say daily this Lent in honour of my virtues.'

The first was the Purity of our Blessed Lady, and she
represented in a very clear manner those words of hers in
her salutation—'How can this be done, since I know no
man?'—and seemed to discourse of this virtue and filled
my whole heart with a knowledge much clearer than ever
I conceived anything before of the dignity of this virtue,
and of how much in all perfection she excelled all the
saints and angels, and possesseth it in all perfection. When
I had said the ten *Aves*, our Blessed Lady bid me say a
Laudate in thanksgiving for all the privileges she hath
in this virtue. And then she secondly represented her
Prudence, and in the same manner bid me salute that
virtue of hers with ten *Aves*, and said and made appear
those words, 'She considered how great this salutation
might be,' and in the like manner went on imprinting upon
my soul with much tenderness the perfection she possessed
in this virtue, and the necessity of it for all those that
pretend to serve God in perfection. In like manner as
before, bid me say a *Laudate* in thanksgiving. Then, thirdly,
I saluted her Humility with ten *Aves*, and our Blessed Lady
represented those words, 'Behold the handmaid of our
Lord,' and showed me the very great fulness she possessed
of this virtue, and how much it pleases her the endeavouring to imitate her in humility, and said, 'My child,
to the end that you become disposed for the effects of
my graces, you must become little and even nothing in

the sight of yourself and my servants, and not only esteem all above yourself, but even be a servant to all in your heart, by exalting and esteeming their virtues, and in your actions by serving them, and doing humble offices in my mitation.' Then I said the *Laudate* as before in thanksgiving.

The other ten *Aves* were in honour of her fourth virtue, Fidelity in faith, and our Blessed Lady represented those words of St. Elisabeth, 'Blessed are you because you have believed,' and so went on showing me how she was all replenished with a lively faith and divers particulars of the benefit and necessity of this virtue. And she said, 'My child, it is not enough to beg it and esteem it much, but thou art obliged to exercise the acts, and since I command thee, not to believe me but as far as thy confessarius approves it. It is, if thou didst understand it, even the greatest pride the devil can tempt thee to, not to believe; and be ever submitting and adoring me in my favours and graces towards thee, and though none can ever attain my perfect imitation, yet to those that praise my Son for what He hath bestowed upon me, I do obtain much;' then a *Laudate.* Her fifth virtue our Blessed Lady represented to be her Gratitude to God, by these words of her *Magnificat* — 'My soul doth magnify our Lord,' and in like manner as before went on showing me in how large a manner she possessed that virtue, and showed me how much I want it, and said, 'My child, see how my heart is still rewarding the least *Ave* that is said in my honour; and and how very much am I bestowing upon thee which still thou art afraid to acknowledge from me.' Much more I might say upon all this which I understood of the perfection our Blessed Lady possessed in this life in these virtues; but it were too long to write them. But she said I would always receive a particular grace from her, if in her imitation I do either towards her or creatures exercise any act of gratitude, so great a patroness she is of that virtue that she will not fail to show herself apparently to them that, as I have said, do imitate her therein; then the *Laudate* as before. Her sixth virtue our Blessed

Lady represented as her Obedience, in those words, 'Be it done to me according to Thy word,' and on this she seemed to inflame my heart with a desire to obtain the perfection of it, and our Blessed Lady said, 'Obedience hath cured thee, and as long as thou art a lover and practiser of it, I will always be ready to help thee.' In particular I understood the dignity of that vow, and the favour our Blessed Lady hath done me in making me endeavour the practice; then a *Laudate*. The seventh virtue she represented was her Poverty, and how she exercised it in the Nativity of our Blessed Lord, all which was in particular showed me, and our Blessed Lady gave me her Son in my arms and bid me say a *Laudate* in thanksgiving for the perfection she had in that virtue. Her eighth virtue was represented her Patience, by those words when she sought and found our Lord in the Temple—'Your Father and I have sought you in much sorrow,' and this was showed me by our Blessed Lady with much clearness, and how I should imitate her by patiently expecting in time of aridities or troubles, till our Lord pleases to show Himself; but she said, 'My child, I dare not leave thee one instant to thyself, so very apt art thou to fail, and so weak in bearing anything; but say the *Laudate* in thanksgiving for my patience.' The ninth was her Charity, on those words of the Gospel, 'They have no wine,' all which was most clearly represented to me and practically applied to myself, which would be too long to set down; after, the *Laudate*. The tenth virtue her Constancy, by her remaining with our Blessed Lord under the Cross, and she said, 'My child, those that imitate this virtue of mine, and love in their thoughts and affections to accompany me under the Cross of my Son, shall participate of my glory and power in disposing of those sacred merits of His.' After I had said a *Laudate*, our Blessed Lady embracing me, said, 'See, now, I have taught thee how to pray and say thy beads, contemplating me and my virtues, and whosoever uses this way I will communicate great graces to, and favour them, and will give them the gift of prayer; and whosoever shall say daily ten *Aves* in honour and memory of these ten virtues,

I shall find myself obliged to make them participant of those virtues, and will make it my care to imprint them in their hearts.'[1] Our Blessed Lady bid me tell your Reverence this devotion, and said, 'I will communicate great light and favours to him by this devotion,' and also said that when you visit her at the Slues,[2] if you salute her with this devotion, it would be most grateful to her, and that you should find it is so. And she said, 'My child, this is no such thing as any fancy of thy own, but a means I take by the exercise of this devotion, to teach many to know and consider my virtues and to imitate them; and those that love me already and know my virtues, to them it shall be a means to receive from me much favour; and others it shall teach to know me, and by this devotion thou shalt receive more light and grace than by all thou hast known heretofore. Fear not to tell this' (*Paper by Mother Margaret*).

[1] These ten *Aves* in honour of our Blessed Lady's virtues were revealed by her, more than a century before, to Blessed Jane, Duchess of Berri, an Annunciade religious and descendant of St. Louis, almost in the same order, but not so fully explained, as to Mother Margaret. Their recital was enriched, by the Pope, with great indulgences; but Father Bedingfield has left in his own handwriting an assurance that Mother Margaret had never heard either of the devotion or revelation.

[2] Our Lady of Slues (Cluyes) was an image held in great reputation at Lierre (where our monastery then was). It used at times to be brought to our convent in great solemnity, and was the one that cured our venerable Mother Ursula (Mother Margaret's sister) when sh was dangerously ill (*Note by the Religious*).

CHAPTER XIV

She speaks of the advantages of frequent Communion, and receives from our Lord instructions how to profit by it. He admonishes her to visit Him frequently in the church, and with her heart in other churches which are least frequented. Our Lord sometimes communicated her Himself, and showed her Himself in her heart, and in the hearts of all the Sisters. She saw also on different occasions saints and angels adoring the Blessed Sacrament, and our Lord pierced her heart with a little spear.

On a particular occasion she found herself very much importuned the whole morning with her usual temptation, as she says, to leave Communion, but knowing it to be contrary to her duty, and against obedience, she endeavoured to prepare herself as well as she could after her cold manner. But as the time of Mass drew nearer, she became less able to help herself, and more oppressed with fears. Yet, as she could not discover in herself any just cause for them, only some apprehensions that she deceived her confessor, she resolved to overcome herself and to communicate. She remained, however, in a sort of wavering suspense till after the Elevation, when she again renewed her resolutions, thinking that if she was to be a lost soul it should be through obedience. In this strife our Blessed Lady appeared to her, with her Infant Son, who said those acts of obedience had brought them to assist her in preparation, and strengthen her against the like temptations for the future. As soon as she had received the Sacred Host, in which she saw our Lord distinctly, He told her He would show her the dignity and benefit of communicating, and how every Communion worthily received would appear in Heaven.

After this, as she thought, she saw our Lord all glorious and bright, or rather all Heaven in Him, and understood that all glorified bodies are made glorious, and receive their splendour from His Sacred Humanity, and as His Sacred Humanity shall shine in every glorified body, so shall every Communion give new lustre to our bodies, so that the more frequently we communicate, and according to the fervour and love with which we dispose ourselves for it, so we shall partake of the glory of the Sacred Humanity, and by this to a proportion of His Divinity, which the soul shall see and enjoy more or less according to its fidelity in corresponding with the influences of light, and graces that have been communicated to it in the Sacrament. Then our Lord said to her in a most sweet manner, 'Now, My child, I hope you will ever be eager and solicitous to receive Me often, and dispose yourself thereto, to the best of your power, since every Communion, as you see, and every act of virtue you then exercise, shall be so abundantly rewarded.' The beauty and glory our Lord appeared then in was to such an excess, that nothing she thought could possibly surpass it; and immediately our Lord showed her in Himself the impression of priesthood, the glory of which so far exceeded all she had seen before, as entirely to extinguish even the remembrance of it.

After this our Lord admonished her not to put herself so much in pain on occasions when she was not so sensible of fervour and devotion, nor even when oppressed with the contrary, since the benefit of Communion no ways depended upon it; a simple though obscure faith that He is always the same, as great, as powerful, as merciful, and as good in the depth of aridity as in the height of consolations, will abundantly recompense all other deficiences, and by approaching the Sacraments in these humble sentiments, after having made use of the proper prayers for that purpose, although in the greatest dryness and insensibility, the same graces and benefits may be received as when they are performed with the most lively sentiments of devotion, which are sometimes more apt to deceive than sanctify us. Nay, oftentimes a Communion received without any apparent effects of devotion, only because obedience requires it, surpasses many others in which we feel satisfaction, and is far more grateful to God, and will be rewarded with a much greater glory in Heaven. 'Never, therefore, be anxious,' said He, 'for past sins and imperfections, when you should be preparing yourself to receive Me; for it is a mere illusion of the devil, who, under the specious appearance of a false humility, would dissuade you from approaching so often to this sacred table on account of your unworthiness, or if he cannot effect this, to hinder you at least from that devotion which you might otherwise attain; and by this throwing you into perplexities deprives you of the exercise of those loving and affectionate desires, which he knows to be so pleasing to Me. You may be assured it is not what is past that puts an obstacle to My graces, since all that by a simple act of the will is entirely effaced. But it is the present disposition the soul is in that renders it fit or unfit for the receiving this Divine food, so that a wilful attachment or affection to any venial sin is a greater obstacle than all the other sins of your past life once repented of; and a disposition to be careless or negligent in little things, however small they may be, is more displeasing to Me, and hinders the effects of grace in your soul more than if you came to receive Me with divers venial sins with a due sorrow and resolution of amendment.' Our Lord said He let her know this in reward of her obedience, and assured her that all those Communions she had made with so much repugnance and difficulty on account of the bad dispositions she imagined herself to be in, were highly grateful to Him, and had gained great glory, which He forbore to let her see clearly, because He knew it would give her affliction, by putting her in mind of certain occasions she had let pass, in which she might have gained such immense treasures. On all these occasions obedience and submission frustrates the devil's designs, and satisfies for many imperfections one may then be guilty of through their own frailty, anxiety, or inadvertency. She was much comforted at this, and resolved for the future to believe and practise whatever her confessor should advise her to, and our Lord assured her that such was the secure means of knowing His will, and that she had in part overcome the difficulty, and should not for the future be so much tempted in that kind, but that she might with a moderate endeavour help herself so far as easily to master all contrary dispositions.

If therefore at times she found herself in a changeable disposition, or to fall into some imperfections, she was not on that account to be dejected, but rather humbled : ' for it is beneficial to My servants,' said He ; 'and no small effect of My love towards them, to let them see thereby that in this life there is no security, nor any perfection so firm, but if I leave them to themselves they will soon become as poor and bare of all virtue as the most miserable. Therefore you should endeavour to draw profit even from your imperfections, confessing and acknowledging your failings and your sins to the effect of your own weakness, and your rising up again from them a singular mercy of Mine, Who with so much goodness and patience am ready to receive and pardon you. If you be only faithful in this practice, you will neither be much dejected at your imperfections nor fail to be truly humbled by them; because you will clearly see that all good proceeds purely from Me, and the contrary from yourself and the devil, whose illusions can never hurt you, so long as you follow that secure road obedience.' Then our Lord said He knew full well our weakness, and how apt we are to fail in all occasions, but His patience, love, and desire to unite Himself to us is such that if we do but know we are poor, and believe in our hearts, as well as say in our words, that we are miserable indeed, and that all our good must come from Him, He will not fail to help us; although at times He takes a satisfaction to see a soul borne down by her frailties and those indispositions which our human condition cannot always avoid, in which painful situation the more she is humbled, and the more she is resigned to her own misery, the nearer she draws Him to her, and forces Him to remain with her. She understood at the same time that it was not His design, nor any way pleasing to Him, to see a soul give itself up to over-much concern for their frailties and weaknesses, such a solicitude being very prejudicial, and a great hindrance to their spiritual progress : 'therefore rather cast your care upon Me,' He said ; 'and though your imperfections be numerous, they shall not diminish your crown as long as you are humble and obedient.'

On another occasion, upon a Saturday, being to communicate, our Blessed Lady appeared to her at the beginning of Mass, and said : ' This is a day particularly dedicated to me, on which I am much honoured by many little devotions of my servants, on whom I also bestow many favours, as you shall experience. Let this day be ever much esteemed by you, for you must know, that out of a special kindness I have for you, it is in your power to obtain much from me upon it.' She saw at the same time the angel, as before mentioned, with the names of Jesus and Mary in glory, who stayed by her all the time of Mass, and at the Elevation she saw our Lord in the Sacred Host, Who remained visibly there till she had communicated, and then He was most clearly represented unto her with all the sufferings of His bitter Passion in her heart, on which our Blessed Lady said to her, 'I have procured you this impression of the sufferings of my Blessed Son, that so you may know how proper it is for His servants and spouses to embrace and love what He so willingly underwent for their sakes.' Then our Lady let her see a great number of angels adoring our Lord in her heart, and said : 'So these heavenly spirits adore and reverence their Lord in the hearts of all who worthily receive Him. But they have such a horror of those who approach him unworthily, that if His goodness would permit it, they would instantly tear them in pieces, which indignation to a proportion is also raised in them, even by those who receiving Him in a state of grace, through distractions or idleness of spirit, neglect to entertain Him in a manner due and suitable to His Divine Presence.' The hearing and seeing of this cast her into great apprehension and terror ; and as she was considering on the goodness of God towards mankind in thus veiling His greatness, and patiently bearing with their ingratitude, that so all may receive and enjoy Him, our Lord answered her that, although according to the common course of His Divine providence His mercies and judgments were kept in a certain obscurity, suitable to our situation in this life, yet to such souls as are faithful unto Him, who with much love, faith, and purity of soul frequently receive Him, and accompany Him in His solitude in the Blessed Sacrament, He often unveils in part His greatness and makes Himself more clearly known, thereby to stir them up to more earnest desires of enjoying and conversing with Him : 'For you must know, My child, there is no devotion more grateful to Me than to salute Me frequently in the Blessed Sacrament. Let it therefore be your constant devotion, both in your own church as often as duty and spare time will permit, and with your heart in those churches where I am the least thought of ; for by sending your desires thither, you will become enumerated amongst that glorious train of angels who are always praising and adoring Me wherever I am, for there is all Heaven, as I have let you see. But whilst I remain in the world, comforting it with My presence in this Holy Sacrament, I expect that My servants in particular should pay Me that homage of faith and love which is due to so singular a favour, thereby to repair in some sort the ingratitude and insensibility of so many poor souls who neither will know nor take notice of those graces and blessings I am desirous to bestow upon them.'

She understood more of Christ's solitude in the Holy Sacrament than she can find words to express, for our Lord seemed in a most compassionate way to show her how, if it was possible for Him to suffer again the contempt with which the world treats Him, by neglecting to make use of the treasure He affords it by His Sacramental presence, would reduce Him to the greatest extremity. 'For I am not only abandoned by the ignorant and libertine,' said He, 'but even by many who are consecrated to My service, and seldom think of Me. Did souls but know how desirous I am of entertaining Myself with them, and love to be forced, as it were, by their desires to make Me remain in their hearts, they would not so sluggishly let pass those precious moments which procure them such inexpressible blessings. For as far as depends upon Me, Who seek nothing more than to be lavishing My favours at that time, it would be impossible that any one Communion should not make them perfect.' She felt a very sensible impression of this truth in herself, and understood that the reason why souls, when they receive His favour in one kind, do not receive it in all, is because they are not at that time disposed for more, and therefore are not made perfect in all, so that although He has visited them Himself, and with all that abundant goodness of which she had been witness, yet it works but some one effect, according to the soul's capacity. So that if we find not the effect of all graces, it is either because we are not disposed to receive them, or too weak and feeble to advance in more than one virtue at once. On Communion mornings she was frequently wakened by her angel guardian, and admonished to prepare herself for Communion, and if she happened to be unmindful for any time of saluting and visiting the Blessed Sacrament in her heart, as our Lord Himself had taught her, she was reminded of it by her angel guardian. And sometimes our Lord Himself would suddenly appear and show Himself to her in the Holy Sacrament, which excited in her most fervorous desires of Communion, with which our Lord sometimes favoured her, communicating her Himself, especially when indispositions hindered her from receiving Him at the hands of His priests.

This favour, as He assured her, was one of the

greatest that He ever did His servants in this life : and that she might not depend upon her fancy, nor her desires, however fervorous, He let her see on some occasions, that though her desires were as great as ever she had experienced them, and He equally near and familiar with her, yet she could not enjoy this favour, nor even think she had received it, only when He out of His extreme desire to be imparting His favours to her, and uniting Himself with her, really, and so sensibly communicated Himself to her, that she could no ways doubt of it, although she could not express it. Neither was it always in the same manner, for sometimes she saw streams of glory dart from the Blessed Sacrament into her soul; in which manner our Lord said, He was often communicating Himself to pure souls, although they do not perceive it, 'for to know it,' said He, 'is a very different favour from possessing it.' Once being something more than usually distracted before Communion, she was severely reprehended by our Blessed Lady, who said, 'How comes it you are so negligent in disposing yourself to receive my Son, whilst He is so solicitous to be doing you particular favours? you should be always adoring Him, as you see those angels.' And amongst them was her angel guardian, who did thereby satisfy for her deficiences, and moved her to great reverence and devotion.

After she had communicated she saw our Blessed Lord in her heart, who showed her much favour, and said, 'Know, My child, you are now no more in your own power, for I have taken your soul from you, and given you Mine,' on which, as she has also sometimes before experienced, she saw the Soul of Christ in her, and hers in Him : and He said, 'Do not doubt of this, for I can show favours and work wonders where I please, in those that will but know I am omnipotent.' Then

she saw her heart in the Heart of Christ, and He said,
'See now your heart is lost in Mine, yet I will shut
up Mine in this little poor heart of yours.' She then
saw our Blessed Lord in her heart, and all the mysteries
of His Sacred Passion were engraven in it, and all His
pains and dolours were so sensibly impressed upon it,
that she felt inexpressible torment, and our Lord assured
her that she should always retain this impression of His
Passion in her heart, though not with the sensible
feeling of His dolours; for He made her understand
that it was not possible to live with that knowledge
constantly, since one single instantaneous sight of the
extreme glory and purity of Christ's Soul, or sense of
His dolours, as she had experienced them, was sufficient
to deprive a person of the use of their senses for many
hours. 'Therefore, although on these occasions you
find difficulty to perform your exterior duties,' a thing
which often troubled her, 'you have still great reason
to be thankful to Me; for I then do you a greater
favour, in not permitting you to be taken wholly out of
yourself by these graces and favours I impart to you,
than by giving them you, which as long as you gratefully
acknowledge shall still be granted to you by a supernatural strength, necessary on these occasions to support
nature, unless your humiliation or My honour require the
contrary.'

At another time as she was kneeling in the choir with
the Sisters at prayer, and calling to mind her many imperfections, and the divers proud thoughts and desires
of esteem, with which she was often molested, she
earnestly importuned our Lord to free her from this
temptation, that so she might not offend Him by her
pride, saying, 'My dear Lord, let me not ever be so
ungrateful a creature, but give me an humble heart like
Your servants here.' And suddenly our Lord showed

J 26

her all their hearts and said, 'See your heart is ready to lie under all their feet;' then He showed Himself to her, in her heart and in all their hearts, after which she found herself surprised with a most clear light of her innumerable failings, and beheld the many times she had received the Holy Communion irreverently, and the many distractions she had often been guilty of in presence of the Blessed Sacrament; moreover all her grievous sins were in an instant present to her, which cast her into so much affliction and trouble that it seemed her heart would have found ease if it could have been rent in a thousand pieces. In this anguish she was comforted by a vision of St. Francis the Humble, who promised her the virtues of humility and simplicity; assuring her he had been much glorified by a devotion of hers, which was often to perform acts of humility in in imitation of him. She saw also many saints adoring the Blessed Sacrament, amongst whom she particularly distinguished St. Ignatius, St. Francis Xaverius, and St. Aloysius, who she understood had greatly helped Sister Aloysia,[1] and was assured at the same time, that it was very pleasing to our Lord to be devoted to this Saint, who had great power in Heaven, and has a particular privilege to obtain for his clients a true devotion towards the Blessed Sacrament, as also to help them through with any difficulties they may have in

---

[1] [Sister Aloysia Francesca of Jesus (Morgan) was daughter to Sir Edward Morgan, Bart., of Monmouthshire, and his wife, Mary Englefield, daughter of Sir Francis Englefield, Bart., she was among the first novices that joined the Lierre community. She entered at the age of seventeen in 1651, and had remarkable good heath till within two years of her death (1672), observing the Rule in its full strictness, when she earnestly implored our Lord to send her here her purgatory. In answer to which prayer, she was visited by several most painful and fearful diseases, all which she bore with great patience, earnestly sighing for the happy moment when death would unite her to her Divine Spouse. She had an extraordinary devotion to her patron St. Aloysius.]

opening their consciences, which she acknowledged to have experienced in her troubles on that head, whilst she lived at Antwerp.

The glory of this and the above-mentioned saints had made such impression on her, as to draw her insensibly to interior wishes that it were in her power to merit also so much. Whilst she was entertaining herself thus, St. Teresa appeared to her and said, ' My child, all this you may obtain if you be but faithful to God, and courageous, and let not a false humility prevail over you, so as to hinder you from aiming to do much for our Lord, for although of yourself you are poor and unable to do anything, you can do all in Him, and by your prayers and good works have it in your power to do great things towards the salvation of souls, of which I ever had a great zeal, and have obtained also the same for you.' Afterwards being much afflicted with regard to these visions, once in particular, in time of Mass, at which she saw angels of a superior kind, as she thought, attending, after Communion our Lord showed her again her heart, as He has done, formerly in His Heart, and said, ' I am now resolved to add one impression which never shall be forgotten by you,' and immediately He seemed to pierce her heart with a most curious dart like unto a little spear, which filled her heart and breast with a most vehement pain, of which she afterwards remained very sensible, and saw at the same time a bright flame of glory as it were ascend out of her breast, and the streams thereof did seem to reach to the Sacred Side of our Blesssed Saviour, from whence also she reciprocally again received new glory. This vision she had some-times renewed, and was constantly more or less sensible of the pain.

CHAPTER XV.

She sees her little sister as an angel, is favoured with a vision of some of her patrons in Heaven, and of Religious Orders. She sees also the mystery of our Lord's Incarnation, is assured of the great merit of religious vows, and instructed how to rectify her intention even in little things.

On a certain occasion finding herself in a very distracted humour, and troubled and down-hearted at being so, she endeavoured to help herself by acts of humiliation, acknowledging her infirmity and insufficiency to attend to anything that was good. In this situation an angel appeared to her with the name of Mary, who said he was sent by our Blessed Lady to comfort her, and assure her that she was much better pleased with her humbling distractions, than if she had prayed with more peace and recollection; and for her reward had sent her another angel, who on other occasions had brought her many favours from our Blessed Lady, though she knew it not. This angel was of extraordinary beauty, and let her know she was her little sister, and although she had not known her upon earth, she should be happy with her in Heaven, where her father was also, and she said that one of his greatest comforts was to see her who died in her childhood possess as much glory as many others who had served God for a long time, and that upon account of the intention he had, in case she was but inclined to it, to dedicate her to the service of our Blessed Lady, in her holy Order of Carmel; 'but as this would not have been if I had lived, so our Blessed Lady was pleased to take me to herself, before I was capable of displeasing her.' Then she said : 'How happy are you who may merit so much;' to which Margaret replied : 'But, dear sister, shall I do so?' who said again, 'You are happy,' and embracing her desired her to praise our Lady for what she had done in her behalf : 'For I having done nothing upon earth whereby to receive continual glory, our Blessed Lady gives me this privilege, because I was even above the knowledge of my years devoted to her, that when she is glorified and praised, I receive an accidental glory, and additional joy.' Having said this, she repeated again, 'You are happy,' and so vanished, singing the praises of our Blessed Lady at her departure.

Having been favoured at another time by our Blessed Lady with a transient sight of some of the saints in Heaven, particularly St. Joseph, whom alone she could distinguish, and saw that our Lady and he received from and communicated to each other mutual glory : she conceived a desire of seeing the state of her Patrons to which our Lady answered that this favour should be reserved for her till another time, but she now let her know that St. Austin had been a constant intercessor for her, and that the humble devotion she had in making use of St. Peter's words : 'Lord, depart from me because I am a sinner,' was very pleasing to her Son, Who always remained the longer with her on that account. According to this said promise she was some time after favoured with a vision of St. Mary of Egypt, who seemed to possess a glory far superior to divers other saints she had formerly seen. She made her understand that she had a singular privilege to help and obtain comfort for persons who are in affliction, as she herself had experienced, and that she was also particularly powerful in obtaining for souls a true devotion towards our Blessed Lady, which had been her only comfort when in this life. She showed her how her crown and glory did most consist in enjoying a clear sight and knowledge of the mercies of God, which gave Margaret great consolation and made her then sensible how much she had experienced of them. She showed her also, but in a manner she cannot express, how before she died, she was brought again to her baptismal innocency, and enjoyed a crown above that of virgins. She saw also St. Francis of Sales, and understood that he had a plenitude of the Holy Ghost, not inferior to the great St. Austin. He appeared in great glory, which he said was augmented by the good effects the reading of his books had worked in her, and that he had often helped her, in reward of her pious endeavours to bring others to be devoted to him. She saw at the same time St. Peter of Alcantara, whose glory although extremely great, was very different from the glory of the Bishop of Geneva. This Saint assured her, that for her imitating him in what he used to say, and desire in this life, namely, the humiliation of confession, she should also feel the recollection and mortification of her cell, and become many ways greatly beneficial to her neighbour. She then saw St. Francis the Seraphic, and all his whole Order. The glory of this saint resembled much to that she had had seen St. Joseph in : she distinguished clearly his stigmata in his hands and feet, which did not appear as she had seen them in pictures but as rays of glory, though very different from those which environed him. She understood that the devotion of Sister Margaret of St. Francis to him, had obtained his particular care over this community, and was assured that any person.

who is truly devoted to him will obtain the virtues of humility and simplicity, in which he is singularly privileged.

St. Francis said, though he had in his Order many most eminent saints while he was upon earth, yet there were still living many as great, and in some kind greater, which she understood to be a privilege granted to all Founders of Orders, who merit even in this life, that Almighty God of His goodness raise up from time to time other saints to uphold their spirit, and to do that which oftentimes would not have been fit in the beginning of the Order, and afterwards contribute to its preservation and greater good. The splendour of this Saint, and the glory he received · from all the different branches of his Institution, for all that profess his rule seemed equally near him, was so great that she seemed in a manner out of herself in beholding it, and in amaze began to think that there was no glory in heaven comparable to what this Order enjoyed : but being favoured also by our Lord with a sight of other religious Orders, she was equally astonished, for every one did seem to possess, though in a different kind, so much glory that those she actually looked upon, she thought them so far surpassed all others that nothing else could be greater, or any way comparable to it. 'This,' said our Blessed Lord, 'is Heaven, and this the glory I impart to My servants :' and if there were as many millions more of different Orders, He could as easily glorify Himself in giving them different degrees of glory. She observed that the crowns of all these Orders were not only different, but some far superior to others in glory : and that those Orders whose principal Institute is recollection and union with God by prayer, were in a particular degree glorified in seeing and knowing more of Almighty God than others, which made her think the happiness of a Teresian to surpass all others; which our Lord gave her to understand was the happy situation of the blessed in Heaven, who possessing all they desire, conceive the highest opinion of their own glory, without envy or ambition to higher, which He let her experience. For when she beheld the Order of Carmel, she thought there was no glory like unto what it enjoyed, though when she looked upon others, it seemed to her that nothing could be greater than theirs, yet she had no ambition or desire of any other but that of a Teresian. She observed, however, that though the crowns which distinguished each Religious Order were common and uniform to all those who were of that Order, yet as they were rewarded each one according to their own private merits, they were quite different from each other in point of glory, exceeding one the other beyond all comparison according to the various virtues they had excelled in, and the perfection they had attained to during their life.

She saw also many other saints who had not been of that state, or were particularly affected towards any Institute, were favoured with a participation of the glory belonging to the Order to which they were devoted. She beheld amongst these Master John of Avila; this venerable priest seemed to have a glory nothing inferior to any of the rest, for she understood that he had divers crowns as of Apostles, Founders of Orders, and in some sort of Martyrs, because he had a spirit and desire to have glorified God in all these states, if His goodness had so ordained. As she had often found much comfort from reading the books of this holy man, she had a singular devotion towards him and was overjoyed at seeing him in so much glory, which being augmented with that of priesthood, surpassed all that she could express or imagine.

She received this favour on this occasion to make

her in some manner comprehend the dignity of religious
vows, with which our Lord was pleased to comfort her,
because she had been much tempted in point of her
vocation, assuring her that they were in dignity and
reward next to priesthood, and that the glory of a priest
independent of any good works, that dies but in the
state of grace, exceeded the glory which Lucifer lost.
But a thought occurring how that could be, since she had
always supposed that there was no higher glory to be
obtained, we being only destined to fill up the place of
those fallen angels, our Lord assured her it was not
so; 'For,' said He, 'My glory is Infinite and without
limits, so that there is as much difference between the
glory of My Saints, and that of the highest angels, as
there is betwixt a poor soul in the state of grace, and the
greatest saint in Heaven, in glorifying of whom I am
glorified, rewarding each one according to their merits,
so that if they deserved a new Heaven, it would be as
easy to Me to give them that additional glory, as to
create a little fly, and My power, if you did but understand it, is as much concerned in the one as the other.'
Our Lord let her then see how one did enjoy more than
another, which she can no other ways express than by
comparing them to a variety of Heavens, only that she
observed that the difference betwixt the superior and
inferior glory consisted in a more or less clear sight and
knowledge of God, and that the highest saints not only
see, but also enjoy the glory of the lower, who without
knowing what those above them enjoy in particular,
rejoice to see Almighty God honoured by their glory,
which gives them constantly new satisfaction. 'Thus,'
said Our Lord sweetly to her, 'as you see, that what
I show you is always new, and whether it be in itself
greater or less, you always think nothing is comparable
to it, even so it is, but in an infinitely more angelical high

degree, with My saints in Heaven, who always find My glory new and surpassing all they can imagine, and though each one enjoys it in a different degree, yet this causes no envy or trouble, because their happiness is to rejoice in My will and glory, which are displayed by communicating to My servants a reward adequate to their merits, which makes that one saint is greater than another, because by their labours and faithful correspondence with My inspirations, I was more seen and honoured in them whilst they were on earth.'

Here it seemed as if her soul was taken from her and placed before the Blessed Trinity, where all Heaven was present, and the mystery of our Lord's Incarnation was clearly represented to her, and she understood how the merits and graces communicated to the saints and martyrs where all obtained by our Lord's becoming Man, which she was assured to be the most potent work of God, wherein the mystery of the Sacred Trinity was most clearly expressed. And it appeared to her that the glory of the saints was a reflection of the glory of God which they received from Him, and that His Throne was the glory of the saints and angels. She understood also that there were now as many saints upon earth as ever, and that daily God did communicate greater, and greater heights to His Church, but that there were not so many saved by innocency as formerly; that in all states of life there were some highly grateful unto God, Who bore Him so much love, that His desire to enjoy the just with Him in Heaven does more hasten the end of the world than the sins of the wicked. Then our Lord showed her a book and asked her if she knew what was written there, to which she durst not answer anything, for she apprehended least it should be her sins; but He smiling upon her with much sweetness opened it, and showed her her vows written in a most clear hand, and underneath this little act, which she was frequently accustomed to make in these words: 'Lord, what I have promised you is pleasing to me.' Which seemed to be expressed in much more glorious and brighter characters than her vows. After this our Lord mildly reprehending her said, she had often for needless fears omitted to repeat her vows, yet, without reflecting of it, had often renewed them by this act, which He here showed her written in the book of life, affirming that He Himself was this living Book. And immediately as she thought, she saw her vows written in Him, with her usual act somewhat changed, affirming thus, 'What you have promised to Me is pleasing to Me.'

Having understood all these things from our Lord, He also added: 'See now, I hope you will ever have an esteem of religious vows, by which so much may be gained, for though religious persons should often offend Me, and that even by breaches of their vows, yet if at their death they have the happiness to be found in the state of grace, their places in Heaven will be above the angels, and by the impression alone of their sacred religious vows will be ranked next to the priesthood. What, then, do you think will be the glory of a faithful soul, who possessed of this high prerogative goes on daily advancing in perfection and seeking in all to please and honour Me? Let this, therefore, be your constant aim, not so much because thereby you shall ever see and enjoy more of Me, which however is a very good intention, but because the more glory you merit, the more you glorify Me, which intention, as being the most perfect, will give more lustre to your actions and render them more pleasing and acceptable to Me; for by it they are more purified from all self-interest and the soul becomes more closely united to Almighty God,

Who cannot fail to reward it with mutual affection and all kind of celestial graces.'

The more she understood of this truth, the more she became inflamed with affections and desires to regulate all her actions by this sublime rule, and resolved never to deviate from it, but to endeavour to be faithful unto God as well in great as lesser things, that thereby rendering herself more capable of His graces, she might continually augment His glory, and eternally honour Him by eternally receiving His favours and benefits, of which the more capable we are the more He is pleased and glorified in us.   Here our Lord encouraged her again to be assiduous in mortifying all selfish inclinations and affections, and warned her to set a great value on little things, and esteem nothing of small account, whereby so much may be gained, as to see Him more clearly, love Him, and glorify Him more for ever.   As He said this He seemed to increase in beauty and splendour, and so vanished from her sight, leaving in her mind a deep impression of all she had seen and heard.

CHAPTER XVI.

How on a feast of Pentecost she was wonderfully favoured by our Blessed Lady, St. Teresa, and Mother Anne of the Ascension, who assist her in preparing herself to receive the Holy Ghost, of which she had some apparent sign in the motions of a natural dove.

IT being Margaret's custom before all principal feasts of the Church to prepare herself for them, not only by offering up her ordinary actions, which she then performed with more than usual assiduity, but also by set devotions adapted to the times, so on this occasion she endeavoured to dispose herself with the greatest fervour, in hopes of receiving thereby such lights from the Holy Ghost as might enable her both to regulate discreetly her conduct, and clearly discern His Divine inspirations, and thereby safely avoid being deceived in these her extraordinary favours, which, however convincing they might appear, whilst she received them, failed not to give her constant uneasiness afterwards, not being able to persuade herself that such things could ever agree with her miserable and imperfect life.

Being full of these thoughts, and what people might reasonably think of her, our Blessed Lady appeared to her and reprehending her, let her understand it was highly displeasing to her Beloved Son to see her in so much care and fear of being censured by the world.

If she therefore intended to keep herself in His favour, she must be willing to appear anything before the world, and be faithful to Him, by neither desiring honour nor dishonour, comfort or tribulation, but leave all that care to Him, and accept of what He pleased to give her, which disengagement from herself and all that is earthly was chiefly necessary to receive the Divine Spirit, Who breathes when He pleases and knows no human respects. 'Such a pure and humble heart, which desires nothing but His will, and by faith to love and serve Him as He pleases, are the true dispositions towards receiving the Holy Ghost, with His celestial gifts, as I am now come to teach you.'

Then she said that, after her Blessed Son's Ascension, she was endowed with a plenitude of faith, and by a pure gift of God, with a consummate perfection, that her faith did bring the Holy Ghost in greater abundance upon the Apostles, and upon the whole world, than all the labours and the dispositions of the Apostles put together, and according to the faith she did exercise here on earth, so is now her power in Heaven to help and strengthen the weak in faith, who may more easily obtain relief and assistance through her means, than by applying to her Divine Son without her aid, for a lively faith is only planted in an humble heart, in which virtue as she exceeded all other saints, so she surpassed them in all other perfections, particularly faith, therefore she received the plenitude of the Holy Ghost in as full proportion as is possible in this life, and in a degree superior to what any other creature ever will attain to, or even be able to conceive. 'It shall therefore now be my care,' said she, 'on this approaching solemnity to obtain for you such an overflow of graces, that all which I and my Beloved Son have hitherto done for you shall appear only as a shadow when compared to them. For since you see how poor and void of all good you are, I need not fear but all that I bestow upon you will be acknowledged as mine, and will oblige all, who hear of them, to confess that my Son is wonderful in His works; by which we shall both be glorified. If, however, at any time we seem to absent ourselves from you, it is only in appearance, for we are still equally with you, and to give you an occasion of greater merit: for by such vicissitudes of favours and trials, my Son brings His chosen souls to be daily more and more humble and disengaged from all things created, and even from any desire of enjoying His extraordinary graces; which desire is often a real hindrance to their further progress in virtue, insomuch so that numbers of souls are kept from greater degrees of perfection, by nothing else than pretending to know and understand much of God, whilst their imaginary favours are merely the effect of their own speculations, by which they become so wise in their own conceits, that my Son, Who reposes in a sincere humble soul, can find no place in them.' Margaret at this time thinking she had no other desire than not to offend God by pride, and by abusing His favours, our Lady said to her: 'Remember that, as I have told you, all virtues are exercised in the practising of any one with perfection, so in the same manner when receiving my Son you are favoured with any one principal grace or gift, He makes you at the same time in some sort partaker of all, for by giving you Himself He gives you also His Divine Spirit, in Whom all are included.'

On the vigil of Pentecost she was awoke as usual by her angel guardian, and was also favoured with our Lady's blessing, who accompanied her to prayer, where as she was acknowledging her great unworthiness and incapacity to prepare herself for so great a treasure as that of receiving the Holy Ghost; importuning our Lady for her assistance, the Sacred Virgin appeared in a more clear manner, thrusting the little Infant in her arms, said : 'Here is my Son, observe Him, and He will teach you how you are to prepare yourself. St. Joseph gained all his sanctity by contemplating the eyes of this Blessed Child, and now you have the same in your power that you have Him in your arms and heart, let Him not therefore go till you know how to prepare yourself for the Holy Ghost.' Thus the Infant remained with her, and bid her to have but a lively faith, and be humble, and she should receive His Divine Spirit and His gift. As soon as she had communicated she was made sensible how the Holy Ghost was imparted to every one in the choir, each receiving a larger or less share, according to the disposition she was in, and she saw, as formerly she has done, the sacred Soul of our Lord, and her soul was all lost in His ; so that she seemed to have no other soul but His ; for as it appeared to her they were both become one, and yet she saw her soul like a pure white dove in the Soul of Christ our Lord, and He said : 'Doubt not, My child : My Father, and I, with the Holy Ghost are here, and have our throne in your heart, and you shall henceforth confess by the effects that We repose in your heart and soul.' Then immediately she found a most delightful sweet breath breathe into her soul, and it seemed to imprint there all those gifts she has read belong to the Holy Ghost : what made the greatest impression was faith, for her whole heart did confess that great things belong to our Lord. This now prevailed so far over her, that notwithstanding her great unworthiness, she thought it impossible ever more to doubt of His favours, which she resolved henceforth to declare without further trouble or concern, for she clearly understood that an humble, simple heart ought neither to desire comfort nor fear discomfort, but wholly to be contented with the will of God, which is the disposition the Holy Ghost brings and desires to leave in the soul; yet not so as to slacken its recourse to God by prayer, which is to be made use of before every action and undertaking, as well little as great, recommending all to our Blessed Lord and Lady, and leaving the success to them : confiding that whatsoever happens is most conformable to the Divine will of God, in which alone she is to endeavour to place all her comfort, for by it she will be sure to conserve in herself the spirit of the Holy Ghost, and to partake of His direction in all her actions. Here she saw clearly how in every thought and motion of the soul that is pure, the Holy Ghost does operate, and, in some sort obliged to be its director, as long as it continues to be in these dispositions, and believes with a strong faith that what is accomplished in it is His Divine work.

This impression of the Holy Ghost remained with her in a most lively manner till the next morning of Pentecost, on which she was again favoured with the presence of our Lady, accompanied by St. Teresa and Mother Anne of the Ascension, who seemed to be in much more glory than ever she had seen them before, but they let her understand that their glory was always the same, and by appearing so they only meant to augment her joy and satisfaction. Then St. Teresa laid her hand upon her head, and expressed much dearness to her, during which she sensibly felt the effects of her assistance towards receiving the Holy Ghost.

And Mother Anne of the Ascension said that it had always been her custom to prepare herself for this solemnity in a most particular manner, knowing how much it imported to be guided in her actions by a right spirit, of which she was used to receive a particular plenitude on this feast, and was now favoured with a

K 26

singular power to help all those who should imitate her herein, and was therefore now come to comfort her by her presence, and favour her with special assistance on so important an occasion, and said she would always protect and be a mother to her. Margaret, amazed at these expressions and the extraordinary beauty and glory this celestial company afforded her, thought she could not wish or desire anything more, nor share in greater abundance of God's favours than she had done the day before; but our Lady answering her thoughts, said: 'This day I am resolved that all present shall know and be convinced that you have received the Holy Ghost.' In time of the first Mass, she was greatly overjoyed by seeing the priest receive such an abundance of the Holy Ghost; for which she saw he was very well prepared, and had done all he knew to dispose himself, she saw also several persons in the church receive some more, some less, especially a poor old woman, who received a great share. When the hymn *Veni Sancte Spiritus* was intoned at the Mass, according to custom, a wild dove was let fly in the choir, with the gifts of the Holy Ghost written upon parchment, in the form of flaming tongues, which were thus scattered upon the floor. The dove first flew unto an image of our Blessed Lady, and from thence to Margaret's head, where it remained immoveable till towards the Elevation, which drawing near, she began to think how, the dove remaining upon her head, she should be able to put her veil in order, so as to be ready to communicate, and immediately as she had this thought, the dove flew from her head upon the Lectionary before her, and fixing his eyes upon her continued so till she went to Communion, which although she herself did not observe, having her eyes shut all the time, some of the Sisters who had observed it said afterwards that they were as much moved at the posture of the dove whilst it stood looking upon her, as when it remained fixed on her head.

When the Sacred Host was lifted up, the whole church and choir became instantly filled with glory, in which glory she beheld a dove betwixt silver and gold, from which there came streams of glory, and it seemed to descend and light upon her head, on which being desirous to be made sensible of its weight, as she had been of the wild dove, it passed immediately upon her, and, fluttering with its wings, it made a sort of wind, which filled her with a most agreeable air, and this she understood was the same the Apostles had experienced when they received the Holy Ghost. All this time our Blessed Lady held her by the hand, and St. Teresa with Mother Anne of the Ascension stood close by her, and thus encompassed with glory she went to Communion; which as soon as she had received, she saw the same dove in her soul and our Blessed Lord, by Whom as she thought she was carried to the side of His Eternal Father, Who seemed to breathe into her the Holy Ghost; and though all this passed in a very short time, as she knew afterwards by the ending of the Mass, yet by what she had enjoyed and understood in her soul it appeared to her as if she had been long entertained by our Lord, Who seemed to converse with her in a most familiar affectionate manner, assuring her that her soul was one with His, in which was included all the treasures of Heaven, with which she was enriched, and with the gifts of the Holy Ghost, Who should always remain with her, and give her a right understanding. This happened to be the gift written upon her billet which our Lady had appointed her to pick up. When Sext began the wild dove came and fixed himself for a time upon her breast, on the side of her heart, from whence it afterwards flew again upon her head, and seemed with his wings to cover her once or twice, as if it were taking leave, and soon after fled away, and became so wild that it was near a quarter of an hour before they could catch it to send it home. All the day after she was favoured with the presence of our Lady and St. Teresa, so that in company it was as much as she could do to contain herself, or dissemble the interior joy she experienced, for every place seemed full of God, so that she thought herself as it were in Heaven, for wherever she was, in choir or recreation, she heard angelical music, notwithstanding her endeavours to divert and amuse herself, lest the Sisters should perceive anything. Here St. Teresa said to her: 'My child, be not in pain on account of what others perceive in you, for you must know you have in this the advantage of me, and divers others, who have received these or the like favours from our Lord, for half of what He has bestowed upon you, is enough to make any person, who is not supernaturally assisted, as you have been, out of themselves many hours, if not days; therefore, although some little inconveniences may ensue, you have still great reason to thank our Lord for thus wonderfully supporting you, and therefore freeing you from censures to which I have been exposed on such like occasions.'

On another day, she being to wash her feet, as is customary sometimes, Sister Martha offered to help her, but Margaret with the humility of St. Peter refused to accept of her charitable service; when behold her good angel appeared and bid her condescend to her kind offer, or else he himself would do it in her place, since he envied nothing more than like her to be able to render any service to the spouses of Jesus Christ. This obliged her to submit, and gave the good Sister occasion of gaining an ample reward; for during this action she received a plenitude of the Holy Ghost, which Margaret saw communicated to her in.that very instant, and understood that she was a most humble soul, and highly acceptable to our Blessed Lord, Who assured Margaret at the same time, that whosoever did anything for her He would reward them even in this life; which has been experienced on other occasions to be true.

NOTE VI.

Margaret's account of heavenly music.

'AFTER I had told your Reverence of the music and acknowledged my fault, in not speaking of it before, immediately after, being in the Recreation, I heard the same music, by fits, the whole time, which was heard by none but myself, for at first I questioned those that were with me, but they heard nothing. I could not tell what to conceive the music to be, nor could not imagine any instrument like it. It was sometimes like sweet curious voices, and though it seemed very still and sweet, yet it was so shrill and loud that I heard it above all other speaking or noise; and though I did speak and divert myself, yet it was always distinct to me, and so very grateful that I never experienced anything like it. This morning, which is the 11th of May, all the time of the Hours I heard the same, and our Blessed Lady seemed to be there according to her usual way and said : " Do you know what you hear? I have done you this favour for three reasons. Do not fear, it is I, my child." (For then I was much afraid and it was distinct before my eyes how often I had fed my humour in hearing music.) Our Blessed Lady went on and said, the mortification I did heretofore in telling my confessarius that I did apprehend I had offended God in that point, and doing it, notwithstanding the difficulty I had in speaking of it ; and my fidelity in not pleasing myself afterwards in any of those thoughts, though

I often on those occasions (I mean of music) thought no heaven like it, was one reason. The other was that from this time forward I shall never be able to be pleased with anything of that kind, but shall always know and have this heavenly music so present with me, that what I hear will only serve to make me remember that there is nothing like that ; and all I hear shall sound as praise to God. The third reason was because I shall see all her words and my confessarius' words verified : which was that nothing that I have suffered in or (been) mortified in, but shall be rewarded even in this life.'

She sees the state and condition of several persons then living, both present and absent. And our Lord teaches her that she is not only to receive tribulations with resignation, but even to rejoice in them. She is cast downstairs by the devil, and afterwards beaten by him on account of some narrations concerning Purgatory which are here set down.

As she was hearing Mass one day, she saw a poor woman in the church who, as to the exterior, seemed to be in much misery, yet she was encompassed with very great glory. And our Lady, who was there present showing her the condition of this poor creature, said, 'This woman scarce knows what she says, and as little thinks of the favours I and my Son are doing her; and yet her devotions, as simple as they are, have more power with us than divers high acts of many contemplative souls; and were it necessary, she could speak with more knowledge of Heaven and heavenly things than many learned divines.' So pleasing to God is simplicity, which gives Him a free communication with the soul.

At the Elevation our Lord showed Himself unto her in the fulness of His glory, as He is oftentimes pleased to do, and He let her see many particulars of the priest's condition that celebrated, and withal how He went clouding His greatness, and even the effects of His extraordinary greatness, according to the perfection of the priest, who, although he was in His favour, on account of some gross neglects in which his ignorance excused him, he rendered himself incapable of receiving any singular benefits from that great Treasure he had so very near him. This excited her to most fervent prayers for some priests she had known when she lived in the world, and who were reported to lead but imperfect lives. As she was thus recommending all such persons to our Lord, those she particularly reflected upon she saw most clearly, and the state of their souls; and our Lord gave her to understand that He did her this favour to the end she might be convinced of the fallaciousness of this world, and how different the judgments of men are from His. For He let her see that those of whom she had the least opinion were much more in His favour than several others of whom she had a greater esteem, and as she became more clearly enlightened with the particulars of both, she understood that a good meaning and the humiliation persons receive in being censured by the world, if they bear it but with patience and are careful to avoid any gross disedifications, supplied for many lesser defects, especially in persons of small capacity. She saw at the same time the condition of one for whom she had a particular respect, at whose hands she had received her first Communion, and she understood that his soul was in much danger, and some particulars were represented to her which moved her to be earnest with our Lord in his behalf.

But unexpectedly and without any thought of hers was placed before her, as it were, Father Andrew White, S.J., who had been Confessor at Antwerp Monastery whilst she lived there, and his soul appeared to her in a great degree of glory, and our Blessed Lord and Lady, who were still present with her, assured her that he was a

very great servant of theirs and had been brought to
Antwerp by them, and of particular favour to the Religious there, where he had effected their designs, and
had done more for that house by his humble prayers
than a person of greater abilities would have been
capable of. She understood that he had suffered much
in several kinds and that still he had a continual cross,
which daily crowned him with glory with the special
assistance of our Lady, to whom he has frequent recourse, and receives from her more help than he is
sensible of or is able to understand, because she has
much for him to do in her service, who by his prayers,
in which he is more powerful than in words, does convert more souls than many others with preaching and
such laborious works, and draws down many benedictions
upon his whole Order. As she had never been inclined
to have this opinion of him, for she thought he never
understood her spirit, being always inclined to think
too well of her, she seemed to doubt of what she saw;
but our Blessed Lady assured her it was so, and all he
had said to her on those occasions was true, and if at
any time he did not understand her it was when our
Lord did not permit that he should; for if he had, it
would have proved a great obstacle to her coming to
this foundation, because he would then have endeavoured
to have kept her at Antwerp.

Being once in the choir at Vespers, she saw Sister
Agnes of St. Joseph encompassed with devils, who were
tempting her, some to uncivil things of different kinds,
some to despair, and others to make away with herself,
which moved her to pray much for this good sister,
for she seldom came near her but she beheld something
or other of this kind, although not always so distinctly
as at present. Whilst she was recommending her to
our Lady she was pleased to appear to her and assured

her she would not fail to assist her, provided she only endeavoured to help herself, which on all occasions was the first step in searching relief, in which ordinary means and natural industry are to be made use of. As these devils, by their frightful postures and menaces, seemed to take delight in making offers to do her harm, our Lady said, 'In this you see the mercy of my all-powerful Son, Who has so limited the devil, that although he has permission to tempt, yet he has not the least power to hurt either body or soul: trust therefore in me, and be assured that this good sister is under my special protection, and so dear to me that nothing shall do her harm.'

Another time after Communion, as she was again praying for this dear sister, our Blessed Lord appeared to her, and standing close by her, as on other occasions He has done, He seemed to embrace her and said, 'This is a pure act of obedience and charity, and you shall see how pleasing it is to Me, for although you have no great affection towards this sister, she is most dear to Me, and I will make her so to you, and will teach you how to rejoice and take content, even in the afflictions and sufferings both of my friends and your friends, as much as in their prosperity and greatest blessings, because both are equally pleasing to My Father and depend upon His Divine will and disposition, Who is as much glorified and honoured in exercising His servants by tribulations and crosses, as in bestowing favours and rewards upon them.'

Here she understood how, though by every little sufferance we bear with due patience, a great reward may be gained, yet if we neglect or make ill use of them, our Lord will not therefore cease to be still glorified, Who gave the inspiration or occasion of so great merit, and Whose will is as much accomplished

in our punishment as in our reward ; 'for,' said He ' My
Father has all the sufferings which both you and all
the world have passed, are passing, or will pass through,
now actually present before Him, and is taking glory
and content in seeing His will accomplished in all, which
is what you are to reflect upon, and then all crosses
will be sweet, because you will look upon them all as
conformable to My will, which is the perfection My
servants are to endeavour at, to rejoice and take content
in all things. And though this be a pure gift of Mine,
and not attainable in perfection without My extraordinary grace, it being a privilege belonging to Heaven
and a part of the bliss My saints and angels enjoy
there, yet by My grace and your endeavours much
may be procured, and by fidelity in aiming at the
practice of it much is to be gained; for according to
the conformity and habitual joy which the soul, by
rejoicing in the Divine will, attains to in this life, so
in equal proportion will her glory and knowledge be in
the next.' Then, laying His hand upon her heart, He
said, 'You have long laboured to accept of all as My
will, but when you meet with afflictions you know not
how to look upon Me, in sign therefore that it is I,
and this favour I do you a free gift of Mine, your heart
shall henceforth never entertain any joy than in My
will, and it being Mine, and I in it, as you see, I will
fix My reign there, and be known by the title of King
of your heart. To the end therefore that My abode
may be in peace, you must also, as far as is agreeable
with human frailty, refrain from grieving at anything
but in Me, and for Me, which is to be accomplished
by reflecting, in time of troubles, of what kind soever
they may be, whether they may happen to yourself or
your neighbour, that it is the will of My Father Who
is in Heaven, and Who, according to the merciful views

of His unsearchable providence, sent such a cross, or permitted that other affliction to fall upon you or your friends,
in which, as He is ever taking complacency and satisfaction, so that on that head you are to rejoice with Him and
in Him. This is the joy which will make your crosses
light, and though it does not take away your natural
sensibility, yet the act itself, though made in an insensible manner, it is so grateful and pleasing to Me, that
it unites you to Me more than much greater suffering,
and gives you a closer union with Me when borne with
patience and resignation that are not attended with this
act of rejoicing in My Father's will, which was My constant occupation whilst on earth and still now the same
in Heaven, as well as of My saints and angels, whom
my servants upon earth are to imitate. If you are but
faithful in this, I promise you, to a proportion, a share
of this peace of mind which never any one but My
dear Mother did perfectly enjoy in this life, so as neither
to be overjoyed nor so much afflicted by what happens,
but to moderate both by turning peaceably to Me and
rejoicing in My will, which I will make both sweet and
easy to you. And since I have assured you of establish-
ing My seat in your heart, doubt not but whensoever
you make this act, I will be sensibly with you and make
you understand how pleasing it is to My Eternal Father.'

After this and many other things of the like nature,
which she cannot well express, our Lord assured her
that Sister Agnes was a soul very dear to Him and
His Blessed Mother, that she was of a most innocent
life, and had been brought hither by them in order to
perfect her and make her a great saint. She had indeed
been greatly deceived by the devil in her devotions, a
snare which some pious souls are easily caught in,
especially when they are attended with self-satisfaction
and content, on which account He had permitted the

devil to tempt her more, that so she might the sooner come to know herself and have recourse to proper help. 'For it is long before well-meaning people, who aim at virtue their own way, can otherwise be kept within bounds, or made to understand in what true virtue really consists, which is obedience, a virtue I exact of all My servants, because humility will be in the obedient man.' Our Lord continued to express much love for her, and said she had as yet much to suffer, which would turn to her greater good, since He had brought her hither to save her soul, which, if she had remained in the world, would have been exposed to many great dangers.

The devil, envious still of Margaret's happiness, seeing her daily thus favoured and cherished by our Blessed Lord and His Sacred Mother, sought to vent some part of his spite against her by casting her downstairs, which he did with great force, before she had time to make the sign of the Cross. But all turned to his greater confusion, for Margaret, without being hurt, was received at the bottom by our Blessed Lady, who stood there with her good angel, and showed her the enemy in a terrible shape. Then throwing her mantle about her, of which we have before spoken, she let him see he had no power to hurt her, although he suffered more in seeing her thus protected than if he were in Hell, which indeed he seemed to signify by the howling and hideous noise he made at his departure, of which one of the Sisters who was then passing by was also witness. His malice, however, did not end here, for some time after, Sister Margaret praying, as she had been desired, for Reverend Mother's intention, which was, to know if her mother was in Heaven, she understood she was there, and had been freed from Purgatory by a Mass which was said for her at Antwerp; she also came to know

that her father was likewise there, after a short stay in
Purgatory, from whence he was soon freed, through the
many prayers and Masses procured by his friends, and
all her sisters except one, who wanted twenty-five Masses
to free her from Purgatory; of which particulars having
informed Reverend Mother, as our Lady had ordered
her, the night following the devil appeared to her in a
threatening and hideous shape, saying he would teach
her to tell stories of Purgatory, and beat her most cruelly.
But after some time our Lady appeared and comforted
her, saying she had done well in obeying her, and then
showed her this poor soul all in flames, which made
such impression on her that, though she can say little of
them, she thinks she shall never forget them, as they
seemed equal to those of Hell. Only she observed that
the soul enjoyed a singular peace and submission to the
will of God, though it did not mitigate her torments.
She was so much wrought upon by this sight, and what
she had suffered from the devil, that she could not settle
herself to anything all the morning, although she had the
presence of our Lady, and many comforts from her, who
asked her if she was not willing to suffer a little to free
this poor creature, and bid her offer it all up to God for
her soul. This was the mother of Reverend Mother's little
niece,[1] who lived then in town, a girl about eight years of

---

[1] [This girl was afterwards Sister Mary Teresa of Jesus. She was
daughter to William Warren, Esq., a Protestant gentleman and his
wife Anne, daughter to Thomas Downes, Esq., and thus sister to
Mother Margaret of St. Teresa Downes, Vicaress and then first Prioress
of the Lierre Monastery. This child, dedicated from her birth to our
Blessed Lady and St. Teresa, had been given by her pious mother
their names at her baptism, which she retained in religion. Mrs. Warren
only survived the birth of little Mary Teresa a few months, and on her
dying bed confided with great earnestness the little orphan to her
maiden sister Martha Downes' care, conjuring her by all the bonds of
affection and charity, to bring up her only daughter a fervent Catholic
in solid piety, and as soon as she could send her to her sister at Lierre.

age, and was promised by her mother at her birth to our Blessed Lady and St. Teresa, who now assured Sister Margaret that she should have the happiness of clothing her in this monastery, which afterwards fell out accordingly. After this, going to the convent Mass, little

When the child was six, her aunt Martha died, and the father's Protestant relatives wished much to obtain possession of the child, but she was sent beyond the seas to her aunt, Mother Margaret of St. Teresa, then Prioress of the Lierre community, who placed her with good Catholics for her education. The last of the twenty-five Masses for Mrs. Warren's release from Purgatory was said at Our Lady of 'Clouse' (Clues is Dutch for Cloister), a Dominican church at Lierre, where a miraculous statue of our Lady was venerated (hence the name of Our Lady of the Cloister). Little Mary Teresa aged eight was present, but did not know for whom the Mass was said, but of a sudden towards the end of the Mass, she swooned away, being very much frightened ; coming to herself she called out to the Devôtes (pious women of Lierre, similar to Beguines), under whose care the child then was : ' I see my mother all in white go up to Heaven, and she says I shall come to her,' and something of her being religious, which she could not well relate. What confirmed the belief of what the child said was, that though she could not possibly remember her mother, who died when she was only a few months old, she minutely described her person and every feature, with other circumstances so very clear, as if she had known her, nor had she ever heard of her mother being in Purgatory, or that the Mass was said for her soul, nor did the maid of the monastery nor the Devôtes know anything why they were sent with the child to hear Mass at Our Lady of the Clues, but to hear it for our Reverend Mother's (Prioress) intention. The little one was as one transported the whole day, relating to the Sisters what she had seen and heard. It wrought on her so much that she got a great fever. When only fourteen Mary Teresa earnestly besought the Prioress of Lierre, then Mother Margaret of Jesus (Mostyn) to admit her as novice. Difficulties being made on account of her tender age, she pleaded her cause so well with the Bishop (who had come to the monastery for the elections) whom she accidentally met, that he dispensed with her age, begging the Prioress (Mother Margaret) to receive and take great care of her and not allow her to observe the full rigour of the Order. She was admitted into the convent and at fifteen received our holy habit, and made her profession two years after, aged seventeen. She was a most sweet, innocent, and fervent soul, and seemed never weary of praising God for His great mercy in bringing her to religion. She died at the age of fifty-four in 1696, after a life of habitual suffering most courageously endured.—Extract from the Book of Lives of the Sisters.]

thinking that the soul was to be freed then, as soon as the Gospel was ended, she saw it stand close by the priest, where she also saw our Lady and St. Teresa in great glory, and seemed to express much joy. The soul looked very red and much inflamed till the time of the Elevation, after which she changed all pure white and clear, as she had seen all other Saints, and, making a bow in thanksgiving, bid her tell Reverend Mother she was now in Heaven ; and the other devotions her Reverence had procured, besides the Masses, were applied by our Lady to two other souls, who should soon be released. These Sister Margaret, after Communion, saw ascending into Heaven in great jubilee ; they had both been saved by their devotion to our Blessed Lady. One was a person of her acquaintance, who had been much devoted to and helped by St. Teresa, the other was a devôte who had made vows, but had been very negligent in keeping them. Here our Lady let her know that, when persons do any good works in behalf of the deceased, it is most grateful to her that such be left at her disposal, in case the souls for which they are offered stand not in need of them.

Another time, hearing Mass for a relative of Reverend Mother's, lately deceased, a wild young man, she had knowledge from our Lady that he was in Purgatory, and would not be freed by this Mass, but if as many Masses were offered up for his soul as there are days in the year, and the money given to some poor priest, he should presently be freed, otherwise he is to remain in Purgatory till the day of his anniversary. Our Lady said also that, for his father and mother's sake, she had obtained his death, for if he had lived he would have been a lost soul, so that they might think themselves well off for having lived to bury him. She understood also at this time that Sister Eugenia's brother was in Heaven, and her sister-in-law in Purgatory, concerning whom she had these particulars—that for her releasement the following devotions should be performed, namely, that she procure our Lady of Duffel to be three times visited, because her sister-in-law had promised three pilgrimages to St. Winefride's Well, and had not performed them; and that twenty-five Masses of the dead be said, and one Mass for her soul, which, being duly accomplished, she is to go to Heaven the Saturday following. She was likewise once ordered by our Lady to let Sister Margaret of the Angels,[2] then Subprioress at Antwerp, know that her mother was in Purgatory, where she suffered no other pain than that of not seeing Almighty God, which she cannot enjoy until these following things be performed, namely, that the Subprioress procure nine Masses to be said for the souls in Purgatory, which her mother had promised during the sickness of one of her sons and not complied with; that she send one in her name to make a pilgrimage to our Lady of Montague, where is to be offered the value of ten shillings; and that there be a Votive Mass of our Lady offered up and heard by Mother Subprioress, in thanksgiving for this favour done to her in behalf of her mother, who, if all is performed, is to go to enjoy God in Heaven upon Trinity Sunday. On this day she appeared to Sister Margaret in time of morning prayer, and in a most joyful manner said the time drew near wherein she was to enjoy God. At Prime our Lady appeared in her usual way, with this and fifteen other souls all in great glory, who were adoring the Blessed Sacrament, as she had formerly seen other saints do. This glory continued with her till Mass, during which they remained till the

---

[2] Margaret of the Angels (Walton). See an account of her in an Appendix to the Life of Catharine Burton (*An English Carmelite*), p. 272.

L 26

priest had communicated, and then vanished, she having left Sister Margaret a charge to inform the Subprioress her daughter, and assure her that her merits had been a great help towards her deliverance, and that she would amply reward the penances and devotions she had performed for her, the want of which would have detained her a long time from the enjoyment of God.

In the midst of these and many other favours, which Sister Margaret at times continued to enjoy, though not always with the same frequency, she went on advancing in the practice of the most solid virtues, knowing well that all other things without these were no more to be looked upon than a sounding brass or tinkling cymbal, to which as the Apostle compares all that is not animated with charity, so we shall here include all her virtues in this same life-giving virtue of charity, to wit, in the love of God and her neighbour, in which two things, as our Saviour says, the fulness of the law is contained. How fully they animated all her actions will clearly appear in the following pages, where we propose in short to show that so many celestial instructions, favours, and admonitions, which we have seen so copiously sowed in the field of her soul, fell not, like the seed mentioned in the Gospel, by the wayside and was trodden on, or upon a rock and withered, or amongst thorns and was choked up, but upon good ground—a very good heart, which yielded fruit a hundred-fold in patience.

[**** The notes which follow are extracts from the papers written by Mother Margaret, which have not all been used in the compilation of her Life.]

NOTE VII.

On visiting the Five Wounds.

THIS day, which is the 10th of May, being doing my ordinary devotions, which is usual with me at that time (the Elevation of the Mass), that is visiting the Five Wounds of our Blessed Lord, praying and offering to every one of them these five things : The conversion of souls to the Right Hand, to the Left the distressed Catholics in England, to the Crown of Thorns the necessities of the Church and the peace of Christian princes, to the Sacred Feet all the humiliations and mortifications which shall happen to me that day, and to His Blessed Side for all friends and particular devotions—and when I am troubled and cannot do this mentally, I say five *Paters* and *Aves* for these intentions, and endeavour to accompany our Blessed Lady under the Cross—as I was doing this devotion this day our Blessed Lady appeared in her usual way in a white cloud, and showed me our Blessed Lord all glorious, His Blessed Wounds seemed all in glory, and said she took my constancy in using that devotion so well, that for that reason I should see her Son in glory, and that whoso-ever doth it, and accompanies her as under the Cross, re-membering the sorrow she then suffered, should be sure of the last sacraments and their senses at their death. I was much altered and comforted, but from His Blessed Wounds there came such a glory that I could not behold them, and I was afraid yet comforted. And our Blessed Saviour gave me a sweet countenance and said : 'As often as you use this devotion, at this time in the Mass, I will give a particular benediction to what you ask, and if there be not a most pernicious disposition in those you pray for, they shall find an evident comfort when you pray for them at that time. You see, and shall find daily more and more, how pleasing it is to Me to serve My Blessed Mother and suffer for Me.' . . . As soon as I had communicated our Blessed Lady appeared in a great brightness, in her silver cloud, with her Son in her arms and said : 'You were afraid of

my Son in His glory, but now I hope you can see Him
a little child for love of you in my arms. I am resolved
to let you see what I have prepared for you in the next life,
if you serve me.'

———

NOTE VIII.

On great humility as to God's favours.

BEING at the Hours in the choir, I found myself inclining to
be distracted and weary, and lifting up my heart to our
Blessed Lady, I said, ' Most sacred Mother, I do not desire
devotion, nor any extraordinary favours, only permit me not
to be so distracted and carried away with toys as to offend
you this great feast.' And immediately our Blessed Lady
appeared, and said, ' My child, thou hast asked what I could
and did wish thee to desire ; that humble act and desire is
more pleasing to me and my Son than all the high acts of
contemplation, as the world calls them. There are many
abuses amongst those that pretend a spiritual life by their
desiring to know much and to be exercising of divers high
acts, and this keeps more from perfection, than any one thing
besides ; and if my Son did not favour them by withdrawing
His favours from them, they would run much hazard.' She
said there were two kinds of ignorance, the one doth make
us saints, the other makes us devils. She said that which is
worst is to be wilfully ignorant of points of faith, of what
Holy Church teaches and commands, and how to direct our
conscience, and what we are bound to believe ; but that
ignorance which makes us saints, she said, is this, that we
must not only know ourselves ignorant of all good, but that
we must endeavour ever to be rather exercising ourselves in
the humblest acts, and longer, than our Blessed Lord doth
exalt us by His favours—rather to be telling ourselves that
we are to desire nothing, and to know that the favours of
His extraordinary Providence are abundantly above our
comprehension and deserts to understand. ' And then,' said
our Blessed Lady, ' shall such a soul, the more she goes·

admiring and acknowledging my Blessed Son in His gifts
that are ordinary to all, and believing that she is ignorant of
all good, and yet desires nothing but still to remain so,
supposing that His will is accomplished in her, in that kind
(is) both more filled with His graces, and when He finds it
fit for her and agreeable with His own honour, He neither
will nor can forbear to be doing her favours in abundance,
for such a soul will even draw Him out of Heaven by her
humility, and when He bestows His graces in earnest He
will be sure that the soul shall not only in words say, " Lord,
all that is good comes from You," but He will have this
stamped upon her heart, and every motion of her mind shall
be still inclining to think, and would be glad, endeavouring
to make all the world know, that she deserves not anything;
and that when a heart can with much peace say and wish to
be deprived of all extraordinary graces and comforts it
possesses, merely because she conceives herself unworthy of
all favours, then that soul is in a disposition ready to receive
the Divine impressions of my Son, Who, when He bestows
His favours, doth not do them because we should conceive
we are prepared and have served God long, and that therefore He hath rewarded us. No, this would make us think it
in our power to command His favours at our pleasure ; but
we must do all on our part, then know that His favour is
given and taken at His own pleasure, and that an humble
act draws Him more to us than many high speculations.'
She said that there were many as great saints now upon
earth as ever, and that daily God did communicate greater
and greater lights to His Church, but that there were not so
many saved by ignorance as formerly ; that of all sorts there
are some that are highly grateful to God, but that there is
nothing that keepeth even millions of souls from great
degrees of sanctity, but that pretending to know, or to
understand, and to be favoured by God, when it is merely
their own speculations, and endeavouring for such high acts,
'that my Son,' said our Blessed Lady, 'Who rests in a
sincere and simple soul, can find no place, they are so wise
in their own conceits.' She said that the love which our
Blessed Lord had to a soul was such, that one which is

truly humble hath power even to convert nations, so much
may she obtain, and that the love and desire He hath to
enjoy the just with Him in Heaven doth more hasten the
end of the world than the sins of the wicked.

———

NOTE IX.

Revelations of the spiritual state of certain persons.

BEING in the choir at Mass, I saw in the church a poor old
woman, that in the exterior way seemed to be in much
misery, but she was all encompassed with glory, and our
Blessed Lady, who then I saw present, told me and showed
me the condition of that poor creature, and said, 'This poor
creature little cares or knows what she sayeth, and what
great favours my Son and I do give her, and yet her devotions, as simple as they are, have more power with my Son
and me than divers high acts of contemplation, and can obtain more of me, and if it were necessary, she could speak and
know more of Heaven than divers learned men, and those
that compliment more with my Son.' I did understand much
by this how pleasing a simple way of prayer is to God, and
that there He can freely impart His graces. At the time of
the Elevation our Blessed Lord showed me Himself, as He
is oftentimes pleased to do, and I did see many particular
parts of the priest's condition, and withal how our Blessed
Lord—though I saw Him in the same greatness and glory
as ever before, and rather more—for always it seems to me
that the present favour, when I see Almighty God in that
kind, is always the greatest, and so very different, and even
new to me, that though I am able to say nothing but what I
have said before by way of expressing what I see, yet my
soul understands such a strange difference, and it seems
always both so new and so much more (oftentimes) I mean the
glory and clarity of what our Blessed Lord shows that I
have no words to express it—but now, though I did see our
Blessed Lord in the fulness of glory, and knew all Heaven

to be there, yet He was pleased to show me how He went clouding His greatness, and even the effects of His extraordinary graces, according to the perfection of the priest ; and though his soul was in His favour, and what he did would have been gross in another, his ignorance did excuse, but yet made him incapable of any extraordinary effects of that great treasure He had so very near him.

This gave me a very particular desire to be praying for some priests that I, when I lived in the world, had an opinion were of a very imperfect life, and as I was recommending them, and all such persons, to our Blessed Lord— all those I particularly reflected upon as the most imperfect —I saw them and their conditions clearly, and our Blessed Lord gave me to understand that He did me this favour because I should see how little the judgments of men and His decrees are alike, for those whom I had the least opinion of He let me see were so very much more in His favour than those, at least, I more esteemed, that I know not how to express it. But I did see clearly even the particulars of both, and I understood that a good meaning and the humiliation which such persons receive by being censured by the world, if they bear it with patience and endeavour but to edify the world by not doing any gross things, oftentimes when it is in persons that have small capacities, is all our Blessed Lord requires. And that those I had a more particular respect to were not as I conceived them. I did see very clearly the condition of one at whose hands I did communicate the first time I ever did receive, and I understood that his soul is in much danger, and some particulars were represented to me which moved me to be earnest with our Blessed Lord in his behalf.

And this put me in mind of a favour which our Blessed Lord did me at that time, which was this : I now remember perfectly I did see our Blessed Lord in the Blessed Sacrament, like as I have seen the pictures of our Lord like the Good Pastor, and all that day I did see Him in that manner; and I perfectly remember I told my confessor that I must be a religious woman, and he said, ' You must not think of any such thing, that is merely a devout humour you are now in.

I was myself never so altered as when I gave you the Holy Communion ; but do not think of any such thing as being a religious, God will never give your friends such a cross. If I had thought your communicating would have caused such an effect, I would not have permitted you to have received. Your grandmother would give me little thanks for your devotions.' Upon this I thought no more of any such course, but rather was wholly set upon the contrary, and fell into all those ill affections and vanities I have spoken to your reverence of formerly. But I perfectly remember this, and that all the house did observe a strange alteration in me at that time, though it had no other effect, but so passed as all good ever did with me. And I know not how, nor upon what account, for I was not praying for that person, but rather recommending some particular friends of mine whom I conceived to be great servants of God and of the Society, but of all those for whom I prayed I saw at this time nothing ; but there was clearly showed me Father Clayton, of whom I had not at this time the least thought ; and I did see him in much glory, and our Blessed Lord and our Blessed Lady, Whom I then did see present, told me that this degree of glory his soul is now in, and that he is a very great servant of Theirs ; that our Blessed Lady did bring him to Antwerp to deal with that monastery of ours, out of her particular favour to those religious ; that he had effected Their wills and done more by his humble prayers for that house than a person of much more abilities could have effected ; that our Blessed Lord and our Blessed Lady both give a particular benediction to his undertakings. And I did see that he was much more favoured of them than he ever conceived himself ; that he hath a particular gift in discerning spirits, and shall never be deceived, if those with whom he deals have a sincere meaning, and this he shall find easily out if he have his recourse to our Blessed Lady. I did see that he had suffered much by way of temptations of several kinds, and that still he hath and carries a continual cross of this kind, but that it daily crowns him with glory, and that though his recourse to her hath been frequent, yet she hath ever been more at hand to help him in all necessities, and in all his former troubles, and even at present, than he will ever come to understand ; that she was the cause of his being of the Society, and that she hath much for him to do in her service ; that his prayers do convert more souls than the preaching and much endeavour of others ; that in occasions both his prayers and his words shall be omnipotent with both God and man.

I was all amazed, and could have doubted of what I did see, because I never was inclined to this opinion of him, and besides I thought that when I dealt with him he did not discern my spirit, but always thought infinitely better of me than I was, and though I had all those troubles yet he perceived them not. Our Blessed Lady told me all he said was really so. 'And what he told you was true, and all those favours which he said were the Spirit of God were so indeed, and I had particular reasons and ends in not letting him understand your condition of temptation, for if he had known it you had not come to this foundation, which I always intended, neither did I mean to help you by any other means ; and what you did in persuading your sister to be open with him hath done her good, for it hath been an occasion which hath made you both most frequently in his prayers, and he can do more by his prayers oftentimes than by his words, for what he doth effect is by my Son's immediate favour and mine, more and above his own abilities ; he is powerful with Us, and doth obtain benedictions for his whole Order.'

I understood that he was of a humour as apt to take hurt by conversations as most, and these were our Blessed Lady's words. She said : 'He is my servant, and although he be apt to take hurt by creatures, and there be some that it must be a miracle that they do not ; yet I have done him this favour, that he hath often done good to himself and others by his conversations, but never taken any hurt, and also hath ever by my graces experienced the contrary in much conversation only, when I have employed him for my greater honour.' I did see clearly all this, and much more, of the merits he would have for the much he hath suffered in his own soul, and that he hath much to pass, even in the same kinds in some sort by fits. I was all amazed at all this, and yet highly comforted, to see our Blessed Lord hath such servants in whom He is so well pleased.

The Mass being done, and as I was going up, and having been with your Reverence, and told you this fancy of Father Clayton, and being troubled and conceiving that I had made it all, our Blessed Lady appeared to me, and comforted me, and said, ' You have done my will, and I will reward you ; ' and showed me a very particular crown for one of those friends of mine whom I had prayed for, when she told me that of Father Clayton, and it was a reward for him, who had been the person who helped me to bring to pass my desires to be religious, and she said that this crown was for that act he did in helping us, and that he did it much against his own inclination. She said that he was much her servant, and had overcome his greatest imperfection very much, which is an esteem of his own opinion ; that he hath in a very great perfection an indifferency to God's will. She bid me not fear that her showing me that of Father Clayton should do me any hurt, or that what I feared should be, which was that which your Reverence told me of being free with him, or going into the Exercises ; for she said I had done all she required in this point, and that I should not trouble myself any more upon that account ; all of that kind should be easy to you, and that she did me the favour of seeing this crown for my friend, because I had mortified myself in telling your Reverence that of Father Clayton.

I forgot when I set that down of the beads, which our Mother gave me, to say how much I was afflicted by the devil for having said that our Blessed Lady had given them a benediction, and he persuaded me that I had made it because I would be thought a saint, and that I should be damned, for our Mother's faith would make them take effect, and she would do well to have faith in them, but for me, I should be damned for it. That I must (not) wonder if they should do miracles, for so did the piece of the ship so long as it was thought to be the Holy Cross. Being much afflicted, and having told my sister something of it, but not that I was troubled, she said, in a jesting way, ' I will give

you my beads to have them blessed.' But before the word
were out of her mouth she was in earnest. I know not
whether she did see our Blessed Lady or no, but I did see
her between us both, and she said, ' Be not troubled, nor do
not fear, I can give what benediction I please ; it is the
devil that tempts you and seeks to disquiet you. I can give
benedictions to what I please, and it is not by nor for your
virtue, but it is out of my goodness. And know that I will
not only give to those beads, but to any others that you ask
with confidence and humility, shall have my benediction ;
and, my child, know I have many blessings for thee.' I do
not know whether this be so or no.

NOTE X.

Some words of St. Teresa, and visions of other Saints.

OUR Blessed Mother did seem to show much dearness, and
told me she would be always with me, and that she would
be served by me and said : ' My child, I will effect by thy
means that in earth which I desire in Heaven should be
effected,' and so gave me her benediction and departed,
leaving her sweet smell. Now your Reverence commanding
me to say all what passed, I must resolve to do it, which
was : Our Blessed Mother said, and showed me, I know
not how, in a cloud, that what she meant of my effecting her
will, and doing that upon earth which she desires in Heaven
is, that I shall, as I understood, pray for England and her
Order there ; and this I did see upon my having a thought,
that certainly it is not our Blessed Mother that would have
anything changed, this must needs be the devil; to which
our Blessed Mother answered : ' No, my child, it is I,' and
then I did see this of England, and she said, the whole
Order would say that her spirit and herself was upon earth
again in me, and that I should have not only that spirit
which she left and planted in those first houses of hers to
the same perfection that she intended and left amongst
them ; but that even what she now desires in Heaven shall

be effected, and that in this country there shall be apparent good spiritually in our own house, and she said : ' My child, fear not, what I have told you shall be true ; our Blessed Lady and I will ever be with you, and have ever pretended much good and glory to God, by what we both have done and will do for you and by you. I ever had a particular favour from our Blessed Lord in both having a great zeal of souls, and powerful both in my words and prayers to do much good for them ; this I have obtained for you, therefore be courageous, for our Blessed Lord hath much for you to do, and let not a false humility make you indeed proud to think that because you are poor and able to do nothing, therefore you cannot do all in our Blessed Lord ; but know though you are poor yet you have the power of our Blessed Lord in your own hands, and know, my dear child, that you shall be esteemed not of one monastery, but of many, and what you shall say shall be esteemed as from myself ; and I, and our great Queen of Heaven, will be as conversant with you as your own Sisters, in all your greatest necessities. Our Blessed Lord hath given you natural parts even to a large proportion, and also He hath given you His graces even more than yourself or any other can see or imagine ; therefore pray much for the conversion of that place, and pray with confidence for you may obtain much. I have ever, when I was in the world, had a great ambition and desire to help that poor country, and now if I could be impatient for anything in Heaven, it would be to obtain great blessings for England : and any of that country that use devotions to me in their afflictions I will help them in a particular manner.'

This put me in mind of what Father Andrew White said to me once, that I should go into England,[1] and he also told

[1 With regard to Father White's (S.J.) prophecy of her going to England, it is supposed to have been verified, by her holy remains having been brought over. At the time when our community had to take a hurried flight from Lierre, it is a little striking that Mother Bernard (then Superior) and two other religious, without any remembrance of the prophecy, made their way at once to the ' Dead Cellar ' and secured our two dear Mothers' bones, which they brought over with them to England, and which we keep with great care.—Papers by the Sisters.]

it to the Prioress, who was Mother Teresa of Jesus ; and I did see Father Andrew White perfectly before me, just as I had seen him once before in my troubles at Antwerp. Our Blessed Mother told me that I must not fear anything, but leave myself wholly in the hands of our Blessed Lord, and showed me the Convent of Antwerp, and she said : ' How would you bear this cross, to be made Prioress of this monastery? I must have you indifferent to all, and look only upon my Son's will and honour. Believe me, my child, you have as hard things to undergo, and yet you shall do much, and come off with them all, much to my Son's honour and your own comfort in this life ; because you must have no comfort but His will. You shall never make any person suffer by your occasion, and wheresoever you have to do, believe me, those that have most fear and apprehension of you, shall grow to love you most.' Our Blessed Mother thanked me for what I had done for my sister, in bringing her to her Order, and she told me that she was most dear to her, and that she had as large a share in her spirit as any in the Order, and she said that she should be a comfort to me in all my troubles, and that comfort which I had given my sister shall by her to me be doubly rewarded, and that she will be in a most particular manner served by us both. All this I did see perfectly three distinct times, and when I had humbled myself in saying it, then our Blessed Lady, and our Blessed Mother, did appear and thanked me for it.

I seeing the great glory of these great saints, especially St. Ignatius and St. Francis Xaverius, I was moved to wish that it was in my power to merit such a crown, and our Blessed Mother appearing showed me all what I have written (but still as I have said that of England did seem in a cloud) and said : ' See my child, all these crowns you may obtain, if you be but faithful to God and courageous ; and know, my child, thou hast the same spirit I have had, and know I give it you by a most particular favour, and this to that proportion you have it, none since my time have ever possessed. Be humble and fear nothing ; imitate me in being sincere with your confessarius and there shall be no

danger, you are most secure.' At the time of the Mass, I
had the same, and so till I had resolved to tell it your
Reverence I was still vexed with it ; but as soon as I had
done it I have almost forgotten that ever any such thing did
pass ; but in the writing of it I find a very great difficulty,
and the more because your Reverence hath obliged me to
set down all the ridiculous thoughts I had, which I have
done, though it is clear to me, as I fear, that the devil hath
put them in my mind ; and yet now I have written this our
Blessed Lady seems to command me not to think of it, but to
believe what your Reverence tells me, and then that it
imports not whether it be true or false. I forgot to say how
the devil afflicted me in time of the Mass, and made me conceive that I had made it all to be thought a saint ; and our
Blessed Lady appeared and showed me it was the devil, and
told me I should not fear, I had said nothing but what had
humbled me home. All the time of Mass, and I do see it
very usually, I did see angels, and sometimes they seemed
to be of a very superior kind, I think seraphim, attending at
the Mass ; and this day I did see St. Ignatius all the time
by your Reverence, as I think also Blessed Aloysius, but
that was not so clear to me then as the other time.

———

NOTE XI.

Value of purity and simplicity.

OUR Lord was pleased to make impressions upon my soul of
His Divine attributes and perfections, of which I can say
nothing, but that I cannot understand what I did see. And
our Blessed Lord said that the three first grounds which He
exacted in a soul, wherein He would communicate His
favours, were purity and simplicity, with a plainness of
heart, free from all duplicity and turnings, and He said :
' My child, a soul that is pure hath all the motions of her
mind in her own power, and even those of the body, to
except some little distractions or evagations of the mind ;
and those souls to whom I give this privilege of purity, all

the effects of nature which others experience, they are not sensible of, and even in occasions which to others are dangerous, to them horror appears even before the occasion be apparent, but this is My pure favour and no otherwise to be obtained, and I give it and take it as I please ; for oftentimes I am most glorified in letting My servants see their own weakness, and in letting them carry the misery of their own natures about them ; and then when I free them, though it be but even for a fit of time, they come to see My goodness and power so much the more : and to those that I try in this point home, doth My mercy in giving them peace truly appear, and their crowns are doubled, and even made one with Myself in this life, if they prove victorious over themselves. According to the favour I do, and to the approach which I make to a soul, do I exact that she despoil and decline herself from all things created, and this with a constant fidelity ; for as long as there is any earthly or human respect, as the tie is of a greater or less moment, it hindereth more or less the favours which I would otherwise impart. And thou must know that a pure fidelity is by Me exacted according to that approach (as I have said) that I make to fill the soul ; that if spiritual and ecclesiastical persons do not contest and overcome the pleasure which generally men take to be praised, that they will never know the favours of God in earnest, because they are thieves and rob God of His honour, and their darkness will still grow greater.

'And believe Me, My child, that the least little inutility or idleness of a soul, obscures her instantly to some proportion, and it doth much impeach that true liberty of spirit and heart, a certain old habitual dissimulation, which will needs not understand what it ought, for it restrains it, and makes souls wilfully ignorant of what they are even bound to know. When I work and operate all in the most intimate part of the soul, then know that any little sufferances or indisposition of the body, or any affliction, doth more unite and make Me one with her than divers consolations. I have many servants that have great desires, and even impulses to prayer, which yet are hindered by the indispositions of their body; but if they prove faithful, although they have in this case need of even an angelical kind of patience, I will reward this fidelity with an abundant reward even in this life. To those souls where I communicate Myself in this extraordinary way, every motion of their mind must be disposed of by Me, and they must know when they have done all they know, that all that succeeds well is My work, not theirs; and on a soul to whom I impart My favours, if she do not prove faithful, I grow to exercise My justice most severely accordingly.' And this fidelity consisteth in that she doth in earnest seek to deny and disappropriate herself of all things created, especially whatsoever may incline her to an esteem of herself, or any the least duplicity in her proceedings; that it is not enough to desire to be perfect, but that we must seek it, and that divers do conceive they do much, but if it be much in speculations and desires, it doth rather puff up to pride than please our Blessed Lord. That desires though they be never so great, that have not, and leave not in the soul a plainness and simplicity of spirit are always to be suspected. Our Blessed Lord said: 'I do remain and am pleased in, and will give Myself to be known and understood and felt by, an humble, simple heart, and there will My Father and I, with the Holy Ghost, be always found imparting Our truths, and the true knowledge of all truth which is God, Whose Omnipotency is made a prisoner to such a soul, and she may even govern Him together with all His Divine perfections as her own, for her humility makes her Lord and Master, and having conquered her own inordinate passions, she hath Me engraven upon her heart, and hath power to dispose of My treasures, and this because she hath no disposition but My will, so that I am even forced to make My will hers, that so I may effect My will by her.'

Our Blessed Lord said a world of such things, and yet I cannot say I heard words, but all this and much more was engraven upon my soul, and though I can say little, yet I find there is more stamped upon my heart and understanding than I have words to express. He told me that prayer did consist much more in giving to God, by way of love and affection, than in receiving great consolations from God;

that afflictions and sufferings do much more unite us to God than an abundance of consolations, and our Blessed Lord said : ' Believe Me, to the end that you get up to perfection it will be necessary that you, and all souls that pretend it, should endeavour to know themselves exactly well, that so they may know how to punish themselves in a just way. I mean by that point of knowing themselves, that they be diligent in observing their imperfections, that so they may be able to remedy them ; but this without much solicitude, and always to remedy them more by humbling themselves by seeing their faults, than by the confidence they have in their own endeavours or remedies ; and this humility, with a confidence in Me, will be the ready way to free you from any imperfections, or at least will make your imperfections perfections before Me. It is a voluntary fault in religious persons if they be not perfect, and proceeds from their want of perseverance in seeking perfection and in overcoming themselves.'

CHAPTER XVIII.

Her elevation to the office of Prioress, her humility, self-contempt, and love of poverty.

SISTER MARGARET was so richly adorned with this fundamental virtue of perfection that it gave a lustre to all she said and did, so that if she might be said to have particularly excelled more in one virtue than another it would be in that of humility. This clearly appeared to all that knew or spoke with her, by the low opinion and sentiments she ever had of herself. She was often times heard to wish she was only like the least in the monastery in degree of perfection, then she could think herself worthy of the habit she wore, and many times with tears in her eyes she would stand in a sort of amaze, admiring as she said the immense goodness of Almighty God, in dealing so mildly with her, and forbearing to punish more severely her many and grievous sins, since the horror she herself had of her own imperfect life was as much as she could bear with, wishing she could but declare to the world her poverty and ignorance, that so her nothingness might be manifested to all, 'For truly I am good for nothing but to take up the place of others who would have served His Divine Majesty much better. How is it possible, my dear Jesus, You should still have patience with me, unless it were because You find me really a pitiful object of Your mercies? May Your holy name be ever praised and glorified in me Your unworthy and truly useless servant !'

This mean conceit of herself was universal, and extended as well to what concerned her natural good qualities as her spiritual gifts and graces, neither was it alone contained in an outward show of words, but was real and sincere, as appeared in all her actions and proceedings, in which she ever preferred the judgment and experience of others to her own, and submitted herself with the greatest promptitude and facility to any of the religious either in discourse or other occasions, and was sure to be the first at performing anything that was mean or humbling, as weeding in the garden, carrying wood, or lighting the fires; all which she did with such simplicity and forgetfulness of herself, as if she had been fit for no other employs. But her religious Sisters had far greater ideas of her worth, of which she had given convincing proofs in the easy and complete way of acquitting herself of the different duties annexed to the principal offices she was charged with in the house, where nothing of consequence was done without her advice; and therefore at the third election after the beginning of this foundation they unanimously chose her for Prioress.

When his Lordship the Bishop had declared it to the community according to the usual manner, he congratulated with her Reverence on the choice, who was so surprised and alarmed at it that she could not for some time speak, but kneeling down all bathed in tears, with her hands lifted up, she humbly besought his Lordship not to confirm the election, alleging many reasons, and want of abilities, which rendered her incapable of so important an office, amongst others pleading her want of age, not being as yet thirty. At which my lord smiling said, 'Good Mother, trouble not yourself with that, it will do you no more service than all your other reasons, for

suppose it be so, I can and do dispense with that.
Therefore take courage, my dear Daughter, and accept
patiently of this cross, for the honour and love of God.
He will help you to bear it, for I am sure His hand is in
your election, and I cannot leave to confirm what the
Holy Ghost has done : be confident He will direct you
in all your actions. Why do you weep and afflict yourself
whilst all these good religious are full of joy? Why do
you continue to grieve thus? Truly I think if I had
but your picture it would represent to the life *Mater
Dolorosa.*'

She was some time before she recovered herself of this
dreadful shock, as she termed it, which in one instant
renewed all her former apprehensions concerning the
dangers attending superiority, for although by what she
had understood before of our Blessed Lord she was
sooner or later to expect it, yet it seemed still too difficult a cross to impose upon her young shoulders. But
since such was His Divine will she had nothing left than
to renew again the sacrifice she had made of herself, by
repeated acts of resignation and submission to His
merciful appointments, hoping that according to His
promise He would faithfully assist her, and not permit
her poor soul to suffer any prejudice by it. The remembrance of what had then passed, and some other favours
she received, alluding to her present circumstances, contributed also to restore her to her peace of mind, as they
greatly helped to diminish her fears, for she understood
that Mother Anne of St. Austin, who she saw had a very
high place in Heaven, had suffered no other Purgatory
but the time of her superiority, because it was not only
contrary to her inclinations, but she had met with such
crosses and trials during it, as entirely cancelled all the
punishment due to her sins. She succeeded Mother
Anne of the Ascension in the charge of Superior, and

had a great regard for this our dear Mother Margaret of Jesus, whom she greatly comforted, when bowing to her she said, ' Happy are those Superiors who suffer by their office !' Mother Anne of the Ascension likewise afforded her no less consolation, who appearing once in company with our Blessed Lady thanked her for all the devotions performed in her honour, and pointing towards the Blessed Virgin, said, ' Our glorious Queen will reward them all.'. Then she assured her of her particular assistance in all she undertook, admonishing her to be punctual in little observances, and to maintain love and charity amongst one another, and there would be no danger. ' For,' said she, ' I am crowned with more glory for what I did towards upholding little observances and charity towards each other, than for all those other things you esteem so much, which I did for the good of the Order.' She said that it was fitting that Superiors should exercise their religious in little things of obedience, and also in some small mortifications, for these help to cultivate religious simplicity, and charity. That when she came to die her greatest scruple was concerning omissions of that kind. She also said she was much pleased in this house, and would always assist the Superiors of this and Antwerp monastery, if they did but desire it, which was a thing pleasing to God.

At one of her re-elections, his lordship, who was now become acquainted with the many singular qualifications of this venerable Mother, and a great admirer of her virtues, speaking to the community in her Reverence's absence, said, that in all his life he never met with her equal; for so much wisdom, and so great humility, he must confess was rare to be found in these our days. These were the sentiments of all excepting herself, whose actions gave a more authentic testimony, for in all the time of her happy government she conserved and advanced herself in this fundamental virtue, under-valuing herself to that degree as scarce to admit of the respect due to her office. Much less would she permit herself to be exempted from anything either in observance, clothing, or diet, which on account of her many infirmities and constant weakness she might reasonably have done, but always endeavoured to be served as the least in the house, and according to the Constitutions, to lead her flock in all religious practices. Her Reverence always had a great deference to the Discreets, so that she never resolved upon or asked in any way, although it were but in trifles, regarding the government of the house or those under her care, but by their advice; and though their judgment did sometimes differ from hers, she left her own to follow theirs, in which way of proceeding she always thought things fell out better than they would have done according to her own way of thinking, thus attributing all the good success of her affairs to their prudence. To such a degree of humility and simplicity was she arrived, by a constant denial of her own will, that she could safely say she was never less satisfied than when she met with occasions of following it.

Her Reverence had also so true a neglect and contempt of herself as never to have been heard to speak of, or say anything which tended to her own praise, nor could she endure to hear the Sisters or others applaud or take notice of her actions, and if by chance she overheard any such discourse she would show much displeasure, saying they little knew what they admired, and less reflected on the occasion they gave her to suspect their sincerity, for of all vanities she had the greatest hatred and disgust to flattery, which she could never dissemble. Out of this same contempt of herself she was seldom known to take notice of any failings or omissions which regarded her own person, on the contrary, it was plain

to perceive a kind of joy in her countenance when anything of that kind happened to her, as it sometimes did,
either by negligence or hastiness, our Blessed Lord so
permitting it, for her greater merit and others' example.
And when on such occasions the Subprioress would
reprehend the Sisters for their rudeness and want of
respect to her Reverence, she would be much displeased
with her, saying, 'You cannot trouble me more than in
taking notice of such trifles; if you did but know the
dislike I have to hear anything of that nature, you would
not give me the mortification. How do you think we
shall gain Heaven, or become in anything like to our
dear Lord and Saviour, if we bear not with contempts,
or accidental neglects? for my part I assure you I am
more covetous of these few occasions of imitating Him,
than worldlings are of the greatest honours their ambition
can aim at. For the love of God, dear Mother Subprioress, let us look well to the main point, that
observance be well kept up, and let us give the Sisters
good example therein: as for these punctilios, God forbid
we should be so sensible of ourselves as to value them.'

The little regard she had for herself went so far that
she would not permit the Sisters to kneel or stand in her
presence, if she could possibly prevent it; and she would
suffer any inconvenience rather than give them the least
trouble, for which reason she would use all sorts of
industry and forecast to prevent or hinder them from
moving out of their places or fetching anything that
might be wanted; on which account she often took
round about ways not to disturb the community by
passing them. If on occasions she borrowed any trifle
of the Sisters, as a needle or other such things, she
would be as careful in using it and as diligent in restoring
it as though in itself it had been most precious or of the
greatest importance, and so grateful and in so humble

manner did she return thanks as to cause them surprise and confusion, having ever in her thoughts that point of the rule, 'He that will be the greatest amongst you shall be servant to the rest,' which she humbly observed. When according to custom on particular occasions she spoke her faults in the refectory, it was in so humble a manner, and with such confusion, as if she had been the most imperfect Religious in the house, acknowledging her infidelity and ingratitude to Almighty God with such abundance of tears as often moved the community to the same, whilst she at their feet was begging pardon for her ill example. Such was her extraordinary simplicity and desire of humiliations that on those occasions she would often find out something to say or do that argued a want of judgment. And although her Reverence could not but be sensible she was endowed with a greater share both of the gifts of nature and of grace than is common, yet she was so truly little in her own eyes, and so far from valuing herself upon anything, that according to her own sentiments, self-conceit or vainglory could find no sort of food in her to feed upon; neither could she imagine anything to pride herself in, unless it were her little Spouse Jesus, for Whose sake she desired only to be despised and contemned. For, as she often said, it would be a strange thing to see a God. become so little and humble and not to strive to imitate Him.

It was this virtue of humility which animated her with such particular devotion towards the Sacred Infancy of our Lord, and inspired her with those simple, innocent and familiar expressions which in any other would have often been ridiculous, but in her were accompanied with so much sweetness and devotion, as to render them amiable and edifying: so that her whole person would change while she was entertaining herself with the little image of the Infant at Bethlehem, and she seemed in actions and countenance on those occasions like unto an infant. Once on the feast of the Three Kings, having the Infant in her arms, and admiring His little hands with extreme tenderness and feeling, in one of her usual transports, reflecting on His Sacred Wounds, she said : ' Oh, that I was able to endure the like for You, my dear Jesus : but as that cannot be, my will at least shall be bored in a thousand holes for the love of You.' Out of this motive of mortifying her own will, she was never heard to contradict others in discourse, although she knew them to be in the wrong, nor was she positive in maintaining her own opinion or proceedings ; but when contradicted would acquiesce as quietly and calmly to another's sentiments, as if she had been in the wrong. Nor would she show any displeasure to to any of the religious for being of a different opinion to hers, but would peaceably hear their reasons, and often follow them preferably to her own, and took anything well she was put in mind of.

Although her Reverence was very handy in all sorts of work, and particularly what regarded her needle, she never failed in any the least necessity to employ herself in the meanest offices, such as sweeping, washing dishes, helping the vestieres to fold linen, or darn their old things, in which she took particular satisfaction, and endeavoured to do it in the neatest manner, and as she thought might be most agreeable and easy for the Sisters, of whom she would often learn little things, and afterwards took great delight in telling others, ' This I learned of such a one, such a person taught me this way of working.' In which and all her proceedings she ever showed a great esteem and respect for the religious, whom she looked upon as models of perfection ; and when in Chapter she had admonished any of their defects, she would at the end thereof seek to excuse them, by acknowledging her bad example and unmortified life to be the real cause of their little progress in virtue, annihilating herself beneath all and begging their prayers, by which she hoped to obtain light and grace to mend her faults, which she greatly apprehended would otherwise be a hindrance to the graces and benedictions our Blessed Lady and her sweet Son were ready to bestow on the community.

Her love to poverty was such that according to her own inclination she would have been glad to have lived in a house without income, or anything certain to depend on, that she might the more perfectly practise it. She called it the jewel of a religious state, and the treasure of her heavenly Spouse Jesus, by which He enriched His dearest and best friends: so that she had ever a particular joy and satisfaction in wanting necessaries for her own person, always making choice of the worst and meanest things for her own use, not being able to suffer anything about her that was superfluous. And where she perceived that in clothing or other anything better was given to her than what the rest had, she would find out means secretly to deprive herself of it, and give it to some others she thought in more need. Nor would she scarce admit of what was fit and becoming in ordinary things, as fire and candle, which she could seldom be prevailed to make use of them, notwithstanding her constant indisposition, which rendered her most sensible of cold. She had always such constant reluctance to the evangelical virtue as to practise it to the most insignificant things, even to the picking up of a pin, though she was in never so great a hurry, and so neat and careful of her dress and habit, that she seldom went about the house without ticking it up. Her Reverence was also equally vigilant

to see it well observed and practised by others; for
which end she would not permit those in offices to make
or change anything without her knowledge, and would
also cut all the religious' clothes, both linen and woollen,
herself, lest there should be anything superfluous or
wasted. She could not bear to see anything that belonged to the community lost or broken, nor any way
out of order, and when she found anything cast aside
or neglected, she would be the first to carry it where
it belonged to, being very delicate in point of neatness
and seeing things left in their proper places. For this
reason her Reverence would often take occasions to
make her rounds and visit in particular every one's office,
by which she came to see and know when anything was
wanting to the Sisters: and when she found all things
in good order, neatly kept and mended, she would be
highly pleased, saying all places looked like unto little
Bethlehem, poor and neat.

When any of the Sisters showed a kind of solicitude,
wishing her Reverence's purse could provide them with
new supplies, telling her it was loss of time to mend
and repair the old things, she would reply: ' have
patience, dear Sisters; our Spouse knows best what is
good for us: this is true poverty, by which we hope to
obtain eternal riches. I thank God I never am in pain
or solicitous on this score: and if it were in my own
choice, it should be rather to want than possess plenty.
God forbid that a poor Teresian should ever apprehend
want, since it is poverty must make us like unto our
beloved Spouse Jesus, Who is greatly delighted to see
us clothed with His own livery.'

From this same spirit of poverty chiefly proceeded
the precious account her Reverence made of every
moment of time: saying, there was nothing religious
people would have more to answer for than the loss of

time : therefore, she was greatly remarkable for her economy herein, so that she was never seen to idle one moment away, but on the contrary sought all occasions of gaining. For besides ordinary work time, which she employed with particular diligence and quickness, so as often to despatch more in an hour than many others could do in two, she would frequently sit up late at night to mend and repair what she knew the religious stood most in need of; and when any of the Sisters finding their work so far advanced, seemed to wonder how it was possible for her Reverence to get so much done, she would with her usual cheerfulness and good humour smiling answer them : 'Don't you know that my little Spouse helps me?'[1] It was also her custom to rise at three o'clock in the morning, even in the coldest seasons, which time she usually spent in prayer over and above the ordinary hours thereto allotted : at which she even assiduously accompanied the community, as well as all other duties.

She had so great a forecast in regulating her affairs, that when she had anything to write that was not pressing, she would defer it till Sunday or holy days, so to avoid even the occasion of idleness. And because she loved dearly to be with the community, she sometimes wrote her letters amongst them whilst they were at work in the recreation, in which she had so great a facility that no discourse or recreative jests of the Sisters seemed ever to disturb her, but her pen was constantly upon the run; and she would in a short time finish many letters of quite different business, without study or hesitation, saying to those that wondered at it, she never

---

[1] [The community at Darlington still possesses a very handsome set of elaborately worked vestments, together with cope and antependum, which the Sacred Infant helped Mother Margaret to embroider. All is as fresh as if lately done.]

wanted matter or words to express herself in writing
such poor stuff as it was: for she had such a mean
conceit of herself also in this point, that she would sometimes seem dissatisfied with her own inability and want
of capacity, and when it was anything of importance
would humbly beg of others to make her a copy: though
all who knew her acknowledged that she had a fluent
and grateful style, and so much to the purpose, that
few could equal her.

Even when her occupations allowed her the least
spare time, she had always some pious book or other
at hand to spend it in, restoring her decayed forces by
that heavenly food, as she called it. And she has often
been heard to say there was nothing she took more
delight in than reading, and that, according to inclination, she could leave meat and sleep or any pastime
soever, for the pleasure she took in this exercise. On
Sundays or other festival days, she would find out a
pious historical book, and read it to the religious in time
of recreation, which was the most agreeable entertainment
she could give them, who could not but admire when
the lecture was in Flemish, of which she had no other
knowledge but such as she had gained by her own
private industry, how it was possible for her to read the
same to them in English with equal fluency, as if it had
been printed in the same tongue, without either stam-
mering, or being at a loss for the least word or expression which she interpreted to them in a most easy and
agreeable style ; which made her so far from becoming
tedious by these pious exercises, that all the time seemed
too short, that was spent in them. This profit was no
less than the pleasure, since many have affirmed that
at such times they found themselves more moved to the
love of God, and more enlightened in the ways of perfection than they were able to obtain by their own

labours, in many months, for as they said, although we have often heard and read many of the same sort of things before, coming now from her Reverence, they make quite a different impression on us, which is truly not to be wondered at, when we consider the rest of her engaging qualities.

Such a constant application may perhaps render her Reverence suspected by some of over much austerity or restraint to her community, or of being difficult in giving access, as people much occupied too frequently are. But her Reverence was quite the contrary: for as she was neglectful of herself, so was she of her occupations when she had the least occasion of complying with others' inclinations or desires: so that she has been often known to walk and talk with others at times the most inconvenient to her, with the same cheerfulness and affability as if it had been her own choice, and so long together, that when she came to her cell, she seemed quite spent and ready to faint through fatigue. So in the midst of business, or delicate and curious work, at which she was particularly dexterous, and frequently occupied, either for the church or special friends, she would break up all to give a hearing to the least religious, although sometimes in trifles, and would discourse with them, and listen to their wants and grievances with so much ease and sweetness as though she had no other affairs in hand, never putting them off till another time, or permitting them to go away unsatisfied. In which practices she truly became all to all, and rather a slave than servant to all, constantly sacrificing her whole person hereby to the love of God and her neighbour.

NOTE XII.

An account of Mother Margaret's virtues written by her sister, Mother Ursula.

IN recreation Mother Margaret would, when her affairs permitted, strive to be the first, for she loved dearly to be with her Sisters, being always in a pleasant humour, cheerful and merry, and she received great contentment to see her religious so too, saying it was the Spirit of God, and that our recreations should proceed from the joy and delight we receive in Him, and the celebration of the Divine Mysteries, moving ourselves to those affections which the Holy Ghost did actually suggest as proper for the feast ; at which times her Reverence was always so full of Almighty God that she could not contain herself, of Whom when she was speaking she seemed to be in her element ; especially when it was of the Sacred Nativity, or any mystery of our Blessed Lord's Infancy, she would be so transported that she seemed wholly changed, her face would become so beautiful, that we could scarce behold it, and it seemed also to us that her eyes cast forth such divine rays as kept us all astonished, and we could plainly perceive that her heart was all inflamed with the love of the sweet Infant, expressing in her words the profound knowledge and heavenly visitations with which her whole soul was plentifully stored. There did also at these times appear a great simplicity, goodness, and inno-cence in her countenance and words, and with it so much wisdom and prudence as caused great admiration in us all ; and sometimes when she would be speaking of the Sacred Infant, she became so sweet and affable, that she seemed to us like an innocent child, both in her gesture and words, entertaining the Infant Jesus in so amiable and familiar a manner that we could not but believe she visibly beheld the Sacred Infant in her arms, in Whose embraces was placed all her delight, content, and felicity ; so that all temporal objects and accidents she either beheld or heard, she instantly applied to the praises of her little Spouse, Whose

Divine Goodness was so enamoured of her that it seemed
He vouchsafed to be her constant companion, as her Reverence would with much sincerity often confess, being so
transported that it was not possible for her to contain the
joy of her heart, which was so great that she made us all
participate with her. Particularly at the feast of Christmas
she would find such ways to demonstrate the jubilee of her
soul, so to incite us to admire, praise, and love the infinite
goodness of God on this great festivity, which may be seen
by her most sweet pious songs of this mystery, so full of
Divine spirit as moves all that hear them.

Mother Margaret seemed to us an angel of peace ; her
most familiar discourse was to us upon all occasions, ' Dear
Sisters, let us love one another.' Saying, ' I would have you
strive to exceed in complying, and showing a cheerful readiness to assist and serve each other, expressing love by works
as well as words.' This was her own practice, which she
endeavoured by her example to imprint in the hearts of her
religious, for she would be as diligent in preventing the
Sisters as if she had been a novice. And when any of the
Sisters were never so little indisposed, her Reverence would
steal up to their cells, and make their beds, &c. . . . And if
she thought anything was better or more convenient, about
herself, or bed, she would find some means to change it,
and give it to those she thought had more need ; so great a
dislike she had to have anything more than the very least in
the house.

CHAPTER XIX.

Of her spirit of suffering and mortification.

ALL who have written the lives of saints, and committed their most celebrated actions to posterity, have made particular mention of their sufferings, which, however averse to nature and the ordinary inclinations of delicate Christians, render all such conspicuous who share in any distinguished manner of them. And it is a received opinion of our holy forefathers that there is no solid perfection which is not purified by sufferings; and these truly have chiefly contributed to raise the saints to that inestimable glory they now enjoy.

Suffering is the first lesson given to Christians: witness the Gospel and the holy writings of the Apostles, amongst whom St. James, in his Catholic Epistle to the faithful dispersed amongst the Gentiles, says: 'My brethren, esteem it all joy when you shall fall into divers temptations; knowing this, that the trying of your faith worketh patience, and patience has a perfect work, that you may be perfect and entire, failing in nothing. . . . Happy is the man that endureth trial, because when he has been proved he shall receive a crown of life, which God has promised to them that love Him.'[1] Whence we must take notice that it is by trials and tribulations we come to the perfect work, our sanctification, which must be deficient in nothing; it is by suffering we must manifest our love to God, Who promises here the same crown to those who love Him and those who endure trials for His sake.

[1] St. James i. 2—4, 12.

N 26

Of these our venerable Mother, as we have seen in the beginning of her Life, had an abundant share, being often reduced to death's door by long and most painful sicknesses, some of which were so violent as to leave in her their suffering effects all her life long; which she cheerfully embraced, looking upon them as the purifying instruments of God's merciful hand, being mindful, as the Apostle exhorts us, of the consolation given us by Almighty God, Who, speaking to us as His children, says: 'My son, neglect not the discipline of the Lord, neither be thou wearied whilst thou art rebuked by Him, for whom the Lord loveth He chastiseth, and He scourgeth every one whom He receiveth.'[2] Which He clearly manifested in His only-begotten Son, Who, although impeccable, was exposed by His most loving Father to all kinds of sufferings.

But when, like another Job, she seemed to be given up to the unmerciful fury of the devil, it is incredible to relate the sufferings she underwent. For whilst her body was bruised and broken, and her heart agitated with alarming fears and frights of various kinds, her spirit was oppressed with all kinds of temptations, which brought her to such an uncomfortable situation that, as she herself acknowledged, she was almost reduced to despair, since Heaven seemed shut against her, whilst the rage of Hell had surrounded her, which without supernatural help she would not have been able to withstand. Neither did she here fail to adore the providential hand of God, Who is sometimes pleased thus to try His servants; she submitted herself herein to the secret dispositions of Heaven, supporting all with patience, and conformity to all that could anyways tend to the greater glory of God, Who is noways more glorified than by the soul's fidelity in accepting of these purifying crosses, which sometimes

[2] Heb. xii. 5, 6, from Prov. iii. 11.

deprive it even of the consolation to know or think it makes a right use of them. In these trials Almighty God retires Himself, as it were, and abandons us, as He did His beloved Son upon the Cross. He leaves us in darkness, and not only deprives us of all sensible comfort, but gives us up to the most vehement repugnances to all that is good, permitting all our exercises of piety to be molested with numberless horrid and shocking temptations, in the midst of which the soul seems to itself lost, being void of all sensible hopes of Heaven, and possessed of a certain assurance of Hell.

These are the ways by which Almighty God, stripping us of ourselves, unites us more closely to Him; for by these means He frees His servants from many obstacles that hinder this spiritual communication and separates them from all imperfect attachments to their prayers, mortifications, or other pious exercises, which are but too often mingled with selfishness and desire of satisfaction. A soul in this situation thinks all inevitably lost, when in reality the whole is gained, and so secure that no repugnances or aversions, however lively, cannot hurt it, these being only simple efforts of the inferior powers, which cover the superior and real sentiments of the soul, that lay hidden like glowing coals under a heap of ashes. Our Lord as to His inferior part had such a repugnance to His bitter Passion, that it cast Him into an Agony, in which whilst He lay sweating Blood, the superior part consummated the sacrifice by a most perfect resignation, which He retained till all was accomplished, although some time before He expired He cried out, as one forgotten and abandoned.

Having thus passed through many tribulations, it pleased Almighty God to crown her fidelity by a glorious triumph over her enemies, in putting an end to the devil's insolent molestations, and restoring to her a perfect peace of mind, which was also attended with better health; but as sufferings were chiefly what she aspired after, she was not long before she broke it, by an over rigid and severe mortification; for, as she said, she could not comprehend how it was possible to love God and not delight in suffering for His sake, nor how she could otherwise deserve to be called the Spouse of Jesus Christ, Who, being innocence itself, out of pure love for us, treated His Sacred Body so rigorously, and gave it up for us to all kind of torments. Therefore she thought a religious life, as being a more strict imitation of Christ, ought never to be free from sufferings, and consequently that religious persons should never cease from afflicting their bodies with vigils, fastings, and other corporal austerities, depriving it of all that can give it satisfaction.

This has been the spirit of the saints, always to carry about them the mortification of Jesus, and it is in a particular manner the spirit of Carmel, which in its holy reform renewed all the severe austerities of the ancient Fathers of the Desert, as the lives of its first reformers have manifested to the world, who treated their delicate bodies in so terrible a manner as to move those who were witnesses of their sufferings and mortifications not only to compassion, but a sort of horror, so repugnant and afflicting they appeared to nature. Which is not to be understood alone of St. Teresa and St. John of the Cross, who laid the corner-stone of this most wonderful edifice, but also of their first companions in their foundations, where we meet with such unparalleled examples of poverty, want, and sufferings of all kinds, attended with the most rigid austerities, that they even exceed our comprehension, since according to the delicate notions of these our days they seem impracticable. Which in reality we need not be so much surprised at, since even St. Teresa herself often stood in admiration of the wonders

the grace and love of God worked in His innocent but
ferverous servants ; for as she says, speaking of her religious daughters, the ardour with which they embraced all
sorts of mortfications was astonishing, and she remarked
that the greater these mortifications were, the more joy-
fully they were received, so that Superiors would sooner
be tired in proposing them than the religious in practising
them, since their desire in this regard seemed without
bounds. The same we may truly say of Mother Margaret,
who thirsted, as it were, after mortification which, besides
what has been before mentioned in regard of diet, was
extraordinary, always making use of the meanest and
worst fare, and that in so small a quantity, only once a
day, that it seemed inconceivable how she could subsist
with it. So constant was she in point of abstinence, that she
was never known to take the least refreshment, not even so
much as a little beer, betwixt meals, although she was always
subject to a continual feverish indisposition, nor could
she ever be persuaded in her lesser infirmities, with which
she walked about the house, to mitigate these, or other
corporal austerities, till she was commanded so to do by
her confessor, who no less than many others judged her
too prodigal of her health, and truly not without reason,
as may be easily seen by a petition she once made to
him concerning some penances she desired to perform in
order to prepare herself for the feast of her Seraphical
Mother, St. Teresa. Which were, that for three weeks
beforehand she might rise an hour before the rest of the
religious, and spend that time in prayer, one half of it
kneeling in some painful posture, and the other prostrate
with her arms a cross ; that during this time she might
take ten extraordinary disciplines, for the space of a
Miserere, with sharp wires ; that she might lie upon a
board, and not change for the whole night the posture
she lay down in ; that she might fast three days each

week, and mortify herself the other days all she could in her diet, without being taken notice of; that she might constantly wear a hair-cloth round her waist, and a pea or other troublesome thing in her spargates ; that as often as she found herself sleepy at prayer or Divine Office, she might make use of something so painful as would drive it efficaciously off.

On another occasion obedience, as she said, not permitting her to perform extraordinary penances, to which she still found herself much inclined, she desired to know if she might not at least continue her more ordinary ones, which she could do without any person's knowledge, although they should spend nature and prejudice her health; she having not that, but a good intention, in performing them.

This was indeed but too truly the consequence of her over rigid mortification, by which, and her former sickness, she was already reduced to such a state of weakness that the doctors said it was impossible for her to recover her strength, her stomach being so far impaired that all the sustenance she took turned to catarrhs, so that she vomited daily two or three basins of phlegm and water, which was the cause of many painful and dangerous infirmities, as the griping of the bowels and a constant aching of the back, which was accompanied with other violent pains, all which reduced her to so low a condition that she was nothing but skin and bone,. though she was naturally inclined to be corpulent. Sometimes these pains, together with the colic, would seize on her in so violent a manner that she would be forced to keep her bed for three or four weeks running, not being able to retain anything she took, nor suffered to have any rest either night or day from the vehemence of her pains. Neither could the many remedies applied by the doctors give her the least ease, at which they were

amazed, and no less than the community greatly wondered how it was possible for her to hold out. Notwithstanding all this, her Reverence was ever so present to
herself that in her greatest infirmities she seldom omitted
to perform her daily devotions towards her Heavenly
Spouse, and would never fail to make her daily preparations for Holy Communion, as if she was actually to
receive It; always have a thirsting desire of that Heavenly
Food. And when it was apprehended her too great
application and fervour in preparing herself, either for
spiritual or real Communion hindered her rest, she would
with much sweetness reply, ' Think not so, dear Sisters,
since my God is pleased to come to so poor a creature ;
it is the only comfort in the midst of pains I am sensible
of, and what alone gives me strength to bear so many
afflictions ; truly without this consolation it would be
impossible for me to live, whereas I can do all things in
Him Who strengthens me ; ' which was certainly verified
in the effects. For on these occasions it was ever
remarkable that her face would become as fresh and
well coloured as though she was in perfect health, and so
cheerful was she, and resigned to the Divine will of God,
that she seemed to feel no pain ; which is not to be
wondered at, when we reflect on what has been said of
the extraordinary effects this Holy Sacrament wrought in
her pure soul.

The extreme fastings, and other inconceivable penitential works of many most celebrated saints, have doubtless often contributed to diminish in a notable manner
their natural forces, and sometimes, though indirectly,
also to shorten their lives ; in which we suppose them to
have been directed by particular impulses of Divine
grace, knowing that God is wonderful in His saints, who
in these extraordinary ways are more to be admired than
imitated, and serve more for our humiliation than imita

tion, as they give us an occasion of seeing our own poverty and misery, which may reasonably cover us with shame and confusion, when we reflect on the little we are willing to do for the love of God, whilst His innocent servants seem so insatiable of sufferings as neither to spare health nor life. Discretion, therefore, the right rule of all virtues, is particularly to be observed in this, especially by young beginners, whose fervour is apt to lead them into excesses, and make them prefer their own inclinations to the advice of their directors, whom they either neglect to consult or obey, and thereby expose themselves to many dangers. Of this Mother Margaret was warned by our Lord Himself, Who, whilst she was saying her beads one evening, upon her knees, although quite tired and spent, appeared to her, and after embracing her with much tenderness, asked her why she did not sit down, as she had been commanded to do when she was weary; for she must know that such acts of obedience were more agreeable and pleasing to Him than the respect she proposed by kneeling or standing. When she was set down in great confusion, our Blessed Lord seemed to do so likewise, and said that the moving of a hand, or even doing things which were agreeable to our humour by obedience, were more acceptable to Him than many penances of our own invention; nay, even the greatest mortifications, although done with leave, were often of inferior merit to lesser things, or what might seem trifles, done with the spirit of obedience. For oftentimes people, by taking satisfaction in their spiritual exercises and penances, hinder themselves more in their progress in virtue than those who are remiss in such practices, because the one becomes blinded with their own ideas, and easily forget themselves; whereas the other is sure one time or the other to be humbled, and thereby made sensible of their want of fervour. At this same time He let her know she had lost much by being too eagerly attached to indiscreet penances ; but the condition she was then in, and her good intention, had in some part recompensed it. Therefore for the future her desires of mortification should be mortified by abstaining from all extraordinary mortifications and conforming herself exactly to obedience. This she ever carefully observed, looking upon herself as a useless servant, who was not deemed worthy of doing anything for God, Whom she did not fail, however, daily to honour by constant self-denials in such things as could not prejudice her health. But to say the truth, she had now no longer need to look after mortifications and self-denials, for both constantly attended her, so that at last she was seldom without constant pain and such an indisposition of body that would have made many others in the like disorder keep close confinement. Still she accompanied the community in all duties, and went up and down, taking care of all the concerns of the monastery as though she were in perfect health, which gave each one reason to admire her singular courage and exemplary patience. Indeed she seemed to the community as though she had no feeling of anything which regarded her, ever showing a real dislike to any sort of considerations, although reasonable in her pitiful situation.

She had an utter aversion to whatever tended towards private ease or commodity, constantly disdaining to take the least satisfaction in anything transitory, and treating those things with contempt wherein there was any appearance of self-love, which was what she hated above all other imperfections ; neither could she bear to see it in any of the religious, all of whom she endeavoured, both by words and example, to make lovers of the Cross and mortification. She was so wholly dead to herself, and had so subdued every appetite and inclination, that one

could seldom perceive what she liked or desired, since
everything seemed indifferent to her. It was also equally
rare to hear her Reverence complain, or speak of her
sufferings, and if she chanced to mention them, it was in
a sweet and cheerful manner, accepting of all as coming
immediately from the merciful hand of God, often saying
she could never repine or think anything too much she
had to suffer. Nay, she would confess it even gave her
a thirsting desire for more, and stirred her up to new
and more fervent prayers for grace and strength whereby
to accompany her beloved Spouse with constancy in the
ways of the Cross by sufferings.

CHAPTER XX.

*Of her exemplary patience and charity in suffering
various censures and contradictions.*

As it did ever evidently appear that sufferings were the
only joy and satisfaction of her heart, in which alone she
took delight, so it seems no less certain that the Divine
Goodness was pleased to send her numberless occasions
of exercising her ardent love and charity by them, in
afflicting upon her a variety of crosses, censures, and
contradictions from all sorts of persons. This she had
already been forewarned of some years before by St.
Teresa, who, on a certain occasion of some troubles,
appearing to her, amongst other things commended her
for the esteem and veneration she had showed towards
the Order, and told her that as she had many parts
of her humour, so she must be contented to have part
also of her sufferings, especially in point of censures,
which would be the more sensible to her, because they

will come from persons of respect, whose friendship and esteem she would be glad to cultivate. But since she had a grateful nature, she need not fear, only she should endeavour herein to imitate her, and resolve to employ this talent in making herself grateful to God, then she might be assured He would make all easy to her; though she would promise her she would share in this cross, and that too abundantly before she died. Then she let her know how greatly it imported to love and suffer willingly what her Heavenly Spouse should impose upon her, and to embrace all with a cheerful heart. At which her Reverence being much struck, she earnestly begged for patience and courage, that so she might in all faithfully conform herself to the will of her Divine Spouse; on which St. Teresa said, 'You have courage a great deal more than ordinary, and will have more communicated to you when it is necessary; for our Blessed Lord is so near you as not to let you want anything that may dispose you for His service.'

We have hitherto seen this venerable Mother suffering in body and mind by exterior and interior pains, chastised of Almighty God, and cruelly afflicted by the devil. Heaven and Hell having thus contributed to purify her chosen soul, earth is now to interfere in completing her martyrdom, for as St. Bernard says, 'Persons the most perfect are still wanting in something towards an accomplished sanctity, unless their reputation be also slandered, for till then they cannot be said to be in all conformable to Jesus Christ, after which model they are to be formed and so grow, as the Apostle says, into a perfect man, unto the measure of the age, of the fulness of Christ.' Truly all the interior and exterior sufferings of our Lord, however inexpressible and beyond comprehension, are nothing when compared to what His Sacred Person endured by the loss of His reputation. By those

He was brought indeed to a corporal ignominious death, but by this He died in the hearts of all, even His dearest friends, to whom He became as it were a scandal, so that His chosen disciples durst no longer own Him, seeing He was looked upon by all, as the most vile of impostors.

By penances, mortification, sufferings, and self-denials, we are brought in some sort to die to ourselves; whilst we hereby live in the highest esteem in the minds of others. But when our character is destroyed, all these admirable virtues fall to the ground; then we become, as Scripture expresses it, dead to the heart—that is, in the hearts of all whose veneration is now turned into contempt, and is the more sensible as the persons concerned are more nearly allied or connected together, which circumstances made the Royal Prophet formally complain, saying, 'My friends and those who eat bread with me, have drawn near, and are risen up against me.'

If ever her Reverence was heard to complain, it might be on this same account, for, as she said, her greatest trials in this time, and what gave her the most affliction, was to find herself abused by those whom she esteemed her most intimate friends, with whom she had been so cordially free as to disclose to them the secrets of her heart, acquainting them, as her directors, with the state of her soul, who had not only approved her spirit, but greatly admired the effects of Divine grace, which they saw so abundantly in her as to look upon her elected by Almighty God for one of His choicest servants, and a most proper and fit instrument to promote and advance in herself and others the honour and glory of God. To find, I say, these same persons become so opposite to her, that it seemed they made it their study to blame her, and lay many strange aspersions to her charge, such as were even scandalous to externs; and all only because she had contradicted them in some things, wherein the progress and welfare of this monastery, which was then in its beginning, did greatly consist. In the supporting of which her Reverence, with a more than heroic patience, withstood such reproaches, scorns, and ill-treatment, as is not fit nor proper to be related.

In what regarded her own particular she was condemned as a hypocrite, and one that loved changes; that her pretended zeal of perfection was nothing but an effect of pride, cloaked with a counterfeit resemblance of virtue; that she was deluded by the devil, and gave just reason to apprehend for the state of her soul; and many things of the like nature, which her Reverence heard with singular patience, receiving from them many reprehensions, contempts, and slights, with an admirable humility, and equality of mind, charitably endeavouring to excuse their rashness. What was most wonderful, and which indeed touched her to the quick, was that many things regarding her conscience, and interior graces, and favours communicated to her soul, were divulged and made public, not only to several of our English monasteries, but even as far as England; where they came to the hearing of her secular friends, to their great concern and uneasiness, she being now become the talk and ridicule of certain devotees, for all who heard of her took the liberty to condemn her conduct and to deride her manner of prayer, saying it was fantastical, and a mere temptation of pride. That in place of aiming at true mortification and solid virtue, she sought rather to delude the world by exterior appearances, desiring to be looked upon as humble and a saint, whilst her only ambition and satisfaction was to govern. Many even pious persons proceeded so far as to reprehend her in their letters, saying she wanted experience, and that her proceedings would soon spoil this new monastery, and

reduce to nothing the spirit of St. Teresa, to the great
discredit of the Order. They would also, by a feigned
compassion, bewail the misfortunes of the poor religious,
who they doubted not were put to great sufferings and
inconveniences by her unsettled way of government.
That she was certainly deluded with regard to her high
contemplation and pretended favours, which the effects
would not fail to show, with many other misbecoming
and impertinent reproaches, which her Reverence bore
with such a steady and unalterable patience, as truly
convinced each one that she was entirely dead to herself
and to every sensation of passion or resentment; for in
all these occasions she was never heard to complain, or
murmur at such unreasonable proceedings, but always
preserved her usual peace and quiet of mind ; nor could
she ever be prevailed upon to vindicate herself, or even
so much as to take notice of these or any other uncharit-
able aspersions, though they were manifestly contrary to
truth.

If at any time it was represented to her that not only
her own honour but also that of her family and the
general credit of the house was concerned, she had no
other answer than to refer them to the judgment of her
Seraphical Mother St. Teresa, who speaking of this point
of honour says, ‘It is a thing which causes furious
ravages, in so much that there is no sort of poison more
efficacious towards destroying the body than this is to
corrupt the perfection of the soul ; that the least point of
this execrable honour is worse than the plague ; that any
person who is led by it is in a wrong way, and it is impossible for them ever to become united with Jesus
Christ ; nay, they have great reason to fear lest they
should become a second Judas.’ Finally, she earnestly
begs of God to deliver her from such people, who think
of serving Him, and still remain solicitous about their

honour, fearing to fall into discredit, and lose their reputation. The worst is, as she adds, that the devil would
make one believe that we are obliged to take care of our
honour, on which account there are many who still value
themselves upon it, because as they say it is prudence,
and a means to preserve their authority by which they
may do much good, which she calls a pitiful blindness,
and the miserable effects of our sins ; since there are few
people who are not affected with this too great discretion,
which hinders them from making any advancement.

Her Reverence, who had frequently been so favoured
by this her holy Mother, and received so many salutary
instructions from her, had imbibed no small share of her
holy spirit, so that in this point she was entirely conformable to her, both in her sentiments and practice ;
for we may truly say no ambitious person could be more
eager of honour and esteem than she was of contempt
and abjection, which appeared on all occasions, and
particularly on these. So that in place of justifying herself, or showing any resentment, she made it her
endeavour to be so much the more obliging in her
answers, writing to the above mentioned persons with
the greatest submission, and in a most affable and
friendly manner, which she also observed when occasions
offered of conversing with such as had been any ways
against her. An example of this had happened to a
certain virtuous, learned, and holy man, whom Almighty
God had permitted, through the persuasions of others, to
persecute and contradict her in many occasions, by
which he had conceived such an aversion against her
and her proceedings as not to afford her a peaceable
word, which was the more sensible to her because he
was one she valued much, and had formerly contracted
a particular friendship with, on whose judgment she had
greatly depended. The prejudiced opinion he had of

her Reverence continued for some years, but at last, casually passing through the town, he was moved to make a visit to the monastery, where he called for the Reverend Mother, who seemed to enjoy the pleasure of seeing him, and received him in so courteous and cordial a manner, expressing the respect she had ever for him, and acknowledging with so much gratitude his former favours, that he was quite astonished, and as one in the utmost consternation, remained a long time before he was able to utter one word, finding himself so struck with confusion at what he had done and said to her prejudice. Falling then upon his knees, his tears gave testimony of his sensible regret, whilst with all humility he begged her Reverence ten thousand pardons, acknowledging his own rashness and want of judgment; saying he found now he was deceived by the persuasions of others, and saw clearly they proceeded wholly from passion; "our Lord will meet with them, and make appear where the error lies." He confessed it grieved him much to think how he had been imposed upon, and said that one of his greatest crosses would be the remembrance of the many unreasonable troubles he had by misfortune caused to her Reverence. Here our venerable Mother, with no small confusion, replied, 'Our Blessed Lady and her Infant Son has permitted this and much more from others for my greater good, perhaps I should have been a lost soul had it happened otherways, you know my sins and wicked life deserves much more than all that has been said about me. I beseech you, dear sir, to believe this truth. I have never yet repined at, or thought the worse of those who blamed me, though I could not but know I was innocent of many things laid to my charge, since I was not ignorant, but very sensible of my faults, on which account I did not wonder the world should have so bad an opinion of me, for did they but know my poverty and imperfections as they are manifest to yourself, they would far exceed all that has been said of me. And if it were lawful for me to declare them, I would expose myself to still more grievous censures, that so the mercies of my God might be the more adored and admired by all.'

Such was the happy meeting and cordial reconciliation of these two venerable souls, who remained some hours together, treating of spiritual things, with mutual profit and satisfaction. In this time her Reverence gave him a clear knowledge of the state of her soul, and the happy and flourishing condition of the monastery, at which he was much edified, saying it gave him just reason to praise Almighty God, and to rejoice with the Blessed Virgin and her dear Son, Whom he found so perfectly served amongst them. His chief concern and amaze was, to think how among all these visible signs of the Spirit of God being with her Reverence and community, it was possible for him and so many others to be so long deceived; which he could attribute to nothing else than a special permission of Divine Providence for her increase of merit and greater good. He also made use of this occasion to encourage her Reverence in the pursuit of the virtue and perfection she was aiming at, assuring her she was in the right way, and that her conduct evidently appeared to be in all conformable to the Spirit of God, Who would accomplish all His designs in her to His own glory and the spiritual progress and profit of many; but that she must still expect to meet with crosses, both at home and abroad, and from those she least expected them, which afterwards wonderfully fell out as he had foretold, to her great surprise and increase of the esteem she ever had for this holy man, by whose friendship and correspondence she received singular satisfaction, and solace in the midst of her tribulations, till such times as it pleased God to call him out of this world, which happened shortly after, and was a heavier cross to her than all the other mortifying trials he had given her in his lifetime.

But why should we wonder that externs and such as were not thoroughly acquainted with the virtues and good qualities our venerable Mother possessed should abuse and treat her harshly, since even those who knew her worth and perfection by daily conversing with her were often moved to cross and contradict her? Nay, her own religious, who loved and reverenced her as a saint, would be tempted to dislike and murmur at her proceedings; so that she has sometimes been heard to say in confidence, she had most to suffer from those she treated best; and that such persons, for whom she had laboured most, and endeavoured to oblige by particular favours and charitable indulgences, were those that proved her greatest cross, since she observed that their return was often the height of ingratitude, which of all things she was most sensible of, it being the most contrary to her own nature, which was obliging and grateful.

In fine, she was so thoroughly dead to her self-interest, and to all satisfaction in anything created, that she has been often heard to affirm that to her knowledge she never did anything, although it were according to her own desire, in which she did not find a cross some way or other, yet so invincible was her patience in suffering them, that they were never able to alter or diminish that quiet repose and peace of mind which seemed to have taken entire possession of her soul, and aided her to go through all with an admirable fortitude and courage, never complaining, or showing any motion of the contrary disposition, either in words, gesture, or countenance, which was ever so serene as to evidence her entire resignation and conformity in all things to the

Divine will of God. So that she might truly say with St. Paul, 'I live, yet not I, but Christ Jesus lives in me.'

CHAPTER XXI.

Of her mildness, affability, and tenderness towards her neighbour.

COULD I describe or draw out to the life the amiable features of this our venerable Mother, it would in some sort spare me the pains of compiling this chapter, which is only to declare and lay before the reader, what each one might plainly read in her countenance, which had something in it so angelical and elevated, mixed with a cheerful, mild, and attractive grace, that the sight alone of her was sufficient to convince any one that she possessed in an eminent degree the above-mentioned qualities and virtues, as many who had the happiness, as they said, to behold her, testified with no small admiration and wonder. These her attractive looks were still heightened when any charitable offices towards her neighbour presented themselves; the joy of her heart then shone in her countenance, and added such a lustre, that those who had to converse or treat with her on these occasions could never sufficiently express themselves in speaking of the amiable qualities which God had been pleased to adorn her with. These engaging endowments this community had the happiness, not only personally to behold, but also experience, for her Reverence was ever so loving and tender a heart towards all her religious Sisters, that it seemed her all content-ment was to strive at becoming all to all, that so she might gain all, which was so effectual that it seemed as if God had placed her in this life to make them happy by her means.

Her affection towards these her children was most sincere and equal, never showing more or less regard for one than another, so that she has been sometimes heard to say that if she was put to her oath to know which of the Sisters she loved most, it would be impossible for her to distinguish any difference. How true this was her daily actions manifested to all ; for she was ever so careful and tender towards each one, attending with a most watchful eye on all their concerns, that she would prevent them even in the least things, with all imaginable comfort, both spiritual and temporal, professing there was nothing could afflict her more than those under her care should want anything in her power for their consolation, saying she would rather lie in Purgatory for too much mildness and indulgence than cross the religious by harshness or any seeming neglect or want of care, of which her great solicitude for all that concerned the community as to diet, clothing, and other necessaries was a clear proof. And when those about her would admire her industry, and to their thinking her over great care of the Sisters, she would sweetly reply : ‘ It is my duty to serve the spouses of my Infant Spouse. He will have it so ; I must not let them want for anything, because having left all for Him, they have no longer any care of themselves.’ On all occasions this general love did clearly show itself to be found in a high degree of Divine love and charity towards which her natural disposition seemed constantly to incline her. Her great desire of charity and union amongst her children was so singular and admirable, that her Reverence spared no pains or endeavours to increase that treasure in the community, saying it was impossible they should truly love God without loving one another. To which purpose she was used on many occasions with much fervour and tenderness, earnestly to recommend to them that sweet sentence of loving one another : ' Then,' said she, ' our Lord and His Blessed Mother will love you.' So deeply was this sentence imprinted in her heart, that it seemed to be the life of all her actions, and kept her always in the same mild and condescendent disposition, in such sort that when any of the religious had given her any cause of offence, great or little, there was no need to wait for her Reverence's being pacified before they came to speak to her, or ask her pardon, for she would herself prevent them, either by calling for or seeking opportunities to meet them, with a countenance so full of goodness and motherly love as to make them at the same time sensible of their fault and of her affection and compassion for them, never permitting any one to go away from her unsatisfied.

Her Reverence was never known to refuse speaking with any one of the Sisters, though she should happen to be full of business, preferring their satisfaction to all her other employments, how urgent soever they were, not being able to bear that they should suffer any inconvenience or disturbance by her delay. And if it accidentally happened that any of the Sisters were forgotten, or had met with any want of attention in their necessities, she seemed to be undone, attributing the fault thereof to herself, and showing her grief by her tears, saying, ' What else could I expect, since I am so lazy as to employ others in what I should do myself ? Poor Sisters ! what have they to suffer from my want of care for them !' Yet all well knew she never spared herself, day nor night, sick or well, but was continually labouring with the greatest vigilance to supply every one's wants. Her Reverence loved dearly to be with the Sisters, and when affairs would permit, was always in recreation with them, giving life to the company by her cheerfulness and mirth, and she received great contentment and satisfaction in seeing the religious so, saying it was the spirit of God, and that our recreation should proceed from the joy and delight we have in Him, and ought at times to be sanctified by reflecting on the chief mysteries of our Lord, especially about their respective festivals.

In this she was ever most exemplary, and could with great dexterity and to the purpose turn all discourses and other accidental things so as to make them a proper subject for any present solemnity the Church was celebrating, in which kind of entertainment she was so transported and overjoyed, as scarce to be able to contain herself, so that her countenance would change, and her heart seem, as it were, inflamed whilst she was discoursing upon them. At the feast of Christmas and such as regarded the Sacred Infancy of our Lord, which was her choice and favourite devotion, she would find out such ways to demonstrate the jubilee of her heart, and express her affections in so tender and innocent a manner, as to excite all to particular devotion. Such was also the effect of her pious songs,[1] which are still sung to this day, and several such like devout practices, as dressing the Infant for Bethlehem, and other little pious things of that nature, on all which occasions, though she appeared quite alienated from everything created, and had her thoughts intensely fixed upon God, yet she was far from being any ways morose or selfish, and would join with the Sisters in singing, dancing, or any other innocent performances. Neither must you think she was inclined to clog or tie the religious to these entertainments of piety, which, as is said above, were only for particular festivals; on the contrary, in

[1] See Note to this chapter.

other ordinary recreation times, she knew how to find out pleasant and merry discourses agreeable and suitable to what she found the company most inclined to speak of, which she did with so much familiarity and freedom as to render her presence agreeable, and void of all restraint. She would never let pass any jest or mistake, either in herself or others, which could serve to increase recreation, and she was greatly pleased to see the religious love to be together, and find out new ways of diverting one another.

At times her Reverence permitted the community to dine or sup out of the refectory, according to custom, on certain particular occasions. She was most solicitous to have things good, and dressed in the completest manner, which were served with so much generosity, as clearly showed the sincerity of her motherly heart, which thought nothing too good for her dear children. When on account of particular indisposition she was not able to eat anything herself, she would employ all her time in serving and finding out new ways to recreate the Sisters with such an equal charity as if she made it her study to oblige each one in their own way, even to the lay Sisters, of whom she would be as careful and attentive to see them well served as the rest. She was also desirous to have these times made use of in an open and free manner with one another, as the chief means for cultivating charity, and was a great enemy to all formalities and preciseness, which she forewarned the religious against, saying, ' When we are in the refectory, dear Sisters, let us mortify ourselves and be contented with what is given us, like good and perfect religious ; but whilst we are here, let us take our own choice, and simply what we like the best, because our dear Lord will have it so, it being the most perfect to comply with the present action we are about, which by a good

intention we may render as meritorious on these occasions, as penances and mortifications are on others.'

Her Reverence at these times would seldom or never
take notice of faults and imperfections that might happen,
lest it should hinder recreation. And at other times,
when she was pleased to find fault with, or give a
reprehension to any of the Sisters, either for trial of
their virtue or for other faults committed, it was seasoned
with so much mildness and compassion, as to render it
efficacious without being disagreeable. Besides, she
would be as familiar and free with them immediately
after as if nothing had happened. As occasions served,
she would endeavour to instil into all her choice virtue
of charity, saying, ' I would have you all strive who shall
exceed in compliance and showing a cheerful readiness
to assist and serve one another, so expressing love by
works, as well as words,' in which she was a most
excellent pattern, for she was as diligent and attentive
to help or prevent any of the Sisters in their wants as if
she had been a novice ; and if any were ever so little
indisposed, she would steal up to their cells, make their
beds, and perform other little necessaries, and if she
thought anything was better or more convenient about
herself or her bed, she would find some means to change
it, and give it to those she thought stood in more need
of it, ever showing a great disgust to have anything
better than the least in the house.

When any of the religious were sick, her Reverence
was indefatigable in giving and procuring them all the
consolation that could be expected, being uneasy when
she was not with them, and so far forgetting herself
as scarce to take time for her meals. To prevent
all mistakes she would if possible give them their
medicine with her own hands, and would frequently
perform all the other things necessary about them though

never so loathsome or disgustful. When there was danger of death, she attended them constantly, and was either praying or encouraging and comforting them with pious discourses and exhortations, exciting them to a perfect conformity to the will of God, and a thirsting after the happy moment of enjoying their heavenly Spouse, which was so moving and agreeable to the sick that they seemed to have lost all apprehensions of death, which were replaced by a lively confidence in God's mercies and a firm hope of enjoying Him soon in Heaven, which, in the midst of all their pains, was visible in their countenances, frequently declaring that to have her Reverence present with them was the greatest comfort this poor world could afford; for by her affectionate prayers it seemed as if our Blessed Lady and her sweet Son were also present with them in these last moments they had to live, for which they blessed Almighty God, esteeming it a particular favour to have died in her arms.

It was also remarked that her Reverence had a particular instinct or knowledge when there was danger of death, even in the beginning of their sickness, when neither doctors nor any one else apprehended it. On this account she would be very anxious and solicitous for their receiving in time the holy rites of the Church, for which she had a most high esteem and veneration. And if any one to comfort her pleased to tell her the doctor had still hopes that the sick might get through, she would answer : ' I have reason to know better, believe me, dear Sister ; this our good religious will die. I cannot therefore rest till she has had the last sacraments, and so dispose all things with our confessor as to be ready,' which always fell out as her Reverence had foretold. Some died immediately after they had received them, others within a day or some hours, to the great astonishment of the doctors and all that heard of it. On which occasions, her Reverence, bathed in tears, with eyes and hands uplifted to Heaven, would bless and praise Almighty God, saying : ' I was well inspired. How good is our Blessed Lord, so to sweeten our loss ; let us therefore return Him most grateful thanks for this favour. I have a particular joy to see that our dear deceased Sister had had all the comfort it was in our power to give her, and that she has wanted nothing for her spiritual consolation, let us congratulate with her in her happiness, and strive to imitate her virtues, that we may deserve the same favour from our Lord when we come to die.' It was her custom to close their eyes with her own hands, and to perform all the last duties to the corpse, during which she carried herself with singular respect and devotion, calling it the temple of the Blessed Trinity, and the tabernacle of the Blessed Sacrament, using many such like moving expressions, by which she excited devotion and reverence in those who were about her. She also clothed the corpse herself, and would never be long from it till it was brought to the choir, where she was punctual in seeing all things duly performed for the happy repose of their soul, and afterwards carefully, as is required, committed to posterity a most sweet odour of their virtues, in the relation of their lives, which she has left written in her own hand.

This her tender and charitable disposition was not confined to her religious only. It extended to all sorts of persons in her power, so that her generous and benevolent heart was constantly aiming at doing good to all in full measure. On this account, notwithstanding her extraordinary love of poverty, she would sometimes wish for more commodity of temporal means for relief of the poor, towards whom she ever carried a great compassion, which she showed in charitably cleansing and dressing their sores, a thing she often practised towards those who were not able to procure any other help, comforting them at the same time with spiritual and corporal food, according to their necessities, in a most liberal manner. When some out of discretion thought this was more than the house was able to support, it being low in circumstances, she would with much cheerfulness and unconcern reply, ' We have had hitherto more than was necessary, let us not therefore complain ; our Blessed Lord and His dear Mother will, I confide, supply our wants, since I am sure they are well pleased and bless this house for the charities we exercise towards the poor, of whom our Lord is pleased to style Himself Father, and has promised a reward to all such who relieve and assist them in His name.' Supported by this confidence, she was never known to deny in necessity, little or much for their relief, and took great pleasure in giving it to them herself.

She was particularly devoted to the most benign and mild prelate, St. Francis of Sales, so in imitation of his virtues she added constant trial and force to nature, and thereby truly became, like him, exceedingly remarkable for her mildness. Her commands or orders were seasoned with so much good humour and sweetness, as encouraged her children to go through the most difficult labours of the house with great cheerfulness and readiness, her reprehensions were softened by a particular mildness and tenderness towards the delinquent, and never given in any heat or passion, nor even attended with the least appearance of resentment, her ordinary discourse was so entertaining and affable, as not to be easily expressed, which all who had any occasion of conversing with her unanimously affirmed, saying they had never known her equal.

Her compassion was universal, and extended like that

of her great patron to the most insignificant creatures, so that she could not bear to see any of them hurt or tormented, nor would she so much as kill a troublesome fly, saying like him, ' Why should I take away that life I cannot restore ?' What makes these her perfections in this virtue more extraordinary is that her Reverence, being of a sanguine complexion, apt to be hot and hasty, so far overcame herself as never to be seen in a passion, though sometimes extremely urged thereto by the indiscreet behaviour and passions of others, forgetting themselves in her presence, which she would meekly bear, without taking any notice of it till she found a fit occasion, when she thought her admonitions would be able to have their desired effect. So in all her proceedings truly guiding herself by the love of God and her neighbours' good.

———

NOTE XIII.

Lines by Mother Margaret Mostyn.

THE following lines are supposed to be the composition of Mother Margaret. Since her time they have always been sung by the Community, to a quaint old tune, every day during Advent, as an invitation to the Sacred Infant, and a preparation for the Feast of Christmas.

> Sweet blessed little Jesus,
> 'Tis You alone can please us,
>   Why stay You then so long ?
> Lord, hasten now Your coming,
> Our hearts do die with longing
>   To be with You made one.
>
> You angels' joy and treasure,
> Our sole content and pleasure,
>   The comfort of our mind ;
> You desired of all creatures,
> You fairest of all features,
>   Oh, that we could You find !

O sacred, precious Infant,
Our glory, joy, and content,
　　Where is now Your abode?
Where are those chosen places
Where You unfold Your graces?
　　There would I be, my God!

Where are Your midday restings?
Where Your delightful feastings,
　　Which You so long detain?
Where's Your sweet habitation,
Your bowers of recreation,
　　Which Your affections gain?

Within the purest lily,
In a garden plain, not hilly,
　　Inclosed on all sides;
In a precious sealed fountain,
On a solitary mountain,
　　Where all perfection bides.

The sacred Virgin Mother
Is Your delightful harbour,
　　Your chosen throne of peace.
Your dove, Your only fair one,
Your dear, Your only rare one,
　　Where love does never cease.

Then, glorious Queen of Heaven,
Make haste, give us the Given,
　　The Treasure of our hearts.
Sweet Lady, stay no longer,
But make our souls the manger,
　　No creature shall have part!

CHAPTER XXII.

Of her zeal for the honour of God in upholding regular observance and Constitutions, which she also generously defended.

WE may also here justly apply to her Reverence these words of the great Prophet Elias, founder of Carmel: 'With zeal have I been zealous for our Lord the God of Hosts.' For as he, in behalf of God's honour and His sacred laws, exposed himself to all sorts of dangers and troubles, so she with no less fervour sacrificed her whole self in labouring to promote the glory of God by a faithful observance and custody of those pious regulations His goodness had been pleased to commit to her charge, in which she was ever so truly zealous as far to exceed the bounds of anything we can describe. She would often say, she could easily put up with accidental faults and imperfections in those in whom she found a true desire and solicitude to serve God, and that she could cheerfully take any pains or trouble to instruct or forward them in it; but otherwise that the least breach of Rules and Constitutions, or any negligence in observance, made a most deep and sensible impression upon her spirits, out of the apprehension she was in lest any relaxations or want of fervour should creep in amongst her religious, in which Superiors cannot be too vigilant. For as St. Peter Damian remarks : ' We can never restore what is decayed of primitive discipline; and if we by negligence suffer any diminution in what remains established, future ages will never be able to repair such breaches; let us not, therefore,' says he, 'draw upon ourselves so base a reproach, but let us faithfully transmit to posterity the examples of virtue which we have received from our forefathers.'

This was her Reverence's constant endeavour, and to accomplish it she proposed humility, obedience, and love to each other, as the virtues she would have her religious excel in, and which she took daily pains to imprint into their minds both by words and example, saying, a Teresian must have a noble, courageous heart, and not be satisfied with an ordinary degree of perfection, but that each one must aim high, because their imperfections would be sure to pull them low enough; at which they were not to be dejected, but rather by humility raise themselves up again with new fervour, and not to be tired in repeating so laborious an exercise, because it imported little whether this life was spent in contentment or troubles, so that all was done purely for the love of God, which they were all to manifest by their fidelity and punctuality in observing holy Rules and Constitutions, according to the Ceremonial, for all which her fervent heart had so great a zeal that she would sooner have hazarded her life than to have permitted any change in them, or any the least practice in which the spirit of her holy Mother, St. Teresa, was concerned, ever making it her constant rule to avoid even formalities or novelties in the practice of them under any pretext whatsoever.

Such were the exact and discreet sentiments of this our venerable Mother, when certain difficulties were raised concerning the Ceremonial, occasioned by some false zealots, who, not contenting themselves with the observances of their respective houses, under the specious pretext of greater perfection, took the liberty to

model and mend, in such a manner as to cause no small
uneasiness. These dispositions began to show themselves in the community, particularly amongst the young
religious, who deceiving themselves by indiscreet fervour,
were running to extremes, which by their headiness
became very perceptible, to the great surprise of our
dear Mother, who was much troubled at it, foreseeing
the ill-consequences that must necessarily follow, if a
speedy stop was not put to its progress. For which
purpose she generously offered up herself to God, resolving to spare no pains or trouble, though she was sensible
it would cost her much of both. She began, therefore,
by procuring a fair correspondence with some of the
chief Superiors of the Order, from whom she might learn
what practices were chiefly in use amongst them, and
how different points of ceremonial were understood by
them. And though this step drew upon her the ill-will
of some who were not too well affected towards her
Reverence and community, having their interests elsewhere, and were consequently against her having such
particular connections with those of the Order ; yet as
she had taken it by prudent advice she resolved to go
through with it, esteeming it the most efficacious way,
not only to quell the present storm, but to establish
things upon so solid a footing as to prevent all future
ones, which nothing but uniformity in the Order could
truly effect. Here she proceeded so far as to procure
one of the Definitors General to come to a conference
with her, and inform her still more in particular of
common customs and practices of the houses under the
Order. This brought things to so happy an exit as gave
universal satisfaction to all, and not only stopped the
mouths of those who were curiously sifting into the
affairs of this monastery, which was suspected of many
relaxations, but, what was most to its advantage, estab-

lished such peace and tranquillity in the community as to render it still more and more united. It also gave much edification to those of the Order, who greatly admired the regularity they saw kept up in this house ; which might in part be attributed to the discreet government of our venerable Mother, whose rare qualifications they could not sufficiently express.

Some time after this her Reverence had another occasion of exerting her zeal in defence of the Constitutions, which having suffered some changes in former troubles with the Order, became now a motive of fresh debates. This difficulty was raised by a resolution his Lordship the Bishop of Antwerp had taken, for what reason is uncertain, to oblige all the Teresians under his obedience to receive the Fathers' changed Constitutions, which differ from the genuine ones of St. Teresa, so far as to forbid successive re-elections, which those by her approved allow of. In the meantime, the election here drawing near, her Reverence gave his Lordship timely notice thereof by the confessor, who found him so bent upon his undertaking that he would not hear of any reason to the contrary, but change they must, and consequently look out for another Prioress, saying he would not allow the same to be re-elected. This news greatly alarmed the community, her Reverence excepted, who humbly desiring to be quit of the charge, seemed at first glad of the occasion, and desired the religious to submit and satisfy his Lordship. But they representing to her Reverence the ill-consequences that would ensue from it, the confusion it would cause both at home and in all other monasteries under the Ordinary, and how prejudicial it would be to their holy Institute, and the privileges they had been so many years in possession of, she began to look at it as a general cause, in which not only the good of the Order but the honour of God was concerned, and therefore, laying aside her own personal considerations, she courageously resolved to undertake its defence, and to stand to the letter of St. Teresa's Constitutions, which allows the religious the liberty of re-electing. Her Reverence therefore communicated the affair to the other houses of these countries under the direction of the Ordinaries, who were all unanimously of her sentiment, encouraging her and the community to stand firm to their undertaking, and they would join in the defence of it. Mother Clare of the Blessed Sacrament in particular, Prioress of Louvain Monastery, was of assistance to her, by her interest with the Archbishop of Mechlin, before whom the affair was carried, and decided in favour of the religious ; the Universities were also of the same opinion, as well as other learned divines, who in different places were consulted by her Reverence, with no small trouble. But all could not satisfy his Lordship, who still persisted in his resolutions ; and though the Archbishop was earnest with him to leave things in their old way, he would not let the religious proceed to an election, always alleging new difficulties and hindrances, seeking by all means possible to bring them to a compliance ; for which purpose his agents in this affair, seeing themselves unable to gain their point with the religious, began to solicit her Reverence.

They advised her, therefore, to resign her office into my Lord Bishop's hands, which they said would be the only way to accommodate matters and to prevent the scandals which were otherwise likely to fall upon her and the community, whom for her own credit she ought at least to persuade to choose another Prioress, and if that would not do, absolutely to refuse their votes. To all which her Reverence replied she was most willing to be freed from the charge of Superior, and had often begged her dismission as a favour, knowing there were many much fitter for the office than herself; notwithstanding she was resolved in the present circumstances, let the world think what they would of her, never to stir a hair from the present practice of St. Teresa's Constitutions, nor in the least to diminish the religious power of giving their votes according to conscience, as had always been the practice of St. Teresa herself. For her part, it was not in her power to be or not to be Superior, it being wholly in the community's hands and choice, to whose judgment she would always submit. 'Therefore,' said she, 'as far as I am concerned in this present affair, what pleases the religious shall also please me, so that they have but their full freedom according to the Constitutions, whose privileges our Superior cannot even diminish, and much less change. I heartily wish his Lordship, and all those who have so much charity as to think of easing me of my burthen, had made use of some other means to effect it; it would have proved much happier for me, and more to the religious' satisfaction; but as things now are, not only our monastery, but all of our Order under the Ordinary, are resolved to join in defending every tittle of St. Teresa's Constitutions, so that I have nothing more to say, only wish these difficulties may have a happy end.'

By this answer, perceiving all their endeavours were to little purpose, they desisted from any further trials, only they kept the community from coming to an election, putting them off with new difficulties and hindrances till such time as, by the solicitation of the abovesaid Mother Clare of the Blessed Sacrament, who had great friends both at the Court of Spain and Rome, an ample Bull was obtained from Alexander VII., confirming the religious in the possession of their holy Constitutions and privileges. The publishing of this Bull put an end to all further troubles, and cleared up all the difficulties and

scruples which my Lord Bishop pretended were the
reasons of his acting so, yet he was some time before he
was entirely reconciled, which he showed on some occasions. But afterwards growing more calm, and seeing
the mistakes he had let himself be led into, he made a
visit, and presided at the re-election of our dear Mother
with the same fatherly affection as formerly, and ever
after treated the religious if possible in a more indulgent
and obliging manner, renewing his accustomed praises
and singular esteem he had for her Reverence and community, whom he regarded as patterns of perfection.
Thus her Reverence after all her troubles had the satisfaction to see things peaceably settled at home, and
established and confirmed abroad, to the great contentment and benefit of all the houses under the Ordinary,
who were in great danger by these beginnings of losing
their privileges and Constitutions, the preservation of
which may justly be attributed to the prudence and zeal
of our venerable Mother, who by her courage and industry in defending it showed herself to be a true child
of St. Teresa, and a worthy member of the reformed
Order of Mount Carmel, which is particularly distinguished for its zeal in renewing and maintaining its
ancient rigorous observances and rules.

These became now the principal object of her
Reverence's care, applying herself with new fervour to
advance the perfection of them, both in herself and
others. For which purpose she was so watchful in
observing and finding out the dispositions of her religious,
taking proper occasions to admonish them of their faults,
especially the novices, whose progress in virtue she had
most at heart, knowing well how much depended on
their first fervent beginnings, and the dangers that attended any slackness or tediousness in them. She was
therefore willing to embrace any trouble or inconvenience

in assisting and instructing them, instilling into them the principle and practice of humility, as the necessary foundation and corner stone by which all other virtues were to be supported, which she did with such tenderness and affection, as to enable them with ease to go through the hardships of a religious life with great cheerfulness and alacrity, so that the practices of mortification and self-denial soon became familiar to them.

Her Reverence frequently took occasion to remind her religious of the benefit of their vocation, by which Almighty God had selected them from amongst thousands, to raise them to the great dignity of spouses of His only Son, saying it was a dignity which required both zeal and fidelity in the practice of those duties that attended it, which were regular observance, the perfection of which she had so much at heart that when she saw any one perform their actions in a careless or negligent manner, it would move her to tears, saying it was a certain sign of their little love to God and a great want of fervour in His service, which if each one did not daily endeavour to renew in themselves by esteeming and being punctual in the practice even of small things, relaxations would soon creep in, whereby they would become a prey to their own humours and passions, and by degrees lose entirely the spirit of religion.

These sentiments and apprehensions made her Reverence most watchful in correcting the least faults, which she often did more severely than those of greater moment, for, as she said, gross imperfections bring their humiliations along with them, and therefore are rather to be treated with a kind of compassion, whereas by being careful in avoiding small faults, greater ones were prevented. As a means to preserve themselves from both her Reverence suggested the necessity of keeping themselves employed, saying idleness was the pillow whereon the devil rested to hatch mischief, particularly discord and dissension, to avoid which it was necessary that each one should apply themselves with great care and diligence to their own concerns, without busying them-selves with the affairs of others, or intermeddling with what did not belong to them. Above all things she was an enemy to busy tempers, and such as loved employ-ments, often saying they were the least fit for them, and that it had been recommended to her by virtuous persons never to employ such if she desired to keep the house in peace, for to make use of them was like raising spirits to infest the community. Silence and recollection, she would say, are the two faithful guardians of peace and union with one another; this virtue of charity towards one another was so fixed in her heart, and had such influence in all her actions, that we cannot recount any of them without frequently repeating it, as she did, constantly recommending to all that golden sentence of the beloved Apostle St. John, to love one another, because, as she added, it was also the favourite virtue of St. Teresa. Therefore she would never permit the least defect or want of charity to pass without a most severe reprimand, and though her reprimands on other occa-sions were tempered with a particular mildness and affability in giving them, in this point her zeal had the ascendant, so that her countenance could not dissemble the grief and affliction such faults gave her. She would speak of them in Chapter in so moving a manner as to move the delinquents to an abundance of tears, and to so real a sense of their fault as to make them ever after constantly upon their guard against such failures.

Her proceedings in Chapter were so replenished with the spirit of God, and so efficacious, that it was clearly to see she spoke not by rote, but according to what was grounded in her fervent heart by constant and assiduous practice, and this truly made appear the great knowledge she had in all the most solid paths of virtue, so that by her discourses and zealous exhortations each one owned to find in themselves a new increase of spirit and desire of perfection. And though, naturally speaking, all persons apprehend time and place where their faults are openly exposed, it seemed to them the most agreeable of all duties, and all time appeared too short that was spent in it, which proceeded from her Reverence's prudent, charitable manner of performing it, convincing all that her only aim was their spiritual good and advancement, and a thirsting desire to see God perfectly served, so that a little before death she could confidently say, and did acknowledge with the most profound sentiments of gratitude to God, Who had been so good towards her, that she had not much scruple of her government, since she could not remember in all her actions to have had any other end or design than the greater honour and glory of God, and the good of the community.

This her ardent charity, though confined within the walls of a monastery as to its effects, had no limit according to her desires. The misery and blindness of infidels and heretics, especially those of our poor country, was a constant grievance to her, and she would often take occasion to expose their unhappy state to the religious in such moving and pathetic terms, that tears of compassion would flow from the eyes of all that heard her, from whence she would proceed to beg and importune them for prayers and mortifications in their behalf, reminding them of the obligation they had to employ themselves in such charitable exercises in their regard. In this she was herself a rare example, performing numberless extraordinary devotions and mortifications for their conversion, so that in her greatest infirmities and pains their abandoned state was constantly before her eyes. How unhappy and disconsolate, would she say, they must be, poor creatures, in their sickness and other afflictions, who have nothing spiritual to comfort them, and who are deprived of the inestimable benefit of the most Blessed Sacrament, which to us is an endless source of all consolation and real strength and support to us in every kind of necessity—which her Reverence by her singular devotion to the adorable Sacrament very sensibly experienced.

She had also a very great and sensible feeling of the necessities of our Holy Church, and took its persecutions extremely to heart, particularly the last of England, which happened in her time. The first news of this breaking out made so deep an impression upon her spirits that she was a long time silent, then raising her eyes towards Heaven, she said, ' If these good men did only suffer it were little, or rather glorious, since they die for their faith, but how many souls in that poor kingdom will run the hazard of being lost for ever ! Dear Sisters, for the love of God let us employ all our force that His Divine goodness may vouchsafe to cast a merciful eye on our friends and country ; let us implore the help and mediation of our most tender Mother, the Blessed Virgin Mary.' During all these troubles she never laid down to rest without some affectionate prayer in behalf of the poor prisoners, compassionating their sufferings, and wishing them her little conveniences to rest themselves upon.

CHAPTER XXIII.

Of her great confidence in God, by Whom she was often wonderfully supplied.

CONFIDENCE is ordinarily the consequence of love, particularly when one is certain of being reciprocally loved; those, therefore, who love God confide in Him, because they are sure He loves them again. We have seen the truly affectionate love our venerable Mother ever bore to our Divine Lord, from whence we pass to a view of the singular confidence she had in Him, which freed her from all concern regarding temporal means, about which she was not the least anxious, being convinced that Almighty God, as He has promised, will never forget His servants, as long as they are but careful and diligent in His service. She would frequently tell her religious that if ever they came to want anything, the fault would be their own, because it was a sure sign they were wanting in their duty to God. This secure confidence made her place her whole dependence on Him alone, and remit all her cares and necessities to His paternal providence, Who never failed to supply her in all more abundantly, as she often said, than she could have wished, or durst desire. She received a kind of satisfaction in finding herself destitute of friends or such human helps which were common to others, and has been seen to rejoice on certain occasions when she was slighted and neglected by those who knew and wanted not power to supply her necessities. These and such like disappointments rather increased her hopes, saying, the less we receive from men, the more we had to expect from God, Whose power and goodness, when He saw it was necessary, would never fail liberally to provide for us; and if at any time He permitted us to suffer small inconveniences or apparent wants, such His favours would avail us more than all the temporal blessings of this world; 'let us, therefore,' said she, 'leave all things of this nature to the care of our Blessed Lady and her sweet Infant Jesus, Who know best what is good for us.'

This her Reverence's confidence was not in vain, for considering some circumstances that attended several extraordinary events which happened during her happy government, we cannot look upon them much less than miraculous. This poor foundation, although the least wonderful of what we are going to relate, may be looked upon as something particular, since, by the special assistance of Heaven, it became in a short time as prosperous and flourishing as any other of our nation, to the great admiration of all, for it not only met with many contradictions and disappointments in its first establishment, but afterwards continued to suffer a kind of persecution from some disaffected persons, who seemed to envy its increase, dissuading sometimes people from entering here to be religious. This, however, was abundantly supplied by the impartial hand of our Blessed Lord, Who particularly inspired many young ladies of good quality to come to this house, and would not be persuaded to the contrary, nor hear of any other place; for it seemed to them, as they afterwards owned, that they were supported in their resolutions by a special impulse of the Divine Spirit, which convinced them that Lierre monastery was the place allotted where they were to work their salvation and sanctification. What confirmed all of the finger of God being in their choice was, that besides being advantageous to the house, they became most serviceable and exemplary religious, and attained to such a degree of perfection, as to render their sanctity visible to all they conversed with. This was what our venerable Mother chiefly aimed at, who was never solicitous about fortunes ; she valued more their personal worth and sincere desires to serve our Lord. Such as these her Reverence was ever ready to receive with open arms, and with much more inclination than others who were better provided with temporal goods. And when some would tell her it was also necessary to secure the house of a sufficient maintenance, she answered : ' Hitherto our Lord has abundantly supplied us ; let us only trust in the Sacred Infant and His Blessed Mother, and we cannot fear want. My Infant Spouse has promised me He will take care of our concerns Himself ; be not solicitous on this score.'[1]

[1] [The following is taken from an account of Mother Margaret's virtues, written after her death by her own sister, Mother Ursula of All Saints. She is speaking of Mother Margaret's wonderful confidence in God, and says—' I remember once, in time of the war, her Reverence used to lay her small provision of money in a basket over her bed's head ; being to pay a considerable sum for certain provisions, and much falling short of money, she called Sister Teresa of St. Augustine and bid her fetch more, but the Sister staying something long our Mother went herself. The Sister met her, saying, " There is none there ;" but her Reverence, not satisfied, took the basket down again, saying—" I am sure my little Spouse will not serve me so ;" and taking her little Jesus —(a little wax figure of the Sacred Infant Mother Margaret always kept with her money, and which we still have in our possession and keep as a great relic, from its having worked the above miracle. We always, in imitation of Mother Margaret, keep a statuette of little Jesus with the money we have in the house)—in her hand she found underneath a bag of money, at which Sister Teresa was amazed, and those that saw her only a moment before take all out of the basket, where she affirmed there was no such bag that she could find. " Nor I either," said her Reverence ; " my Infant Spouse has brought it." She found not only sufficient to make up the sum wanting, but there was left a quantity for the present use of the house, at which her Reverence, much transported with joy,

This her confidence in our dear Lord made her charity and liberality, as it were, boundless, for she stuck at nothing when there was occasion of helping her neighbour, as the following example will prove. Whilst his Majesty King Charles II.[2] was in these parts in exile,

said—"See, Sisters, how good is our little Jesus, not only to supply us with what is necessary, but He will always have something in store for His spouses. Oh, let us confide and put our trust in Him, Who hath never failed us yet."]

[2] [The memory of our Stuart Kings, Charles II., and especially his brother, James II., seems linked with Carmel, from the great faith in the prayers, and love of, their royal mother Henrietta Maria from her childhood for the daughters of St. Teresa. At the commencement of the foundation of the first monastery, in 1604, of the Discalced Carmelites in Paris, the brilliant Court of Henry IV. and Mary of Medicis became as it were the nursery of vocations for this Order. No less than twenty ladies attached to the service of the Queen were numbered amongst its first novices. Mary of Medicis was herself much attached to the Teresians, and built for herself a suite of apartments adjoining the convent, where she often spent several days with her daughters (afterwards Queens of England and Spain and Duchess of Savoy), and no week passed while in Paris that she did not visit 'her'—as she called them—'terrestrial angels' two or three times. The unfortunate Henrietta Maria (later consort of Charles I.) imbibed thus from her earliest age the tenderest affection for the Order, and specially for the first monastery of Paris. The day before she left for England she spent with the Teresians, and insisted on serving the religious at supper, and on taking leave of them earnestly commended herself, her future husband, and his heretical country, to their prayers. On her return to Paris after the tragical death of her royal consort, Henrietta Maria, by frequent visits to the monastery, sought consolation from the affectionate sympathy of the Carmelites. She frequently brought her two sons, Charles II. and the Duke of York, to the convent. One day she conducted the latter there, and turning to the Rev. Mother Prioress, Mother Agnes of Jesus (of the illustrious house of De Bellefond, who before her entrance into religion had belonged to the Court of Mary of Medicis), said she gave her this young prince, who was much attached, she added, to the Anglican religion, hoping she would convert him and show him the truth of the Roman Catholic religion ; to which Mother Agnes answered—'It belongs to God, Madame, to change hearts, and I am not clever enough to enter into controversy, but I will most earnestly beg of God to influence the prince's heart.' The Queen rose and left them alone. Then Mother Agnes said to the Duke of York 'that she would not enter into any religious disputes, but only took the liberty of entreating him that he would daily pray to God, with a sincere

there was a great part of a regiment of his quartered
in this town, amongst whom were many distressed gentle--
men, almost famished for want, having nothing to sup--
port themselves withal but the charity of some good
people, which was inconsiderable, the town being poor,
and not able to redress their misery, which was such
as rendered them real objects of pity. Her Reverence
was so moved at it, that it cost her many tears of
compassion, saying, as long as there was a piece of
bread in the house, it was not possible for her to deny it
them. Therefore, after she had earnestly recommended.
the affair to the little Infant and His Blessed Mother,.
she ordered the portress to deny none relief as long
as there was anything in the house ; she ordered also·
beef and other meat to be bought for them, which
she would sometimes dress and cook her own self, and
was always careful to see it good and in abundance.

For the space of some months there were about
twenty persons dined every day in the servants' quarters.
Besides diet, she gave constantly to four others who·
were Catholics, firing, candles, and other necessaries.
She also provided the sick with medicines, and paid the
doctors for visiting them ; and the common soldiers·
were provided with bread and beer, who came in such
numbers, that the tourières said it was as much as they
could do to serve them, so they could scarce find time to

will unbiassed by prejudice, that He would give him the grace of
knowing the true faith in order to follow it, and that she promised to
ask the same favour of our Lord for his Majesty.' The young prince,
touched by her words, agreed to the proposal. He often afterwards.
repeated that he had been faithful in making this prayer every day of
his life, and he believed that he owed in great measure his conversion to
this excellent religious. Forty years after, when, driven from the English
throne for his faith, James II. came as an exile to Paris, he reminded
the saintly Prioress (whom he often visited) of the above conversation,
and its wonderful result for his eternal welfare.—From the Life of
Mother Agnes of Jesus, French Chronicles of Discalced Carmelites.]

say their Office. This lasted the whole winter, which was sharper than usual, and thereby increased their admiration, considering they were then a full community, and were served in the same plentiful manner as usual, and their ordinary provisions of firing, corn, and beer, held out in the same quantity, as if no other had made use of it but their own family, which they could not but attribute to anything less than a miracle. Her Reverence was no less astonished than others at so extraordinary a fact, and doubted not but the hand of God had been in it, which greatly confirmed her in her hope and confidence in His Divine Providence, Who had been pleased in so wonderful a manner to bless and prosper this present great undertaking.

This, we may reasonably suppose, was not the only blessing of the kind her Reverence was favoured with, for besides what has been mentioned, her Reverence was at all times most liberal in giving of alms to the poor, and helping distressed persons, both with money and food, in a most plentiful manner, for being of a generous and liberal disposition, when she did such charities, she was sure to do them abundantly, and to the purpose, all which, together with what was spent in medicines and surgery for the poor, run up to such an expense, as seemed far to exceed the bounds of discretion, and could not truly be looked upon less than imprudent in any other who had not an equal confidence to hers. But the confidence of the saints is augmented by necessity, and is so far from being tied to the selfish notions of human views, that we have seen them often in their own greatest wants employ what little they had in relieving the necessities of others. The confessor, Mr. Bedingfield, considering the great charges she had been at, and the failure of some of the yearly rents, apprehended much lest her Reverence should be in want of money to supply the ordinary necessities of the community, and therefore told her to make use of his, which she had in her custody, to the value of a hundred pounds, saying he knew well she must stand in need of it, and therefore he freely gave it her. But her Reverence replied : 'This, dear sir, will help us when we are in great distress ; now our Spouse must look to it,' which she was never necessitated to, though she had it in her care six or seven years, and Mr. Bedingfield supposed it had been spent. Yet after her death, it was found entire, apart, with a note that it belonged to him, besides a good provision of money for present use, which no one could account for, considering that expenses far exceeded the ordinary income of the house, and the community had always experienced the same plenty, without having any considerable alms or being indebted to any one, a thing her Reverence could never endure, for if she was owing, though never so small a sum, she could not be at rest till it was paid, which made her particularly solicitous at the end of the year to pay off exactly the workmen's bills, of which she had great numbers, on account of the many reparations and changes necessary to make up some scattered old houses into a monastery.

Her confidence in God was not confined to temporal things only, but it extended also to the spiritual, as well in what regarded this life as the next, which she was frequently exhorted to by our Blessed Lord and His Sacred Mother, who on many occasions admonished her to leave all in their hands, knowing that God is still the same—as great, as powerful, as merciful, and good in the depth of aridity as in the height of consolations. Which dispositions, as a pious and experienced author remarked, are often defective, even in virtuous persons, who for want of due confidence in the mercies of God, are

always solicitous for their present and future state, and
thereby throw themselves into many agitations and perplexities of conscience, in which they spend much time,
that would be better employed in an humble acknowledgment of their faults ; and while they are contriving
and laying out all for their pretended repose of conscience, our Blessed Lord permits them sometimes to be
tried by various temptations, which, as a cloud overshadow the soul, and separates it, as it were, from God,
in which situation, St. Bonaventure says, they become
disgusted with all that is good ; prayer, lectures, all sorts
of pious things become tedious to them ; they find no
satisfaction either in earth or in Heaven, neither in conversation nor in solitude ; neither, as St. Teresa says,
can the advice of confessors afford them any consolation,
because the soul in this painful state still remains dry
and insensible.   As the same author continues, whether
these pains be inflicted on the soul to chastise, purify, or
sanctify it, they equally come from the same charitable
and loving hand of our Lord, and turn to the soul's
advantage.   This our venerable Mother frequently
repeated, both for her own and other's consolation :
' God knows best what is good for us.'

CHAPTER XXIV.

Of her last sickness and precious death.

HER Reverence some months before her death was observed to be more than usual retired, and seemed pensive and restless, as if there was something or other she would have done, and could not well accomplish, which made some curious to know, and often question her, what it was that gave her such concern; for she being full of business, and the inclosure open on account of some reparations, it was apprehended some accident had happened that gave her uneasiness. But her Reverence always answered it was not so, and that nothing of this world could give her trouble, if she were but sure in all to do the will of her sweet Infant Jesus; during this time often casting her eyes up towards Heaven, with a deep sigh she would say, 'O my God, what would you have me to do?'

A little before her last sickness the Subprioress surprised her writing in her closet, and seeing her serious and her face inflamed, as she was wont to be in prayer, or when she treated of heavenly things, stood some time to satisfy her curiosity in beholding her. But her Reverence perceiving she was there, laid down her pen and folded up the paper she was writing. The Subprioress desiring earnestly to see it, she was unwilling to show it her, saying, ' It is of no importance, only having little to do I was writing down my thoughts to ease my mind; our blessed Lord knows best what is good for

Q 26

us, let us confide in Him, and resolve to suffer courageously for His love.' After her death this paper was
found amongst others in her box of writings, which
clearly showed our Lord gave her a certain warning of
what He meant to do, and that He was disposing her
for Himself. From this time she seemed to be much
changed in her humour, and as one highly disgusted
with all things of this world, which some supposed to
proceed from her Reverence's indisposition, for of a
sudden she was grown extremely weak, and often com-
plained she found a great decay in herself, and could
not do as courageously as formerly she was accustomed.
Notwithstanding she forced herself to comply with all
the ordinary duties till the 9th of August, being the
vigil of St. Lawrence, a feast to which her Reverence
always had great devotion, it being also her clothing
day. For many years she had been visited about this
festival with some extraordinary pains or crosses, which
she always esteemed as a particular favour done to her,
and a certain sign of the saint's protection, whom she
had chosen for her particular patron in sufferings. Now
finding herself seized upon by a violent fever, she was
forced to go to bed, saying, 'this is more than ordinarily
great; St. Lawrence, help me to bear it, and then God's
holy will be done.' She could get no rest all that night,
and the next morning was found so very ill, that the
doctor was immediately sent for, who thought her in so
poor a condition that he would not permit her to rise
that day, lest she should endanger herself. This was a
great affliction to her, as it deprived her of the happiness
of Communion, after which she eagerly thirsted, yet
passed over it with an amorous complaint, saying,
St. Lawrence was now too severe, for there was no
suffering so sensible to her as the being deprived of this
heavenly food. She continued greatly indisposed all

that day, but the day following the doctor found her without fever, and would have ordered physic, only the great heats and her exceeding weakness caused him to defer it. In the meantime she rose and went to the choir and communicated, though with much difficulty, for she looked like one that had laid a long time sick in bed ; her eyes had grown hollow, and her whole countenance so changed that it struck all with amaze who beheld her. She continued so till the 24th of August, on which, having walked about with some strangers who were casually in the house, and sitting with them in the recreation in the afternoon, she was suddenly seized all over with a vehement pain, which she could not dissemble or hide from the religious, on whom she cast such compassionate eyes, as seemed to foretell it to be the last time she should come there amongst them.

Mr. Bedingfield, the confessor, also perceived it, and persuaded her Reverence to go to bed, which she did, but was so far from finding any ease thereby that her pains seemed rather to increase, and her fever became continual. The doctor finding her very ill, and she being conscious of what would follow, beheld her dear children with the tenderness of an affectionate mother, saying her time was come, and though for their comfort she omitted not to make use of proper remedies for her recovery, one might plainly perceive by her words and actions that she was no longer for this world, yet she bid them take courage, and endeavoured to comfort them with hopes of her life, saying she would do all on her part, and was sure nothing would be wanting on theirs, as she was wholly resigned to the Divine will of God, so she desired them to be so, and leave all to the merciful disposal of her Infant Spouse Jesus and His Blessed Mother, Who know best what is good for us ; ' I beg therefore you will desire nothing else of them only

patience for me to suffer the excessive pains I feel.'
She seemed truly to be on a torture, neither able to help
herself nor receive the least ease from those that attended
her, yet bore all with a most edifying patience. All
remedies proving ineffectual, each one's affliction was so
great that they could not behold her without showing
their grief by sobs and tears, which she perceiving seemed
displeased, telling them there was nothing she desired
more than to suffer, and by suffering, as she hoped, to
come to the enjoyment of God. 'Why would you,' said
she, 'deprive me of that happiness I have so long
thirsted after? What is it to live ten or twelve years
more, death must come at last, it is a debt we must all
pay to nature before we can come to live eternally. I
had lived but too long, except I had made better use of
my time.' She frequently adored and praised God for
His great goodness towards her, particularly in bringing
her up a child of His holy Church in the heart of an
heretical country, and calling her from amidst the snares
and dangers in which she began to be entangled, to
become his handmaid in a religious state. Then
humbling herself she would say, 'My ingratitude, O
Lord, is truly great, but Your mercy is still greater, in
which I wholly confide, since I have at least endeavoured
to love You above all things, and am not sensible to
have desired any thing, but to do in all Your blessed
will.'

Mother Subprioress[1] coming to tell her that her old
friend Father Morgan, for whom she ever had a particular
regard, was come to see her, said if she had anything
that gave her uneasiness, she knew her Reverence could
open herself to him, which might be a comfort to her.
But she replied, 'I thank my good Saviour I have
nothing that troubles me, or gives me the least disturb-

---

[1] [Her sister Ursula of All Saints.]

ance; yet I should be glad to see him, but before he comes in, let him know I am not able to speak much on account of my extreme weakness.' When he entered she raised herself as well as she could, and begged his blessing, then fell into discourse with him, which lasted a considerable time, till finding herself fatigued she was obliged to make her excuse, saying she was sorry she could not satisfy her inclination to partake longer of his company, that she hoped for and earnestly desired a share in his good prayers.

When the Subprioress came to her again her Reverence sent her back to take care of the community, charging her to see there was nothing wanting, and to do her best to comply with the good Fathers. 'For,' said she, 'I always had a real value and a true affection for them, and next our own confessor esteem them above all the men in the world, though I know they do not think so. God's holy will be done; when we meet in Heaven they will know how much they were mistaken in me.' At these words the tears fell from her eyes, and seeing the Subprioress also greatly affected by them, she said with much tenderness, 'Weep not, dear sister, Jesus will not have us resent it, He permits all for our greater good; take courage, it is necessary we should suffer in this life, our dear Lord walked the same path, and we must not think to gain Heaven by any other.' Mother Subprioress fearing lest a continuance in such discourse might do her harm, drew the curtain, and desired her to try if she could get a little rest, but it seems she was not to expect any more in this life. Finding her pains increase, amongst many acts of resignation and devout aspirations, in which she passed the whole night, she often expressed a great desire to have the last sacraments, charging the Subprioress to take care she might have them in good time. It being St. Austin's day, a saint to whom she had been particularly devoted from her infancy, she asked the Subprioress if she had been at Communion. She answered she had, and begged with many tears a prolongation of her Reverence's life, or that she herself might go in place of her; on which, telling her she knew not what she asked, she said, 'Our Blessed Lady and her sweet Son know best what is good for you and me, and therefore we ought to be entirely resigned to His Divine will.'

The doctor coming found her Reverence worse, and losing all hopes of her recovery, ordained her the last sacraments, at which she seemed quite overjoyed, and said with a cheerful heart, 'How good is my dear Lord to come to me, there is nothing I more desire.' Seeing the affliction those about her were in, she said she did not think herself worth one of their tears, that our Blessed Lord could easily supply their want of her, who was but an insignificant creature, and had nothing to depend on but His infinite goodness and mercy, who had always prevented her with His favour; that she hoped through His sacred merits, and the mediation of their prayers, she should only leave them to become more sensible of their concerns, and better able to assist them; then expressing the tender regard she had for all and each one of the Sisters, who, she said, were all equally dear to her, she immediately began to prepare herself by an humble confession, after which she went on reciting several acts of gratitude, love, and confidence, expressing her thirsting desires of those happy moments wherein she was to partake of her most beloved Lord in His most comfortable Sacrament, which she received with singular humility and sense of devotion, often saying with great fervour, 'Lord, You know I love You above all things, and there is nothing can separate me from You, nor do I desire anything but the accomplishment of

Your blessed will.' She spent all that day in such like moving acts, notwithstanding her extreme pains, and she desired also the holy oils, which Mr. Bedingfield had judged proper to defer a little not to shock the religious all at once, knowing well the impression it would make upon them.

Her Reverence continuing to lose strength and decay apace, he came and told her he was now ready to comply with her desires, which she heard with much joy, giving God thanks he was so well inspired ; and every moment seemed long to her till she had received that consolatory sacrament, hastening her religious to get all things ready, that nothing might cause the least delay from partaking of the strength and comfort she hoped to receive by it. ' For,' said she, ' the doctors are now of very little help, since with all their skill they cannot give one moment of ease.' The community was again assembled, and accompanied the confessor with the holy oils. When they were come in, her Reverence with great humility begged pardon of all her offences, and said by the merits of Christ she confidently hoped for eternal salvation, entreating the Sisters to beg it of our Lord for her. Then she raised herself up, helped to loosen her head-dress, and betwixt every unction, joining her hands, gave God thanks for making her a child of His holy Church, desiring and hoping to die a true one. The ceremonies being ended, she called for the plenary indulgence of the Order, which she received and heard read with great attention, rendering infinite thanks to her Creator for so many favours.

The community being withdrawn out of the chamber, she addressed herself to Mother Subprioress, and recommended to her many particular things. She remembered herself to her brother and her other friends, desiring her to let them know when she was dead, that they might pray for her. ' I had a great desire to see him,'[2] said she, 'for my own and his comfort, but our Lord would not have it so. When I am come to Heaven, I shall do them more good, and shall be always mindful of our poor family. God give them grace to serve Him well ; this shall be my prayer when I shall be so happy as to enjoy my Lord for ever.' Then taking the Sub-prioress by the hand, she said, ' Courage, dear Sister, do not weep, but rather congratulate with me, for the mercies of my God are infinite ; what praises shall I ever be able to give Him for his goodness towards us both ! Have patience ; sweet Jesus and His Blessed Mother will help you to suffer much. Do not think I leave you, because it is their pleasure we must part in this life ; be assured my care shall be more than ever for you, and all that concerns you, in a more efficacious manner than if I were to remain with you. Put your confidence therefore in Jesus and Mary, and give all the interest you have in me into their hands, Who know best what is good for us both. What I desire at present is that you will not leave me this night before you have closed my eyes.'

Towards nine o'clock the confessor, Sir Henry Beding-field, and the doctor came in to visit her, who found her colour and eyes so lively, and voice strong, that they did not look upon her as yet near death. Whilst the doctor was feeling her pulse, she smiled upon him, and said : ' There is now no more to be done,' nor had she any-thing to gratify him with for all his care but her poor prayers. The same she said to Sir Henry Bedingfield,[3] thanking him for all his favours done to this house. Afterwards Mr. Bedingfield asked her if she would not have him stay by her that night, to which she answered

[2] [Sir Edward Mostyn.]
[Eldest brother of Mr. (Canon) Bedingfield.]

that she feared it would do him harm, because she knew he was not well, otherwise it would be a great comfort to her. From this time she remained full of desires of Heaven and most ardent wishes to receive again the Blessed Sacrament before she died, which he said should be allowed her if she could wait till twelve o'clock, on which she replied: 'God be praised; that will not be long, for it is now eleven.' Finding her spirits fail, she asked for something to refresh her and strengthen her till the happy time, and continued so present to herself that she counted every quarter, and each moment seemed an age till it was come. As soon as she beheld our dear Lord, Whom she so affectionately loved, her whole countenance changed, and became adorned with a kind of venerable aspect, whilst with her hands fixed together, she uttered many most moving and amorous expressions to her Beloved Spouse, Whom she received with great devotion, and remained silent a considerable time.

Mr. Bedingfield came again, and kneeling close by her suggested divers acts of love to God and confidence in His mercies, which her Reverence repeated with so great fervour that he was moved to tears, and humbly begged her prayers for himself and all present, saying he would also pray for her all the days of his life, at which bowing her head, she said: 'God reward your Reverence, I could not wish a greater favour.' Then at his request, she gave her blessing to her afflicted dear children, desiring them not to grieve but to pray for her. 'Be but obedient,' said she, 'in all to your superiors, and carefully observe your holy Rules and Constitutions, and nothing will ever be wanting to you; particularly endeavour to conserve and increase that charity and union you have always had amongst you, and believe me our Blessed Lady and her sweet Son will defend, nourish,

Q *

and be always in the midst of you. Let each one take seriously these points to heart, and beware of the least defect in them. It is these, above all, which will increase perfection in your souls, and uphold this house ; to love one another, dear Sisters, you know is our Lord's commandment ; regard not, I beseech you, my ill example, faults, and negligences, for which I humbly beg pardon of you all, and for everything I may have offended you in.' Then she took leave of each one in a most cordial manner, hoping to see them all again with her in Heaven. After this, raising herself on her pillow, she said : 'Although I find myself in my agony, yet, methinks I can better stir and help myself than I have been able to do all the time of my sickness ; neither am I sensible of much pain," and beckoning to Mother Subprioress to draw near, she spoke to her in a low voice as follows : ' My dear Sister, now approaches the happy time of my departure out of this miserable world, in which you have much yet to suffer ; but our Blessed Lord will help you to carry your cross, and assist you with His grace to perform His will in all, whether it be agreeable or disagreeable, it imports little, so we be but faithful to God, and bear with patience what He sends. I desire you for the love of God, and all the affection that has been between us, let me be buried in the poorest habit in the house, and see you do not permit the Sisters to say anything in my praise, but pray for me, your dear sister.' At this, the Subprioress, all in tears, begged of her Reverence that she would obtain for her the favour quickly to follow her ; but she replied : ' Leave that to God, and desire nothing but His blessed will. You may be confident my care of you shall still be the same, and when I am so happy as to come to Heaven, if I have power there, you shall partake of it in that manner as shall be most to your advantage and comfort. Be sure you rely on and obey our good confessor in all. He is a true friend, and will help you ; take courage therefore, the Sisters all love you most dearly ;' and naming some, said : 'Such are very discreet and virtuous, they will assist you; have confidence in them, and endeavour to uphold observance and charity in the community.' Then she asked her what o'clock it was, who told her a little past four. 'Is it no more ?' said she; and begun to count five, six, seven, which was the time she departed, and we may suppose known to her since she then added : 'My dear Jesus, when and as You please.' After raising and bowing again her head towards the community with a cheerful countenance, as though she was taking her last farewell, she fixed her eyes on a picture[4] of our Blessed Lady with the Infant Jesus in her arms, that hung at the foot of her bed, and remained so without speaking for a considerable time, which made all think the hour of her departure was near at hand.

The confessor therefore began the Litany and recommendation of the soul, to which her Reverence answered in so calm and fervent a manner, that all could hear her. But Mr. Bedingfield, fearing she should spend herself thereby, said : 'Good Mother, do not force yourself; it is sufficient you answer with your heart,' which gave her an occasion of practising, even in her death, her choice virtue of obedience, for she immediately bowed to him, and ceased to answer. Her countenance after this, becoming more than ordinarily cheerful, as one not able to express her joy, he supposed she saw something particular, and remembering the promise Our Blessed Lady had formerly made her of visibly assisting her at her death, he was moved to ask her if our Blessed Lady was

[4] [Still in the possession of the Community. It is always brought to the dying bed of the Sisters.]

not there, to which she replied : 'Oh, yes, dear sir ; our Blessed Lady, St. Francis of Sales, my great St. Austin, the humble St. Francis, St. Bernard, and all the Court of Heaven,' after which, with a most sweet countenance, she instantly rendered her happy soul into the hands of her Creator, on the 29th of August, at seven in the morning, in the year of our Lord, 1679.

CHAPTER XXV.

Of her funeral, with some particulars that happened after it, and a miraculous cure.

OUR venerable Mother died in the fifty-fourth year of her age, thirty-four of which she had spent in a religious state, having been twenty-four years Superior. Her countenance retained the same sweetness and serenity it had during her life, which made her corpse so agreeable that all who beheld her when she lay exposed in the Choir acknowledged there was a certain air of sanctity that moved them to devotion and respect. She was buried with a High Mass in music, and all the solemnity the house could afford, which was attended with an unusual concourse of people, who flocked from all parts of the town to do homage, as it were, to her virtues, which were famed and admired by all, each one being ambitious to relate what they had heard and seen of her, universally concluding her to be a true saint. And therefore numbers of people came to beg for pieces of her habit, or anything else that had been about her, which they carefully kept as relics, and for many years persons in affliction had recourse to her, and came

to the church of the monastery with votive candles to
be burnt in her honour; which sort of piety and devotion was often rewarded by sensible marks of her assistance, as they failed not to acknowledge by coming to
return thanks for the favours they had received, which
confirmed them more and more she was a saint.

It is a saying that the voice of the people is the
voice of God, which we have reason to think on this
occasion was undoubtedly verified; for if we only consider all circumstances, her whole life bears the character
of a saint. Her infancy, spent in so much piety and
devotion as not only to edify all, but even to become
instrumental towards the conversion of heretics; her
maturer age, in the midst of temptations, sustained by
such resolution as to bid a final adieu to all the allure-
ments of the world at a time when everything promised
her happiness in it; her courage in undertaking a most
austere life, so contrary to her delicate complexion, that
she trembled when she thought of it; her constancy and
steadfastness in living up to what she had undertaken
in a religious state, not in a common but most exemplary
manner; her patience and resignation in bearing with
all sorts of trials, interior and exterior, of body and mind,
with an unshaken submission to the will of God. To
all which, if we add the remarkable ways by which our
Blessed Lord and His beloved Mother have constantly
favoured her from her birth to her death, and her fidelity
in corresponding with these graces by an assiduous exercise of all kinds of virtues, we cannot forbear saying with
the people, she is a true saint. But in all we conform ourselves to the submission which is due to higher powers.

Besides these distinguished marks of sanctity we have
from her life, our Lord has been pleased to give us
no small confirmation of it after her death—witness
many helps persons in distress were assured they had

received by her means, which they publicly acknowledged by coming to render thanks ; one of the most remarkable we shall here set down at large. There was in the house a young lay-sister, by name Anna Maria of St. Joseph, who was very handy and serviceable to the community. She fell sick of a violent burning fever, which continued without intermission for six days, and put her in so great danger that the doctor despaired of her life, and therefore ordained she should speedily have the last sacraments, which accordingly were administered to her as soon as could possibly be done. After which, finding her much spent and the fever grown worse, two of the Sisters were left to watch by her in the night, who, perceiving her to grow extremely ill, apprehended she was in her agony, and therefore thought to go and call up the community. In this anxiety she spoke to them, and said something of a great light she had seen, by which, imagining she was delirious, they drew the bed-curtains to, intending still, if she did not change, to call the religious. In the meantime she grew quieter, and remained so till the Convent Mass was done ; after which she desired to speak to the confessor, who came immediately, and she gave him this account of herself— That, seeing death so near, she was seized with a great terror and apprehension of it, finding herself but very ill-prepared for eternity, and therefore, having great confidence in dear Mother Margaret, who was best acquainted next to God with the poverty of her soul, she made a most humble and earnest petition to her, that she would intercede to our Blessed Lord for her recovery, to the end she might mend her life and serve Him better. Her prayer was no sooner ended, but she thought she saw this dear Mother in the chamber, and a glorious light about the bed, which revived and comforted her above measure, so that she found herself much at ease till the time of Mass, during which she redoubled her prayer with greater confidence and devotion than before ; when on a sudden there appeared a heavenly light, and our venerable Mother bearing the Divine Jesus in her arms, upon a white cloth, with straw underneath, some of the ears of which hung lower than the cloth ; her black veil glittered as if it were full of stars, but she had her own countenance, though glorious, and said to her, ' My child, your hour of death was come ; but since, out of your great desire of living to serve God more perfectly, you have put your confidence in me, I have obtained health for you.' In which very moment she found herself perfectly well ; and if obedience had not prevented her, to have the doctor's approbation of her cure, she would then have gone about her work. When the doctor came he could not sufficiently express his surprise at so speedy and unexpected a recovery, which he affirmed was more than natural. He also found her so strong and well reestablished, which increased his wonder, that he permitted her to leave her bed the same day ; and, the morning after, she heard Mass and went to Communion with the rest of the religious, and was ready to go to her work as usual. This happened on the 10th of January, in the year of our Lord 1680, and was signed in form by the doctor, confessor, Prioress, and discreets.

The community had also several other manifest tokens of their dear Mother's regard and protection, who, as Mr. Bedingfield has assured us, was often amongst them, which some of the Sisters have also been sensible of by an odoriferous and heavenly fragrancy they found about them, like unto that the whole house was scented with on her first profession day after her death, being the feast of St. Clare, on which, from the beginning of the First Vespers till the end of the Second, there

came, as it were, a hot burning perfume out of the
vault where she lay buried, which so affected the religious that they found themselves touched by it with
an unusual joy and devotion. They also had the happiness to partake of the same agreeable favour on the
day of her anniversary, for the same length of time
and in the same manner here mentioned, which inspired
them with new zeal and fervour in the performance
of their religious duties. At which truly no one can
wonder, if they only consider the lively impression so
many blessings of different sorts must needs have made
upon them. They had lived and conversed with this
venerable Mother, they had been witness of her accomplished virtues, and they now saw them rewarded even
in this world. What would be more available, what
more powerful to excite them to run with alacrity in
the paths she had trodden before them? Since they
were assured she had a body composed of flesh and
blood like theirs, susceptible of the same trials and
temptations as theirs, and every way equally sensible
of the same difficulties to overcome them. So that
all tended to animate them and their followers to a
serious and exact imitation of her example, which was
still deeply imprinted in their hearts, and doubtless had
the effect, commonly attributed to the examples of saints,
that are said to be like unto glowing hot coals, which
being cast into the bosom of a well-disposed soul, heat
and inflame it with most ardent desires of becoming like
the pattern it has before it.

May this small work ever be attended with such happy
effects; may it inflame the hearts of all that read it with
sincere desires of serving Almighty God by an exact
observance of His holy laws, and all the duties belonging to their state; may it kindle in their breasts
an ardent zeal for His honour and glory, and instil into

them a true devotion to the Blessed Virgin Mary, of all which this wonderful life affords so many incentive examples !

———

NOTE XIV.

From the account of Venerable Mother Margaret's death written by her sister, Mother Ursula of All Saints.

IT was something remarkable concerning the dead cellar, which about two years and a half after her happy departure, was to be opened, one of our Sisters being dead. We expected to find it in a very sad condition, by reason of a great flood which happened half a year before, so that the dead cellar was filled full of water, that it could not be other ways expected but the mud and dirty water must needs naturally speaking make an unsavoury smell, and cause much filth ; but on the contrary, when it was opened, it rather smelt sweet and wholesome, and not the least corruption in it, to the great admiration and astonishment of the workmen that opened the door. All the signs that there had been water in it was that all the coffins were wet and mouldy, like soaked in water, only our dear mother's was as dry and fresh as if it had stood in some closet, so that we may piously imagine that her pure and unspotted body even preserved the chest that inclosed it. This several persons of quality were eye-witness of, for the inclosure also at that time happened to be open. Her own brother, Sir Edward Mostyn, was one. We did expect him here before in her lifetime, but he came not till then. He esteemed the dead cellar a precious reliquary, as also the bed whereon she died, so great a veneration had he for this dear sister, attributing all his prosperity to her prayers.

It happened also that another brother of hers had her picture in her religious habit, and it always hung by his bedside. The same night that her Reverence died he was awoke out of his sleep with a great noise in his chamber, but could not imagine what had caused it, for he was much altered and could not rest after, but rising in the morning he found the picture taken down and set in the other side of the room over against the door, that all who came in must see it, and to his thinking it seemed to cast a more resplendent sweetness than ordinary, at which he was much amazed, and called several in the house, who observed the same change in the picture, saying it looked heavenly, but could not tell what judgment to make of it, not dreaming of her death, for this being in England they had not so much as heard of her being sick, but it happened the same night as she died, as we understood after.

———

NOTE XV.

Circular Letter written by the Very Rev. Canon Bedingfield at the death of the Venerable Mother Margaret of Jesus (Mostyn). The original in his own handwriting is still in the possession of the community at Darlington.

VERY Rev. Mother,—

You must not admire that we come so late to give you an account of the most happy death of our dearest Mother Margaret of Jesus ; I say most happy unto her, but the most heavy cross that ever befell us, and so unexpected that, falling sick upon the 24th of August, the 29th following, at seven of clock in the morning, deprived us of so angelical a creature, for even now our hearts are so oppressed that we can afford you tears abundantly but few words, which shows how imperfect creatures we are not to adhere more close unto the Divine will. But I am not much solicitous for words, being that all almost that ever knew her from her first entrance into religion, which was at twenty years of age, did admire her perfections, of which whole volumes may be written ; given me only leave to present unto you a glimpse of one or two of them, all the rest being their parallels. She was such a true lover of humility that she esteemed herself always the least, and preferred any one's judgment before her own, from whence, besides her title, you could not distinguish her from the least of the sisters, refusing no service unto the poorest of them ; having such an esteem of it that, lying upon her deathbed, she desired that she might be buried in the poorest habit, and that the religious should take care how they spoke anything in her praises, and that they apply themselves seriously unto virtue, and not imitate her imperfections.

She was no less wonderful in her charity towards her charge (to say nothing of her inflamed love towards sweet Jesus and His Blessed Mother, of whom when she spoke frequently you might even distinguish the flames of her heart in her face), her charity, I say, was so great towards the Sisters, that all was too good for herself, all too little for them, being not able to admit but only by obedience of any consideration, though her constant infirmities required it, being scarce ever in perfect health, and frequently carrying a fever about with her. And when our Blessed Lord visited any of hers with sickness she would scarce ever be absent day or night from them, as if nobody had been able to serve them but herself, never leaving them if the sickness was mortal until she closed up their eyes. This is but a touch of what may be said of these virtues, and as much may be affirmed of all the rest, for really each one virtue considered in her well apart seems to bear the prize. My dearest Mother, it ever adds unto my affliction that it permits me not to dilate myself more upon so deserving a subject ; howsoever, I cannot omit to tell you that even a half-hour before her blessed departure, having most patiently endured most insupportable torments of the colic during her whole sickness, when all her Sisters were in tears, she only smiled, appearing with as pleasant and cheerful a countenance, as if she were nothing concerned, with a perfect understanding and even speech, almost to the last moment full of acts of Divine love, she yielded up her happy ghost unto the hands of her Redeemer, so sweetly as we could scarce perceive it. By this only that we have said you may well comprehend how much reason we have to be sad, and therefore be pleased not only to pray for our ever dearest Mother, who we confide possesses the rewards of her labours, but also for us, that we may conform ourselves unto His Divine will, and embrace cheerfully the cross He hath been pleased to send.

Ever remaining, etc.

DEO GRATIAS.

APPENDIX.

A short account of the lives of Mother Ursula of All Saints (Elisabeth Mostyn), Sister Lucy of the Holy Ghost (Elisabeth Mostyn, niece of the former), Mother Margaret Teresa of the Immaculate Conception (Margaret Mostyn), and of Sister Mary Anne of St. Winefrid (Anne Mostyn).[1]

MARGARET and Elisabeth Mostyn were two daughters, sisters of the first Sir Edward Mostyn, the head at the time of the family now so worthily represented by Sir Piers Mostyn of Talacre. Margaret was the elder by rather more than a year. She was born in 1625, on the feast of the Immaculate Conception of our Blessed Lady. The two sisters, who were extremely fond of one another as girls, and who afterwards lived together as religious of the same convent, were not brought up together as children. Elisabeth lived at Greenfield, at that time the seat of the family, with her parents, but Margaret was so great a favourite with her grandmother, in whose house in Shropshire she had been born, that that lady would never part with her, and brought her up until the time of her own death. Margaret was as a child full of piety and virtue, and began early in her life to desire to enter religion, but she was opposed in her wish by her confessor and her grandmother, who, when she came to die, begged her pardon for this opposition. Meanwhile Elisabeth Mostyn was growing up at her home

[1] Reprinted from an article in the *Month and Catholic Review*, June, 1878.

in Wales, with dispositions to piety and religion very like those entertained by her absent sister.

'She was most particularly devoted from her infancy (writes one of her nieces, like herself a Carmelite nun) to our Blessed Lady, and all her little devotions tended to increase the honour and glory of this great Queen, and by these to make herself entirely her servant. What a religious state was, her tender age could not possibly permit her as yet to understand, yet a religious she would be, and where our Blessed Lady would be best served; neither were these early inclinations to piety confined to herself alone,—if she were to be servant to the Queen of Heaven, her little brothers and sisters must be so too, and to make them such she teaches them to say their beads, and other little devotions she thought would be most pleasing to her, and would often take them to visit the old ruinous chapel at Greenfield, which the ancient piety of Catholic times had dedicated to the honour of our Lady. Thither would she lead her little brothers and sisters, and instead of playing would, by her engaging manners, get them to say prayers with her, and perform little devotions with so much order and innocency, creeping round about the chapel on their bare knees for penance and mortification.'

We have already mentioned the opposition which Margaret Mostyn met with from her confessor and grandmother when she first conceived and expressed her desire to become a religious. In one of the papers which she left behind her, written at the desire of her confessor many years later, she tells him that, at the time of her first Communion, she saw our Blessed Lord in the Blessed Sacrament as He is represented in the pictures of the Good Shepherd, and that the sense of His Presence remained with her all that day. Her confessor at the time discouraged her wish, and she then gave herself up more than before to girlish vanities. Something very much of the same kind happened to her sister Elisabeth.

' Being arrived to eleven years of age, and communicating the first time on the feast of the glorious Assumption of the Mother of God, with a great deal of interior devotion and fervent desires, to give herself entirely to her by resolving never to marry, and to dedicate her virginity to our Blessed Lady's honour, were the inspired thoughts and firm purposes of her heart, wherefore she resolved to conform exteriorly with her lips what interiorly she felt inspired with. Immediately she was assailed with extreme contradictions, seeing by it that she made herself incapable hereafter of following the world, and embracing those lawful pleasures and amusements it afforded to young ladies of her age. With these and other cheating thoughts did the enemy endeavour to frighten her from proceeding to fix her generous resolution, when presently the venerable Mother of Mercy appeared visibly before her eyes most glorious, all in virgin white, and told her that she was already hers, and that her promise, proceeding from her own free choice, would but only make her more pleasing to her.'

She was at once filled with joy and consolation, and for nearly three years remained in her resolution without disturbance. But when she was nearly fourteen, and the time approached, according to what was then usual, for her to appear more in the world, her mother, who wished her to marry, thinking that she was very delicate, and that her other daughter, Margaret, would probably think of entering religion, proposed to her a very advantageous match, and would hear of no refusal. The child, for she was hardly more in age, resisted firmly, and casting her eyes upon a picture of our Blessed Lady which hung in the room, seemed to receive fresh strength from Heaven to keep her promise. She told her mother that she was firmly determined to be a nun. The mother sent her off at once to her confessor, who made very light of the promise to our Lady, and told her to give it up. Thus Elisabeth as well as Margaret was turned from her purpose. She began to take

pleasure in dress and company, and, to set her conscience
more at rest, she gave up spiritual reading, and even took
care that the famous book of Father Jerome Platus *On the
Happiness of a Religious State*, should be sent out of the
house, that she might not be tempted to read it.

Soon after this the grandmother with whom Margaret
Mostyn had hitherto lived, came to die, and the two sisters
became inseparable companions at their home at Greenfield.
They were so tenderly attached to each other, that they
made a plan that if either of them came to marry, the other
should try to get married to a gentleman in the same neighbourhood, in order that they might still be united. It is
probable that each really helped the other in what was the
secret though resisted impulse of God concerning them.
They went on appearing in the world, but all the time their
hearts were very ill at ease, and their mutual affection
seemed likely to oppose a fresh obstacle to their vocations.
It was not so, however. Margaret's hesitation was brought
to an end by an apparition of our Blessed Lady in the
garden at Greenfield, and though she kept it to herself for
some time, and was in much danger in consequence, she at
last spoke openly to her sister, and was delighted to find
that she had in truth the same desires with herself. They
had to wait a year before their design could be put into
execution, but their mother was too good not to give way
when the drawing of God's holy Spirit became manifest.
The story of their journey to Antwerp, where the Teresian
convent to which they were destined was placed, is very
interesting. It was in the worst time of the great civil war,
when things had turned irrevocably against the King, and it
was with great difficulty that they escaped the Parliamentary
army which lay round Weymouth, the port at which they
were to embark. Their ship sprung a leak while they were
in mid channel, and they were also chased by a hostile
vessel. But they reached Havre in safety, and after visiting
Pontoise, where the remains of the famous Mary of the

Incarnation—the lady known in the world as Madame
Acarie, who had introduced the Teresian reform into France
—were laid, and to Paris—where they seem to have been
received by one of the daughters of Madame Acarie, at that
time Superior of the Carmelites there—they made their way
to Antwerp, where the Prioress was a lady renowned in the
Carmelite annals as having been the first English nun of
St. Teresa's reform, and the foundress of the convents of the
Order for the English nation, Mother Anne of the Ascension. She received them with the greatest joy, discerning as
she did, by a peculiar gift, their great qualities, both in the
order of nature and in that of grace. Margaret was known
in religion as Margaret of Jesus. Elisabeth took the
name of Ursula of All Saints.

It would take us far too long to attempt to draw out the
spiritual history of these two choice souls, and the details
as far as they are known and traced for us in the pages of
the volume before us are better left to its students, of whom
we do not doubt there will be many, though we cannot hope
for such subjects the interest of every class of our own
readers. The early noviceship of the two sisters was soon
clouded by the death of Mother Anne of the Ascension,
who had received them, and for a moment they were discouraged by a loss which they must have felt in a peculiar
manner. They soon recovered, and became at once eminent,
even in that 'enclosed garden' of select souls, for their zeal
in self-conquest and regularity in observance. At one time,
Elisabeth, or as she was called in religion, Ursula of All
Saints, was in danger of falling under the temptation to
·despondency and melancholy, mainly on account of her
habit of conversing too freely on the thoughts which de-
pressed her with another of the nuns, who was of a similar
disposition with herself. Margaret was also in some danger
from a like temptation. Her engaging and kindly disposition made her a sort of resource to others who were in low
·spirits, and neither side gained by too much communicative-

ness in such matters. All these difficulties, however, vanished as the time of their profession drew on, and they were both professed with great joy on St. Clare's Day, August 12, 1645.

The two sisters did not remain long in the Convent at Antwerp. Three years after their profession, the community had increased so much that it was thought right to send out a new foundation, and after some hesitation the little town of Lierre was fixed on as its seat. Margaret and Ursula were already conspicuous among their religious Sisters for the perfection in which they had caught the spirit of St. Teresa, and though as yet young in religion, it was thought well to give the new community the benefit of their admirable virtues. It was therefore at Lierre that they spent the rest of their beautiful and holy lives. The foundation of Lierre was made in 1648, and six years after that date we find Margaret elected Prioress, having already filled the offices of Subprioress and of Mistress of Novices. She was continued in her office of government by successive re-elections for twenty-four years, till the time of her death.

She died in August, 1679, and was immediately succeeded as Prioress by her dear sister Ursula of All Saints. Ursula had been her assistant as Subprioress during the whole time of her government, and was extremely beloved by her community. She was noted for sweetness of character, severity to herself, which, even early in her religious life, seriously injured her health, and great humility. She had a very beautiful voice, and was most useful as Subprioress, in which office she had the care of the ceremonies and order of the choir, on account of her great exactness and zeal for all that related to the worship of God. When she was Prioress, she was noted, amid all her wonderful affability, for never leaving unreprehended any fault in this matter. But as long as she was Subprioress, she contrived to conceal her great talent for business and the management of the temporalities of the community so perfectly that when her sister came to die, and it seemed as if she were the fittest person to succeed her, there were some who doubted of her capacity on this account. Their doubts were altogether mistaken, as it turned out that she was equal to her sister in this respect. Under both of them the convent flourished exceedingly. She survived Margaret no less than twenty-two years, dying on the 19th of March, in 1700, at the age of seventy-four, and remaining Prioress till her death.

'She charmed the hearts of all the community [writes her biographer] by her maternal charity, general love to all, ever promoting the spirit of our holy Mother by her own example, for she made herself all to all, and was certainly the greatest blessing that community could possess, appearing to be placed by Almighty God over us to make every one happy. She was singular in comforting those in affliction and that had interior sufferings of the soul : the very sight of her Reverence gave them comfort and satisfaction, and to hear her only speak did appease and calm their troubled minds. One quarter of an hour's conversation with her did generally cause their afflictions to cease. When any Sister had committed a fault that deserved reprehension, and that she perceived her afterwards troubled or concerned, she humbly attributed it to some sharpness in her own words. Her Reverence was never at rest till with double kindness and sweetness she had settled them. Her speech was humble and sweet, yet always to the purpose : she had not only the hearts of all, but even of the most stubborn and the most afflicted, by a certain agreeable compliance, which was proper and peculiar to herself, by yielding a little, in a sweet compassionate way, to their weakness and infirmities. She could hardly bear with patience that the Sisters should suffer, or the sick want any refreshment or comfort, through any negligence. As she was a most tender mother to those in health, so was she most careful and compassionate to the sick, and never thought anything too costly for them, which might conduce to their recovery, comfort, and relief, and she had so watchful an eye over all the Sisters that she even prevented them telling her they were not well, calling them to her, forcing them to tell her their necessity or indisposition, and all with so much motherly love and sweetness, that it was a pleasure to open their hearts to her, ever receiving the light and consolation wished for. Amongst other obliging expressions she was often heard to say she thanked God for her want of health, since it made her more sensible of the infirmities and weaknesses of others, and that she had rather be in Purgatory herself for too much sweetness to her subjects, than by being harsh to the religious, put them in danger of tying themselves there for having offended God by any unmortified repining against their Superior's severity. "For what have my dear Sisters, but what I give them? and who can they speak to, but to me? They are the Spouses of my Jesus, He has given me the care of them." She was still, if possible, more zealous of their spiritual advancement. No Sister had recourse to her but always returned with a perfect satisfaction, and it was her practice to mortify those the most who were the most perfect, saying they knew how to make right use of it, and thereby would be an example to others : managing each one according to the spirit which God gave them with a wonderful foresight and prudence. She was of a most compassionate nature, deeply sensible of those she knew to be troubled by interior uncomfortable obscurities, scruples, and aridities, never at ease till she could afford them comfort, which those of her children who with the greatest freedom and sincerity discovered to her their interior, experienced. Her words were always of such force, with her compassionate sweetness, that they never departed from her but with their hearts strengthened with intense joy and comfort. Her chiefest delight was to be in the midst of her flock, and she never let the times when we meet in recreation pass without some pious discourse. She could speak of spiritual things and perfection with that clearness and facility, as if every word she spoke proceeded from a particular inspiration, so that all dearly loved her company, and never thought themselves more happy than when she was sitting and conversing with them.'

The account from which this long passage is taken, and which contains a great deal more that we would gladly quote if our space allowed, was written by one of Mother Ursula's three nieces, daughters of Sir Edward Mostyn, who all became Carmelite nuns at Lierre after the example and under the rule of their aunts. Their lives also are contained in the manuscript from which the volume before us has been printed, but it has been found impossible to find room for them, or indeed for the Life of Mother Ursula herself. There is something very touching about the stories of these three nieces of Margaret and Elisabeth Mostyn, who must evidently have heard a great deal about their aunt's virtues and amiability while they were themselves children. The eldest, Elisabeth, was named in religion Sister Lucy of the Holy Ghost, and seems to have belonged to God in a special manner from her earliest years.

'In her infancy she was very delicate and sickly, and frequently subject to convulsive fits. This made her father take her in his arms, and offer her up a sacrifice on the altar, to be disposed of according to God's Divine will and pleasure, Who had given her to him, to live or die as He should please, in Whose adorable Hands were life and death, health and sickness. How acceptable this oblation was to Almighty God, His Divine Goodness did not only most graciously make appear at present by the child's increasing health, but did afterwards more particularly manifest in these early movements to piety. For scarce could she speak when she took a passionate affection to the Infant Jesus. She was not seven years of age when she began to beg her parents she might be spouse to this Blessed Infant. She used every morning on her little

knees, as she had been taught to do, beg their blessing,
and then would she frequently ask (inspired by the Holy
Ghost to beg at that age what she could not possibly
understand) that they would please to give her leave to
cross the seas, and go to make herself a nun in the house at
Lierre, where her aunts were. It was some amusement to
them to see the manner wherewith the child did daily make
this her humble petition, but they had no more thought of
making her a religious, and one great reason was because
they thought she might perhaps have health enough to be
happy if she lived at her ease in the world, but never arrive
to be so strong as to be able to undergo the great labours
and austerities of a religious life.'

However, the child went on begging most earnestly for
leave to go to Lierre, and at last got her parents' consent
when she was twelve years of age. She did not actually
leave her home and go to Lierre till she was nearly thirteen,
and as soon as she entered on her fourteenth year the
Bishop allowed her to take the religious habit. She was
professed in 1670, having then completed her sixteenth
year. She lived thirty-seven years in religion, dying in
1707, a remarkable example of simplicity, humility, and
self-contempt.

The other two nieces of Margaret and Elisabeth Mostyn
who entered the community at Lierre were Anne and
Margaret, called in religion Mary Anne of St. Winefrid
and Margaret Teresa of the Immaculate Conception. The
last named was the elder of the two, but not the first to
enter religion. She was educated in an English Convent
at Paris, and when her education was completed, went
home by Flanders for the sake of seeing her aunts at Lierre.
Mother Margaret of Jesus was then Prioress, and she told
her niece that whatever vanities and amusements she
pleased to follow, she was certainly to end as a Carmelite
nun at Lierre. The high-spirited girl replied that she would
take care of that, and determined to frustrate her aunt's

prediction. She married a widower, a gentleman in Oxford-shire, with whom she lived for some time in great happiness. But after some years she was left a widow, and determined to become a religious, not, however, at Lierre. She entered the community of the Poor Clares at Rouen, but was obliged to leave on account of deafness brought on by walking barefoot. Then she went to the Benedictine nuns at Dunkirk, but although she liked them very well, she could not feel happy, and was at last compelled to betake herself to Lierre, where Mother Ursula of All Saints was now Prioress.

Margaret seems to have been a person of considerable character, very bright and lively, bearing the austerities of the Order with great cheerfulness, and, at the same time, very docile. She possessed also many useful accomplish-ments. Three years after the death of her aunt, Mother Ursula, she was elected Prioress, and as she remained Superior for twenty-one years, the reign of the Mostyns at Lierre extended for nearly three quarters of a century. It was under Mother Margaret Teresa of the Immaculate Conception that the convent was transferred to the site which it occupied until the community had to take refuge in England. This was a very laborious business, as houses had to be bought and pulled down, and a new convent and church raised. We are told that the Duke of Marlborough, who was then at Brussels, helped the nuns very much by his influence and exertions to surmount their many diffi-culties. One of the best houses included in the new convent had been purchased by Canon Bedingfield for his own use, and bequeathed by him to the community. It seems that in those days as well as in our own, the caprices and obstinacy of architects were not unusual sources of annoyance to the religious communities who had the mis-fortune to fall into their hands. 'The expenses,' says the biographer of Mother Margaret Teresa, 'were unavoidably great, but were exceedingly augmented by the architect's unsteadiness of mind; the workmen's employ of one week he would order to be pulled down the next, to be built up in some other form. This frequently repeated was a just cause of chagrin, and though she procured among friends in England a considerable sum towards discharging the expenses, yet it put.her and the community to great straits, notwithstanding her jointure was so great a help.'

However, she carried all through prosperously. There is an interesting account in her life of the ceremony of laying the first stone, which was attached to the famous statue of Our Lady of the Clues, already mentioned in the life of Mother Margaret of Jesus, while Lady Winter placed it in its proper position. The biographer adds concerning Mother Margaret Teresa, that—

'She bore a great respect to her Superiors, and when Subprioress, was exact in seeing the Prioress' octaves and feasts observed with great decorum, inheriting the true spirit of our Seraphical Mother St. Teresa in promoting innocent recreations in their due times. She was a great lover of a polite and cheerful behaviour, and encouraged lively dispositions, disapproving a heavy and dull temper, being far from it herself even to the end of her life. Mother Margaret Teresa had a terrible apprehension of death; we esteemed it a very visible mercy of God to prevent her in these terrors of death, as He was pleased to call her to Himself in a peaceful sleep, without so much as a sigh or a drop of sweat.

She died in February, 1743-4, while the religious were making preparations to celebrate her jubilee, she had been professed in 1694. She was the writer of the Life of Mother Ursula of All Saints, which has been already quoted here.

There remains yet one more of this family of Carmelites to be mentioned, Anne Mostyn, the younger of the three nieces of Margaret and Elisabeth (Ursula). Her mother died five months after her birth, and she was brought up till she was seven years of age by her grandmother,

Mrs. Petre. Sir Edward married again, and his second wife became extremely fond of her stepchildren. She was to take Margaret Teresa, of whom we have just spoken, to Calais on the way to Paris for her education, and Sir Edward took his little daughter Anne as far as Chester to keep them company. When Margaret knelt to her father for his parting blessing, the child clung to her sister, weeping and entreating not to be separated from her, and no promises or arguments would induce her to give up her petition. The parents were obliged to let her go, and she was placed in the Convent of the English Augustinian nuns in Paris. Several years after, when the lies of Oates and Bedloe raised so great a storm against Catholics all over England, the Mostyns with many other families found it necessary to leave the country for a time, and went to Paris, where they found Anne well advanced in her education. When the danger had abated, and Sir Edward and Lady Mostyn thought of taking her home with them, she disclosed the desire which she had for many years of joining her aunts in the Convent at Lierre. They went to Flanders, and after remaining at Lierre for several months at last gave their consent to her desire. She lived in the convent till her death, at the age of fifty-two, a pattern of religious virtue. She had the care of the sacristy, and was remarkable for her skill with her needle.

'As to the spending of her time, [says the manuscript at Darlington,] it was always so precious in her eyes, that she managed it with so much care and industry, as not to lose a moment of it. She was of a most grateful temper, and the testimony a spiritual person (Father Roper) gave of her, will not be superfluous. He said she was one of much candour and sincerity, and had a soul composed of gratitude and generosity. To this testimony we may justly add, that she was of a very compassionate nature, being ever anxious and uneasy to see any of the Sisters indisposed in affliction, and full of compassion and grief at the miseries, sufferings and necessities of the poor and needy, for whom she would frequently be importuning her Superior to assist and relieve them, and would with much feeling do all in her power to aid them. She was also remarkable in readiness to perform any act of charity for the Sisters who required her assistance, being of a very complying and submissive temper, so that even whilst her own sister was Superior, no one would have imagined she had been her sister, by reason of the respectful carriage and submission she always paid her. Great was her devotion to our Blessed Lady of the Rosary, and St. Gomar also, patron of our town of Lierre, had a part of her daily devotions, most earnestly she recommended herself and friends and all the necessities of the monastery to his powerful intercession—and jointly together with these placed a particular trust and confidence in St. Antony of Padua, hoping thereby to obtain that final favour of the goodness and infinite mercy of God, an easy and happy death.'

It is remarkable that she had frequently prayed that she might have the help of Father Roper, already mentioned, on her death-bed. He came to Lierre to see another of her religious, when Mary Anne of St. Winefrid was in good health, but she fell ill at once, and died as she had desired, with his assistance during all her last hours. Her death took place on the 26th of June, 1715.

We end these remarks as we began them, with a reference to the light which these memoirs throw on the habits and training of our old Catholic families under the persecution. It is impossible not to see how much that training had to do with the mature and solid sanctity which characterizes the lives of which we have been speaking. There is not a single instance in which these ladies derived their inspiration to the perfect service of God in the cloister, from the urgent advice of a confessor, or from the excitement, or supposed excitement, of a retreat, or even from a sermon. The confessors, as far as we are told of their action, sided with the parents in dissuading the girls from their self-sacrifice, at least as long as there was any chance that they might be mistaken, or any wisdom in putting their resolutions to the test of opposition. The intense family affection, also, which distinguishes these lives, was an element likely to work rather against the execution of their designs than in favour of it. But we catch glimpses of the family habits—the reverence of children for their parents, the daily routine of piety, the constant intercourse with the resident priest, the frequentation of the domestic chapel, the active employment of young girls in household duties, and their training in useful womanly accomplishments. Perhaps Margaret and Elisabeth Mostyn and their nieces might have seemed somewhat slow and old-fashioned to many a Catholic girl of their age at the present time. But it is of such stuff as they were made of that the human treasures of the Church are formed—souls such as theirs are capable, when fortified by grace, of the noblest sacrifices that God asks of those whom He draws near to Himself, and it is to the prayers of such as they were that we owe it in great measure, that there is the Catholic faith and the Catholic Church in the country in which we live.

H. J. C.